BRENDAN CORBETT

BLOOD

AND

FLAME

BOOK ONE OF THE QUINATE'S FAITHFUL

Illustration © Tom Edwards

TomEdwardsDesign.com

Editor: Celestian Rince

celestianrince.com

Blood and Flame / Brendan Corbett

ISBN: 979-8-9901899-7-3

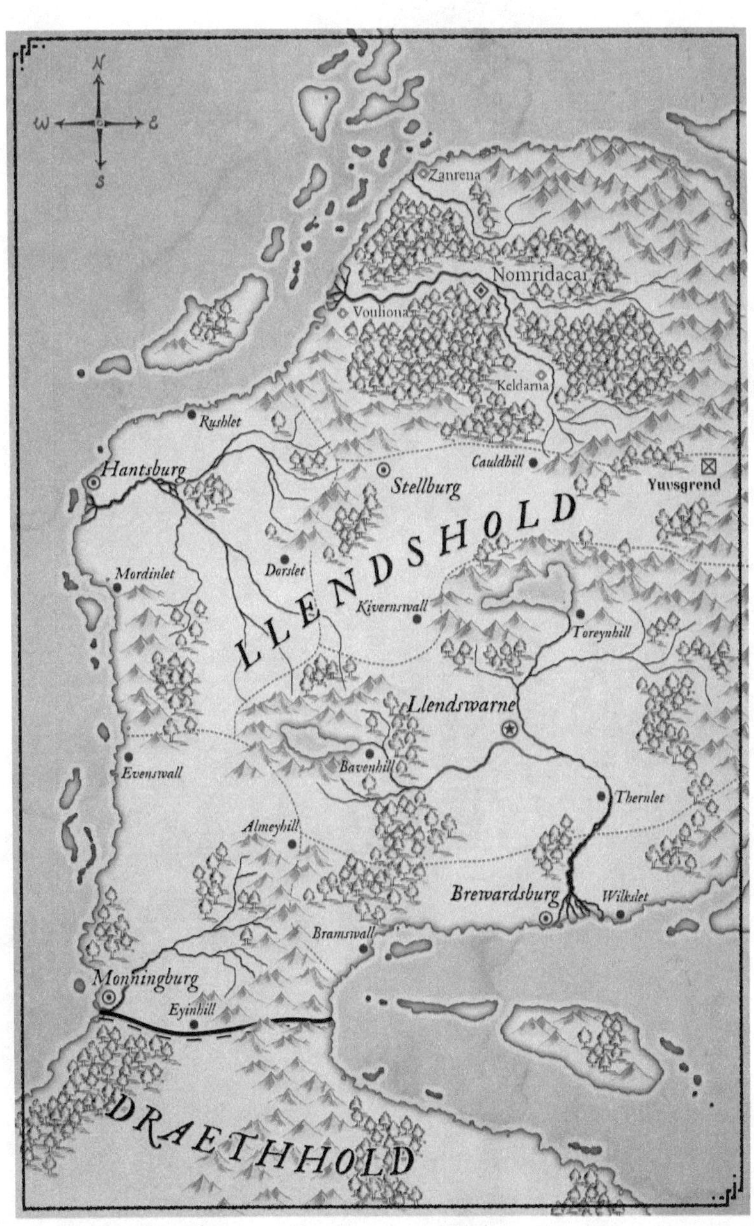

N
W
E
S
Zanrena
Nomridacai
Vouliona
Keldarna
Rushlet
Hantsburg
Stellburg
Cauldhill
Yuvsgrend
LLENDSHOLD
Mordinlet
Dorslet
Kivernswall
Toreynhill
Llendswarne
Evenswall
Bavenhill
Thernlet
Almeyhill
Brewardsburg
Wilkslet
Bramswall
Monningburg
Eyinhill
DRAETHHOLD

CHAPTER 1

Flickering candles mounted on brass sconces cast sparse light in the enormous Temple. Moonlight glimmered in through count-less narrow windows. The ceiling towered more than four stories above, supported by three rows of ten-foot-wide stone columns on either side. A cluster of a dozen Initiates waited before the raised apse at the end of the cavernous worship hall. Illuminated by a single brazier filled with crackling, white-hot coals, their faces brimmed with anxiousness.

A boom echoed through the Temple when a door to the side of the apse swung open. The Initiates jumped, instinctively shifting away from the sound. Moments later, a figure strode in, followed by six attendants wearing simple white tunics and slender pants. The onlookers gasped at the sight of the leader's opulent dress: he wore a white vest with burgundy and purple trim over a pure white tunic which extended nearly to the floor; a braided gold stole rest across his shoulders; white gloves laced in gold and silver covered his hands; a simple band of gold held back curly locks of hair; a solid silver mask hid his face.

"It's the Moderator! He's finally here!" exclaimed an Initiate.

An attendant halted in place and faced the crowd. "You were commanded to be silent!"

The offending boy shrank where he stood as those surrounding him inched away. The Moderator, unbothered, came to a stop behind a stone lectern adorned in gold filigree. Gripping the podium, flickers of yellow danced across his mask. From the darkness behind the Moderator, a Mage approached; her pale linen tunic, cut high at the waist and reaching her knees at the side, bore dark purple trim. A teardrop-shaped bottle, wrapped in bands of silver, hung from her belt beside a cloth gauntlet with steel pads over the knuckles and fingertips.

As the silence stretched from seconds into minutes, the Initiates shuffled from side to side, crossing arms and picking at fingernails. The Moderator finally broke the silence, his voice booming like a drum through the Temple.

"As They speak!"

"So we listen," came a unified response.

The Moderator's shoulders relaxed. "You are a product of the grace of the Quinarium. Our institution took you at the cusp of adulthood and transformed you into what you are today, through training, through nurturing, and by blessing you with the grace of the Quinate itself. Be proud, Initiates, your Instructors have deemed you worthy to face the Rite of the Faithful, through which you might rise, ascend, and join the ranks of the Quinate's Faithful as Mages!"

The Moderator took slow, deliberate steps away from the lectern. He observed the Initiates with his neck craned forward like a falcon in search of a mouse. Heads lowered and eyes turned away from his gaze. Descending from the apse, he walked among the Initiates.

"You stand in the Temple of the fine city of Stellburg, built on ground hallowed by the Quinarium in the name of the Quinate, the Five, our Gods. Ramaia, Almoya, Seraeus, Kosrya, Ilsios, *our* Quinate!" Fury grew in the Moderator. "They bless this place through the labor of the Quinarium. Should you complete your rite, you will be among those fortunate enough to serve. A life spent furthering your skill in magic, dedicated to the Five... a life envied by all."

The Moderator strolled back to the apse, his voice calming. "Some of you will not continue on to your rite, and many do not pass their rite on the first try. There is no shame in failure. Should you be unsuccessful, you will return to your Academy and continue training until you meet our demanding standards. Such is the grace of the Quinarium, an extension of the grace of the Quinate."

Returning to the lectern, the Moderator motioned to the Mage at his side. "Each of you will testify before me, with the assistance of a Mage of Almoya, a seer of the Mind. She will open your memory and I will experience your story, come to know you, and assess whether or not you are prepared for the Rite of the Faithful."

The Mind Mage took the gauntlet from her belt and wiggled her hand almost fully in. She yanked the last inch, seating the glove tightly about her fingers. Raising the silver-bound bottle, she removed its cork and took a deep drink, licking her lips hungrily as she resealed it.

"Dara," said the Moderator, "Come forth. Initiate of the Academy of Ramaia, wielder of Blood Magic, you are the first to be assessed."

Dara took a step forward. Grateful not to be called first, the other Initiates shuffled away as if the young woman were diseased, giving her a wide berth.

"Come," the Moderator invited. "Come, stand before me."

Tension mounted in Dara's shoulders, radiating all the way to her fingertips. She clenched her fists to calm their trembling as she fought the urge to shy away from the attention. Gritting her teeth, she marched to the apse.

The Moderator inspected Dara as she approached. The young woman, though only just old enough to be no longer called a girl, was tall, with muscular shoulders. Her hair was pulled back in a tight bun, exposing an expression of determination painted across her pale face. Skin pulled tight against her pronounced jaw as she gulped.

Dara stopped a few paces away from the Moderator. The mask entranced her; light wavering across its surface cast shadows in tiny pocks and mars, some caused by impurities in the silver while others were signs of wear from years of use. Shadows shrouded the eye holes. When her shoulders slouched, Dara willed herself to stand tall, battling the voice in her mind, whispering that she was incapable, unready.

"The first Initiate is the only one from the Academy of Ramaia, recommended by none other than Okter Bosmun. It is rare for him to send someone unready. I have high expectations," the Moderator drolled, his voice barely above a whisper. "Dara, tell me your story, and let us see if I agree with his assessment."

Dara gulped as the Mind Mage began a long, unintelligible chant. Her gloved hand swayed, fingers pointed at Dara. Finishing her spell, the Mage closed her hand as if capturing the words she had uttered, then opened her palm at the Moderator. A comforting heat filled Dara as if the afternoon sun shined inside her body. A lavender and aquamarine haze drifted from Dara's head to the Moderator. Then a single word enveloped her mind.

"Speak."

Mouth closed, Dara answered with a thought. "What would you have me say?"

"I have already told you. Tell me your story. Start with what you consider the beginning of the journey which brought you here tonight."

Dara inhaled deeply, then slowly released the lungful of air through her nose. "I can still remember my first taste of mana, as if it were yesterday. The warmth flowing into my belly, the sweetness clinging to my lips..."

CHAPTER 2

When she felt the late afternoon sun burning high above, Dara immediately recognized the memory.

Dara staggered forward. Hands pressed on either side of her back. Their touch was neither gentle nor loving; rather, it was purposeful, urging her forward. Glancing over her shoulder, she saw her mother and father. Though the moment took place hardly more than a year prior, and the memory was called forth by magic, their faces were an indistinct blur. The smell of stone clung to them all. Through her tunic, she felt the calluses of their hands.

Quickening her pace, Dara looked at her own hands; she had not been afforded the time to wash away the thick layer of grey dust coating them. Beads of sweat clung to Dara's neck and face, sticky and mixed with powdered stone. The clinking of pickaxes rhythmically striking rock drifted from behind, a reminder of the work waiting in the mines.

The pressure on Dara's back eased as they reached the edge of the hamlet. Beyond a small crowd was an ornate carriage, bearing the sigil of the Quinarium painted in white with red trim—a smaller circle set inside a larger circle, with three arced lines evenly spaced between them. At the heart of the crowd was a Confessor—the head of the Sanctuary and highest-ranking

Quinarium official of the nearby village of Kivernswall—with a Mage by his side.

Dara muttered apologies as her parents parted the crowd, using her as a wedge. They reached the front of the throng to find four Paladins in heavy armor taking hold of a limp body. The boy's head flopped back. Dara recognized Adan, the son of a farmer. She had always thought him vibrant, cheerful, but now his colorless face wobbled as the Paladins dragged him away. Fresh sweat dripped down Dara's face as her eyes blurred and her stomach churned.

A shove sent Dara stumbling to her hands and knees; dust roiled around her. She looked up to see the Confessor, squatting a few feet away. He smiled, deep creases forming at the corners of his eyes.

"What is your name, girl?" he inquired. "Tell me, are you here for the Test of Mana, to drink of the gift of the Five, the lifeblood of the great Quinarium? Perhaps you will be one of the fortunate ones, blessed with attunement."

Dara attempted to speak but her jaw shook, and words evaded her tongue.

"Her name is Dara," said her father.

"Dara!" echoed her mother.

The Confessor stood, one eyebrow raised. His alabaster tunic and vest extended below his knees. "No surname?"

Dara's mother bowed her head. "We are simple miners. First names are plenty, no use for surnames among lowly folk such as us."

"Come, dear, do not think of yourself as lowly!" The Confessor spread his arms wide, sending gold and silver bangles rolling down his wrists. "Whether I am serving the people of Kivernswall in the Sanctuary, or visiting hamlets such as yours, I consider each and every person the same. We are all equals in the eyes of the Quinate, and what is the Quinarium, if not simply a vessel to convey the message of the Five? As the Quinate provides to us, we provide to all!"

The Confessor knelt beside Dara, who was still on her knees. He took her hands in his; his skin was soft, as if he bathed in milk every day. Gem-encrusted rings adorned his fingers. Her face blushed at the thought of her tattered, short tunic being so close to his decorative clothing. After his rousing speech, Dara pondered how equal they truly were. Had he ever spent a night hungry after a day of hard labor? Or had days where blisters on his hands burst with no relief except wrappings of dried linen, knowing the work would continue, come morning?

"Now then, Dara. Are you here for the test? To drink of mana is to pledge your life to the Quinarium, to give yourself over to something greater and more beautiful than you could possibly imagine."

A hand closed over Dara's shoulder and squeezed; a second hand pressed into the small of her back. Calluses dug into her skin through her tunic; the abrasive, hardened lumps irritated her, like pebbles caught in a shoe.

"Yes," she mumbled.

"Now is the time for certainty, for resolution! Before you decide, know that there is risk," the Confessor said, eyeing the trail in the dirt from Adan being dragged away. "Not all can handle such power from the Gods. Though you appear strong physically, strength is no predictor of attunement to mana, and the cost can be total."

The Confessor hopped to his feet, then paced a few times before Dara. The corners of his mouth curled into a smile as the enthralled crowd awaited his next words.

"Should you expire, we will perform the Harvest Ceremony to gather mana from your body. You will become the highest of gifts, living on through the spells of the Mages who serve as the Quinate's Faithful. A noble sacrifice worthy of praise and reverence. While some are found to be attuned and others may pass, most will have no response at all, in which case you may simply return to your life as it was. Though, I of course hope you are sensitive to mana. If you are, you will be called Initiate and sent to one of the five Academies. There you will be trained to one day become a Mage."

Dara wiped her brow. "What of my parents?"

The Confessor grinned. "A kind soul. We, of course, will compensate your parents appropriately. A sum of two hundred Guilders in the case of your ascension, or passing."

"Two hundred?" Dara stammered at the sum, nearly four times what she might earn in a year of work.

Dara's father's eyes widened. "Yes, yes! She has always wanted this! Few are as faithful as our Dara, always praying, always keeping the Five in her heart, mind, and mouth!"

"She truly is a wonderful child," followed her mother. "Never expressed a desire other than to serve the Quinate, through the Quinarium. 'I'll leave you one day, Mother, Father, but don't worry, it'll be for a higher purpose,' or so she always says. Losing our Dara will tear us apart, but the compensation will soften the sting of losing our dearest and only child."

"Come then, Dara. I have heard all I need to hear."

The Confessor brought Dara to the waiting Mage, who cradled a glass bottle enrobed in silver in her hands. Grasping the bottle by its neck, she removed its stopper and presented the bottle to Dara.

"Kneel, Dara, and drink," ordered the Confessor.

Dara expected the bottle to be heavy but found it pleasantly light. The silver bands were cold, yet the glass radiated a comforting warmth, as if a heartbeat pulsed within. Peering inside, she saw a viscous, colorless liquid sloshing about. "How... how much should I drink?"

The Mage smiled. "A sip or a guzzle, the amount matters not. The slightest of tastes will reveal if you are attuned."

"Drink it!" Dara's mother called, her voice shrill.

"Don't be scared," said her father. "Take a drink, Dara. Drink, Dara, drink!"

Dara peered over at her parents. They leaned forward, eyes bulging, mouths open, like cougars ready to pounce on their prey.

"Dara, my child, please drink," urged the Confessor.

Eyes shut tight, Dara raised the bottle to her lips. Before she tipped the vessel, a gentle heat radiated into her mouth. Hesitating for a moment, she tilted her head back and took a deep drink.

It was as if flames erupted over Dara's tongue. An unbridled energy danced down her throat and settled in her stomach. An intoxicating sweetness billowed inside her nose as lingering traces of mana coated her mouth. Despite having worked most of the day in the mines, she felt alert, rested, ready for any challenge which might come her way. Her whole body was suddenly *alive*, as if her every waking moment of life was incomplete until then. A smile crept across Dara's face as she was overtaken by laughter.

"Praise be to the Five!" shouted the Confessor. "She has passed the Test of Mana! Today the Quinate have chosen Dara to be among their most faithful! A glorious day! As They speak!"

The crowd, led by Dara's parents, answered in unison. "So we listen!"

"You good people bear witness that on this day Dara, once a miner, will become an Initiate, destined to become a Mage of the Quinarium. Now, back to your lives, for I must speak with Dara and her parents." The Confessor grabbed Dara's chin and peered into her eyes. "Dara, Dara, my dear child... this is no normal reaction. Your eyes glow with a purity that is rarely seen. Your attunement is exceptional. This response mandates your attendance at the Academy of Ramaia."

"Ramaia?" Dara asked, the sensation calming to a gentle buzz which seemed to flow in and out of her skin. "I am to become a Blood Mage?"

"Yes, you are to study in the ways of Ramaia at her Academy, the highest, most prominent of them all."

A shout and cry followed by sobbing prompted Dara to look back. Her parents embraced each other tightly.

"A Blood Mage. Our daughter!" said her mother.

"Yes, yes! To study among the highest of the Five, Dara, our daughter," her father replied.

The Mage nodded to the Confessor then grasped Dara's shoulder. "You must commit with words as you did actions. Dara, you drank the gift of the Quinate as administered by the Quinarium, and have passed the Test of Mana. Do you pledge to dedicate yourself as an Initiate of the Quinarium, in all you do, in service of the Quinate?"

Dara's head pounded as the sensation of mana waned. A faint tingling settled into her hands. For a passing moment, Dara wondered what might happen if she were to decline, until her parents came into view, still embracing and staring greedily.

"Yes, I pledge myself to the Quinarium."

"We have much to rejoice!" replied the Confessor. "It is a bright day indeed when another joins the fold of the Quinarium. With your attunement as it is, I have no doubt you will call yourself one of the Quinate's Faithful soon. A blessed day this is indeed. Dara, you have inspired my next sermon: we are all equals under the Quinate, and we all can rise to heights never before dreamed. None can deny it when a young miner is bound for the Academy of Ramaia. Come, Mother, Father, let us walk and I will explain what comes next."

The ever-stoic Mage remained and addressed Dara. "You depart in the morning, after first light. Prepare only what you must, but you need not prepare anything at all unless you wish to.

The Quinarium will provide all you need upon arrival at the Academy. Now, the evening is yours. Say your farewells, make your preparations, and be ready in the morn."

After speaking with the Confessor, Dara's parents pulled her to the tavern where drink flowed and cheers rattled the walls. Dara detested the sudden attention and slipped out at the first opportunity, doubtful any would notice she was gone.

Leaving the hamlet, she roamed through the surrounding farms. A piercing shriek followed by soul-wrenching sobs brought her to a stop. Dara crept towards the sounds. She was a stone's throw away when she recognized the farmhouse: it was Adan's home. Through a dimly lit window, she saw the outlines of the boy's parents and siblings clinging to each other in desperate sorrow. Dara sat on the dirt path until long after the family sobbed themselves to sleep, though the sound of their cries plagued her mind as she dragged herself home.

The next morning, Dara waited outside. The air still carried the chill of the night and goosebumps crept up her arms, but she couldn't bring herself to go back inside the run-down, single-room house.

When the rumbling carriage arrived, pulled by four stout horses, the door creaked open behind Dara. The carriage was simpler than the one the Confessor had arrived in: a plain wood vehicle with no markings. Despite its humble appearance, the sight of the vehicle excited Dara, ready for it to take her away to a brighter future, one far from the mines.

The driver hopped down from her perch with a small chest under her arm. Wearing a simple knee-length tunic, a stout crossbow was slung across her back, with a pouch stuffed full of bolts at her side. The carriage driver marched past Dara, nodding lazily, and dropped the chest on the ground in front of her parents.

"As... as They speak," stuttered Dara's father.

"Right, yes, so we listen," replied the carriage driver. "Here's your due. We'll be off then."

The driver opened the door and motioned in. She leaned on the frame as Dara situated herself on the cushioned seat.

"It'll be about two days to the Academy of Ramaia. It's south of Stellburg. We'll be crossing open plains, as easy a ride as they come. Get comfortable, you'll be in there for the most of it."

The carriage driver slammed the door shut and climbed into her seat. Dara scooted over and opened the cloth blinds. Though she didn't expect a fond farewell from her parents, the sight of them huddled over the chest, laughing, crying, and cheering, pained her more than she thought possible.

A whip cracked and the horses neighed, setting off. Dara stared as her parents raised the chest, Guilders falling to the ground around them as they danced giddily like children, without a single gesture to their departing daughter. As the distance grew, they gathered up the fallen coins and then returned to their home, not seeing their daughter's feeble wave.

By the time Dara arrived at the Academy of Ramaia, curiosity had overtaken her sadness and contempt. Stepping out from the carriage, she could hardly believe the building she saw.

Two stories tall, with solid stone walls and tiled shingles, the building stretched hundreds of feet to the right and left. Small windows speckled the simple yet imposing walls, with nothing in the way of decoration. A forest grew in the distance and mountains stretched to the sky, but no other structure was in sight. A few more carriages rolled in, stopping in the field ahead of the arched entryway.

"It'll be your peers coming out from the other carriages. They time the mana drinking across Llendshold so each batch of Initiates arrive on the same day," said the carriage driver. "Quite a coordinated affair, getting you all here. Never as tidy when we take Initiates away."

"Taken away?" Dara asked. "Why are Initiates taken away?"

"I'm nothing more than a carriage driver. You'll figure that out on the inside, I reckon." The carriage driver pointed at Dara's simple cloth satchel, slung over her shoulder. "That all you brought? Not forgetting anything, are you?"

"This is it."

"Well, I'll be off then. I'm expected in Stellburg."

The carriage rolled away, leaving Dara standing alone in the field a few hundred paces from the Academy. She followed the stream of twenty Initiates hesitantly approaching the building. On the way, she took stock of their clothing; all the tunics extended to the knee or further, while Dara's tunic ended below her waist. Further, the tunics of even the most humbly dressed Initiates bore decorative stitching, while Dara's had not a single bit of color.

"You there. Are you a servant?" A boy wearing a tunic which stretched halfway down his calves pointed at Dara. "You must be a servant, wearing a tunic like that. Carry this."

Dara stared at the bags the boy foisted in her direction. The fine cloth had more decoration than anything she had ever seen in her hamlet, yet he swung the bags about as if they were filled with cow dung.

"You're mistaken. I'm an Initiate."

"An Initiate? You? Are they starting us with a joke, Jodrie?" called a girl, her shrill voice sending shivers up Dara's spine.

"They must be, Ffionin," followed Jodrie. "A lowborn like this at the Academy of Ramaia? This little girl must be lost."

Dara's shoulders tensed, and her face flushed. She glared at the boy, who was easily half a foot shorter than her, even accounting for his hair, which was pulled into tall, curly waves. His scrunched face reminded her of a shrew, with thick eyebrows and small eyes.

"Who are you to call me a little girl? Size aside, I doubt our ages are much different if we both recently passed the Test of Mana."

"'Little' doesn't only pertain to age, you simpleton," snorted Ffionin, her crooked teeth bared. The girl's light brown hair was rolled into tight curls, bouncing above her head. "She is right about one thing, though, Jodrie. She is about the same in build and appearance as an ox."

"The Confessor said we are all equals in the eyes of the Quinate," Dara muttered. "Don't we all have the right to learn? To become Mages, and count ourselves among the Quinate's Faithful?"

Laughter erupted at Dara's assertion, with Jodrie and Ffionin doubling over in mockery.

"A lie told to keep lowborn like you appeased, working and toiling in service of your betters," said Jodrie, all humor gone from his face. "You look surprised. Has something addled your brain? Have you perhaps been eating meat?"

"What?" Dara recoiled at the accusation. "I would never-"

Ffionin cut in front of her peer and stomped up to Dara's face. "Poor girl like you, huge as you are, probably can never get your fill. Little animals in the forest must have been tempting, you grotesque beast. Look at her hands! Ugly things they are; brutish, rough. You've done hard labor. I bet you've gone hungry plenty. What a trite idea, going hungry! What animals do you most enjoy eating? Rabbits? Weasels?"

Dara took a step back from the encroaching girl. "No, the Quinarium provides, I always-"

"You smell like dirt," said Jodrie, sliding out from behind Ffionin like a serpent peering around a tree. "Maybe she's telling the truth that she isn't a servant. Probably a farmer, with her hands stuck in the dirt every day."

"I *was* a miner."

A chorus of laughter broke out once again.

"What difference does it make?" Ffionin said, poking Dara in the shoulder. "Disgusting all the same; farms or mines, it matters not. Now we've suffered her presence for a moment, I don't think she smells of dirt so much as shit. Maybe she's been sleeping with horses."

"I'm tired of this. Servant or no, stop pretending you have the worth or right to speak to us openly or deny our commands," Jodrie said with a practiced callousness. "Take the bags. Not only mine, but all our bags. You've boasted about your size. Let's see how strong you really are."

The other Initiates complied, circling Dara and throwing their bags on the ground at her feet; the rhythmic thudding like drums beaten to a song of spite.

"Pick them up," Jodrie seethed.

"You all, stop mucking about! Get inside, now!"

The deep voice was crisp and harsh, instantly commanding attention. A dark-complexioned man stood at a window on the upper floor of the Academy, surveying the Initiates below. His face—with a hawkish brow, wide jaw, and slicked back hair—was emotionless. He wore a broad collar over his tunic, with a border of crimson spirals.

As the Initiates hastily grabbed their bags, Jodrie sneered at Dara. "You've been saved this time, but should you ever forget your place, I'll be there to remind you."

Dara scowled as she trailed behind the gaggle of Initiates heading into the Academy.

Passing through the entryway, they arrived in a round foyer, large enough for a hundred people to roam. An imposing statue cast in bronze, over twenty feet tall, dominated the heart of the space: a visage of the god Ramaia. The feminine face bore a neutral expression and had a mask over its eyes and forehead. A crown of chaotic tendrils radiated out from the god's head, each curl a different length and tipped with a red gem. Columns surrounded the foyer. A garnet banner, with white trim and a white teardrop at the center, hung from each. Black candelabras, positioned throughout, dimly lit the room.

From a door to the right, an Instructor entered. Dressed similar to the man in the window, she wore a tunic which was cut high at the center and flowed below her knees at the sides, with a wide collar. A gauntlet and two mana bottles hung from her belt. Her face was rosy and round, and she offered a toothy smile. Her booming, guttural voice quickly dispelled the notion of gentleness or kindness.

"You are in the Academy of Ramaia, house of the God of Blood," the Instructor boomed, pacing among the new arrivals. "This institution stands above all others, as Ramaia is the highest of the Quinate. With such station comes responsibility, a responsibility we will not let you forget. You *will* become Blood Mages, the greatest warriors in all of Llendshold. As They speak!"

"So we listen," the Initiates replied.

The Instructor paused her speech, staring into the eyes of an Initiate. The young boy wilted under the scrutiny, slouching and averting his gaze. With a huff, the Instructor continued her march, opening bags, grabbing chins and inspecting faces, sparing none. When the Instructor reached Dara, she inspected the girl from head to toe, then sighed audibly.

An impish chuckle broke the silence.

Striding over to Jodrie, the Instructor grabbed the front of his tunic and pulled him close until his face was inches from hers. "Who gave you permission to laugh?"

"It was a reaction, I simply thought…"

The Instructor pored over the boy's face. "I have not asked you to think, nor did I ask for your reaction to *my* work. You are here to listen."

As the Instructor's grip eased, Jodrie's face twisted. "I can't help it. Look at her!"

The Instructor lifted the boy until his toes barely touched the ground. "I was looking at her, as you put it, until you interrupted me. I care not who your father or mother are. Interrupt me again and there will be consequences."

"Y… Yes… what should I call you?"

Dara grinned at Jodrie's panic.

"You will learn and use my name only if you earn the privilege. As is the case with all Instructors." The woman shoved Jodrie away, nearly throwing him to the ground. "You are to address us by our title and our title only. Is that understood? All of you!"

"Yes, Instructor!"

While the Instructor resumed her patrol, Dara winked at Jodrie. He glared for a moment, diverting his head when the Instructor spoke again.

"In this Academy, we have a few simple rules. First, your presence and existence here are at the grace of your Instructors. Act as we command, or face punishment, potentially expulsion, should your behavior warrant it. Second, no one is to leave the grounds of this institution or enter the second floor unless at the direction of an Instructor. Third, and finally, causing harm to each other is prohibited, unless invited to by an Instructor during your training.

"Should you follow these rules and meet our exacting standards, an Instructor will recommend you for the Rite of the Faithful. Should you complete your rite, and we expect all sent from this Academy to do so on their first attempt, you will join the ranks of the Quinate's Faithful. Blood Mages act as protectors, guards, and soldiers, whether with the Quinarium or the armies of Llendshold, a duty you will conduct in a manner that makes this institution proud, and brings joy to the hearts of the Five.

"Now, I will turn this over to the Instructor who will be the face of your training in these coming days."

The man from the window sauntered out from behind the statue of Ramaia, his drooping eyelids exuding boredom.

"Don't trouble yourself with memorizing the schedule; Instructors will keep you on time and task. Each day's training encompasses three elements: physique, combat, and magic. There is also dedicated time for prayer, solitude, and to perform tasks to maintain this institution. There are separate dormitories for each group of Initiates. Yours is through the door to my right, head down the hall to the last door on the left. Deposit your belongings, change your tunics, and meet me in the yard. We begin today by honing your physique."

The Instructor's eyes dwelled on Dara as she walked by, prompting her to hasten her steps.

Once in the dormitory—a simple, long hall flanked by rows of cells separated by wooden dividers—Dara made for the furthest unoccupied space. A uniform, consisting of a simple tunic in the same form as the Instructors, a pair of trim brown trousers, a braided cord belt, and brown cloth shoes, sat neatly folded on a bed. Dara nearly squealed when she touched the clothing, the linen softer than any fabric she had ever held.

A chest and small table were the only other furnishings. An ewer of water and basin sat atop the table beside a small towel and a copy of *The Words of the Quinate*, the religious text distributed by the Quinarium. The wooden dividers provided the only form of privacy from each occupant's immediate neighbors, though the cells were open to those lining the opposite wall.

Dara dropped her satchel and changed quickly, wishing she could see herself in her new outfit. After splashing her face with water, she joined the Initiates funneling back to the main hall.

Once the Initiates had assembled, the Instructor led them to an outdoor yard surrounded by plain stone walls. An assortment of odd objects were scattered across the space, including huge round stones and smooth tree trunks of varying lengths and diameters. The Instructor faced the Initiates.

"Much of your early training will emphasize improving your physique. Strength, agility, control, these are all-"

"Why train like peasants if the power of Blood Magic will fuel us?" Ffionin interrupted.

Jodrie pushed to the front of the Initiates. "She's right. Is this not beneath us? We're in the highest of the Academies, yet we are to move around rocks and logs? What about magic?"

"She's right? Fine then. I will ignore your rudeness this once, and instead we shall test your assertion. Put this on."

The Instructor took a leather glove from a nearby table and threw it at Ffionin.

"A... a gauntlet?" she stammered, admiring the pliable cloth.

"I said to put it on."

The Instructor walked away as Ffionin chirped with glee. She yanked the gauntlet on, the cuff rising halfway up her forearm, but yelped when her fingers reached the tips. Her gloved hand shook as she clutched it to her chest.

Alarmed by the girl's pain, Dara curiously observed her peers' lack of reaction. She leaned to the nearest Initiate, hoping they wouldn't carry the same prejudice now that they all wore the same attire.

"Why did she scream?"

"Are you stupid?" the boy spat. "Oh, it's you, the lowborn. She's wearing a gauntlet. Did you not learn about gauntlets where you're from? There are spines in the fingertips, to release her blood so she can channel mana with a spell."

"She probably never saw a Mage until the Test of Mana," interrupted Jodrie. "Poor, poor little girl. I wager all of us brought poultices to numb the pain in our fingers. Shame, you'll have to deal with the pain on your own. You don't know much, do you?"

"It wasn't as if-"

"Go on, ask someone if they'll share theirs with you. Do it!"

Dara looked at Initiates, who all stared at her.

"Of course they won't," Jodrie continued. "No one wants to waste anything on you. Enjoy the pain. It's fitting for a lowborn."

"Silence, all of you." The Instructor's voice cut like a sickle through dry wheat. He unsealed a bottle of mana and poured a few drops into a pewter cup. "Drink."

Ffionin took the cup and greedily swallowed the mana. "What now?"

"Observe, and move as I do, reciting the words as I say them. Although you are untrained, there should still be a substantial effect." The Instructor moved as he spoke—he touched two fingers to his chin, then held his fist in front of his chest and finally waved his open hand over his chest. "Ramaia grant me speed."

Ffionin repeated the motions, though clumsily, and she stuttered more than once while reciting the spell.

"How disappointing. Your failure speaks of the quality of Initiates sent to us these days," drolled the Instructor. "Take off the gauntlet—I'll take care of this myself. With you empowered by my hand, we will have a proper show."

The Instructor put on his own gauntlet, showing not the slightest discomfort as the spines sunk into his fingertips. Following a swig of mana, he repeated the spell, waving at Ffionin instead of himself. A wispy halo of pale red hovered around her body for a second, then faded.

"Describe the sensation to your peers," ordered the Instructor.

Ffionin spoke so rapidly that the words were barely intelligible. "It is amazing! My blood is running wild. I feel unstoppable!"

"Your speech is uncontrolled—we will correct that in time. A proper mage can speak in measured tone while under the effects of such a basic spell, but here we are, jumping ahead. Why not give your peers a show? Run to the end of the field and back."

Ffionin took off like a horse raging over an open plain, crossing a hundred yards and returning in little more than half the time Dara thought possible.

The Instructor picked up two sticks, each about three feet long and an inch in diameter, suitable replicas for training swords. "Now, for the show. You asked why training of physique is important. Take one of these. Imagine it is your weapon. Strike me as many times as you are able, as hard as you wish. I am under no spell. Per your assertion, the task should be trivial."

Ffionin leapt forward. She feinted left and then right, her moves as quick as a trout darting in a stream. As she lunged, stick outstretched, the Instructor deftly stepped to the side and smacked Ffionin behind her knee. She stumbled to the ground with a gasp.

"Again."

Ffionin charged with the stick overhead. She slammed it down, but the Instructor comfortably dodged to the side. Swinging wildly, she ran after the Instructor, but he stayed well out of striking range as he backpedaled with ease. Finally he countered, parrying her stick and smacking the girl cleanly in the ribs as he stepped past. Ffionin cried out in pain, doubling over.

"Again!"

Ffionin breathed deeply, clutching her side, scowling at the Instructor.

"I gave you a command. Again!"

Unsteady and grimacing, Ffionin ran to a boulder. She kicked off the stone and soared through the air, fast as a diving hawk. The Instructor struck her hands as she flew past. Before she regained her balance, he kicked her leg, sending her rolling across the ground. He walked over and raised his stick.

Crack!

As she attempted to stand, he hit her back so mightily that his stick broke in two.

Ffionin squirmed on the ground, crying in agony as blood seeped through the back of her tunic. The Initiates stared, mouths agape, in silence. The Instructor threw aside his broken stick and faced the class.

"I trust you all have learned why we must train both in physique and combat. Blood Magic has limits. The spells you learn will augment and enhance you, but they cannot create perfection from the imperfect. You must develop your body and your mind to create a foundation upon which magic will blossom, as the Five intended." The Instructor sighed at Ffionin's groaning. "You there. Quit your babbling. Go to the infirmary if you must, but do not interrupt my lesson, which we are about to begin now that you have properly shamed yourself."

Dara sat alone in the canteen, hunched over her bowl of coarse porridge, studded with beans and roughly chopped vegetables, with a hunk of torn bread on the side. While older Initiates ate enthusiastically, many of her peers poked and prodded their food in revulsion. Dara hardly tasted the meal, entirely overwhelmed by her first day.

After the rebuke of Ffionin, the morning's training progressed without incident, though the running, climbing, tossing of logs, and rolling of stones were foreign compared to her work mining. The strain of combat training further exacerbated the aching of her muscles, though Dara found it enjoyable despite never having been in a fight before.

The day had ended with lessons on magic. The classroom session enthralled Dara, and her mind lingered on the experience. From selecting the gauntlet which hung from her belt to drinking mana and learning to draw the magical essence from her fingertips, it had all been intoxicating. Dara set her spoon down and looked at her hands, which just hours earlier had glowed with the power of mana. Itchy red dots stained her callused fingertips; she snorted at the other Initiates' worry over poultices, when the pain was far less than she had experienced in the mines.

Having eaten her fill, Dara examined the canteen, her gaze eventually landing on the Instructors' table. The same Instructor had taught all their lessons, and Dara found him staring intently at her. She looked away for a moment, not wanting to draw his attention. A cautious glance back found him still fixated.

Dara took her bowl to the kitchen then made her way back to the dormitory, head down to avoid the attention of Initiates and Instructors alike. She exited the canteen when a voice called out.

"Dara, a moment."

She froze in place. "Yes, Instructor?"

"Come with me."

Dara's head pounded, wondering what the Instructor could possibly want with her. She silently complied, tracing the Instructor's footsteps through a narrow doorway and up a spiraling staircase. He never glanced back, his steps reverberating through the drab, undecorated hallway. They passed a few other Instructors, none of whom had any reaction to the sight of their peer leading Dara in the upper level of the Academy.

The Instructor opened an unassuming door and entered. Dara paused outside, biting her lower lip.

"I didn't think an invitation was required when I already told you to come with me."

At the Instructor's behest, Dara entered. The room, more than twice as large as the house Dara grew up in, contrasted sharply with the rest of the Academy. Bookshelves lined one wall, stuffed with tomes, scrolls, loose parchment, and maps. Paintings of pastoral landscapes, surrounded by delicately carved frames, covered the opposite wall. Moonlight flooded the room through grand, floor-to-ceiling windows at the far wall. The Instructor sat at a wood desk with his back to the windows. With a wave of his hand, candles around the room burst into flame.

"Come closer." The Instructor tapped his foot until she neared to his satisfaction. "Stand up straight—you're a Human, not a frog."

Dara stood upright, lips pursed, hands clasped, eyes focused on the window pane over the Instructor's shoulder.

"Why are you here?"

Dara shook her head at the question. "I thought you would tell me, Instructor."

"Call me Okter," he said with a chuckle. "While in my office, you may address me directly as such. I don't ascribe to the silliness that is hiding our names. It does little to reinforce the balance of power, especially when I can hold a demonstration as I did this morning, don't you think? As for the question of why you are here, I don't mean in my office. I mean, why you are at the Academy of Ramaia?"

"When I drank the mana, the Confessor said-"

"That is what happened, not why you decided to drink, why you said yes."

Dara stared at the soft shoes covering her feet. Though dusty from training, they were immeasurably cleaner than if she had spent half a day in the mines. Her mind drifted to days past, how she hated being in the dark while the sun climbed high, hated the stench of pitch torches, hated how pickaxe handles wore smooth while her fingers grew rough, hated sharing a single room with her parents, hated that they always smelled of the mines, hated that they never showed her affection, hated...

"I see," Okter said knowingly. "You came here seeking escape. A good a reason as any, if not a touch uninspiring. Fine, I will train you. Here, in the evenings, as a supplement to the training of the day."

"Train me?" Dara crossed her arms. "I don't want pity. I want to earn my place."

Okter grinned. "Look at yourself. A young woman, barely old enough to lose the title of 'child,' with skin so pale it's as if you've never seen the sun and hands as tough as an old black-smith's. If I were to make a wager, and I am not one to waste my guilders frivolously, I would wager a hefty sum that you were a miner. I would further wager that you leapt at the opportunity to taste mana to save yourself, risk of death be damned. You already lost your childhood in the mines. How desperate were you to not lose your adulthood too?

"And so you are here now, and I have made an offer to you, which you question. Tell me, do you miss the smell of the mines? Do you miss going hungry? Do you miss being invisible? Did your hard work on its own help you rise above your station? Do you not want to be something more? I offer you the chance to seize your future and rise in a way you have never dreamed."

"The Quinarium provides," Dara mumbled.

"There is no need to lie to me. You and I both know that not all are provided for equally. Maybe the Quinarium supplemented your meager wages, kept you fed a few more days of the year, but it is far from sufficient. Did they see how hard you worked? No, because effort doesn't always lead to reward. Far more often those nasty, wealthy little idiots like those you met today, shit out from the wombs of petulant Lords and Earls and Elders, find success despite their lacking ability—unless they squander it away. You, however, you found the thing most needed for someone of your birth to succeed: luck. And what luck to find yourself at this Academy, with me as your Instructor. I saw your motivation today, and it was singular."

Dara's face burned at both the accuracy of the assessment and the cynicism. "It is pity, isn't it? Why else would you train me further? Were you also poor before you became a Mage? Reaching down to help another poor person rise, to feel better about yourself?"

A smile crept across Okter's face. "On the contrary, I am the son of an Earl. My childhood was one of ease, and my rise to a role such as this would have happened regardless of my capabilities, which are excellent."

"I... it's..."

"Before you answer, and I presume accept my offer, please understand that this will make your life harder. After grueling days spent training with your peers, long days will become longer still. You will find neither kindness nor affection in me. And yet, through my tutelage, ever pressed to rise higher, reach further, you will become powerful in ways you might otherwise only dare to dream of."

Dara stared at Okter. The Instructor made no attempt to hide his enjoyment, like a cat toying with a trapped mouse. "Why?"

"Have I not answered that question already? I grow bored of teaching idiots lacking both in ambition and talent. I want to tutor someone who is hungry, someone who yearns to be *more.*" Okter rose and walked to the front of his desk. "You seek escape, but I wonder if that might translate into motivation to become great. I see potential in you, Dara, and I would see it realized. Potential for what? I am not sure, but it makes me curious."

The word 'potential' repeated in Dara's head. A tear ran down her cheek. "I... I think yes."

"Oh, stop crying," Okter groaned. "Tears are for children. You are to become a Mage. I need a resolute answer, an absolute commitment. If you are only so invested as to consider my offer, then leave, and I will wait for a suitable Initiate to tutor."

Okter strode past Dara.

"Train me."

"Did you say something?" Okter said, his voice rising.

"Train me!" Dara yelled, fists clenched and neck strained forward.

Okter smiled, stopping by a shelf and taking down two glass bottles with liquid sloshing inside. "Take these. First is an oil, for your fingertips. Something actually useful, not those disgusting poultices which many Initiates insist on bringing with them. Second is a potion of revitalization. Take a sip, and only one sip, before sleeping. You'll be refreshed in the morning. I rarely condone this type of indulgence, but what you are about to embark on warrants it. We begin tomorrow."

The ensuing months flew by as Dara trained from first light until deep into the night. She learned to ignore the threats and insults of Jodrie and Ffionin, and in time they lost interest as Dara proved herself a capable student, accelerated by Okter's tutoring. The Instructor further imparted knowledge on a range of topics reaching far beyond magic. Through his tutelage, Dara broadened her understanding of Llendshold, from economics and trade to the intertwined nature of the Regency and the Quinarium.

Nearly a year passed when a voice roared into the dormitory one morning.

"Initiates, rise! Assemble in the Main Hall!"

Dara scrambled from her bed and pulled on her clothing. She eased into the mob which pressed through the doorway.

"What could they want?" asked a groggy voice.

"This kind of summon means one thing," replied Jodrie.

"We are ready for our rite!" squealed Ffionin.

In the Main Hall, Initiates crowded in front of the statue of Ramaia. An Instructor paced before them, hands behind her back, while other Instructors lined the perimeter of the room.

"One of you has earned the privilege of traveling to Stellburg, where you will present yourself before the Moderator. If he deems you worthy, then you will go on your rite, that you might count yourself among the Quinate's Faithful. For the other Academies, it is acceptable to be sent back without being assigned a rite. However, I expect all from the Academy of Ramaia to exceed the Moderator's expectations.

"The Rite of the Faithful will see you paired with an Initiate from another Academy. No matter who they are, no matter where they hail from, you *will* show them what it means to be a Mage of Ramaia, a wielder of blood!"

Okter stepped away from the walls. "Dara, gather your belongings. The carriage is waiting outside. Everyone else to the canteen."

Initiates frowned as they trudged away; Jodrie and Ffionin were too shocked to comment. Dara waited for further guidance but the Instructors, Okter included, left the hall.

Hurrying to the dormitory, Dara hastily stacked a few changes of clothes, then realized she had precious little else to take. Searching for a pack, she took out the satchel she had brought on her first day to the Academy. The coarse material felt strange, but lacking other options, she stuffed the clothing inside and left.

The carriage waited a short distance from the Academy. Dara enjoyed the warmth of the sun on her skin as she walked until Okter appeared from behind the carriage.

"You are more than ready," he said, opening the door.

"Are you hoping I will make you proud?" Dara quipped as she entered the carriage.

"Dara, it has never been about making me proud. This was all about you fulfilling your potential, which I believe you are prepared to do." Okter smirked and tilted his head down. "As They speak."

"So we listen."

Okter slammed the door shut and the carriage driver cracked his whip. Dara shut her eyes in quiet contemplation, the wheels grinding over the dirt road to Stellburg.

Chapter 3

Dara shook her head as the sounds of the rolling carriage faded. She opened her eyes and the emotionless silver mask of the Moderator greeted her.

"Return to your fellow Initiates," he said coolly. "Next, from the Academy of Seraeus, Keian."

Dara slinked down the steps, passing the next Initiate on her way. A sideward glance revealed fear and nervousness in his wide eyes and open mouth, a modest comfort following the Moderator's lack of comment on Dara's recounting.

Back among her peers, Dara stared at a flickering candle. Based on the melting wax, only a few minutes had passed while she stood before the Moderator. Questions plagued her. How could they have seen so many memories in so little time? What was the Moderator looking for? Had she done enough to move on to her rite? Had the additional training with Okter jeopardized the assessment?

The Moderator's voice broke her from the daze when he called for another Initiate. Feet shuffled and fingers dug at nail beds as the minutes crept by. Up and down, the Initiates flowed; Dara mindfully counted those surrounding her, and soon realized only one remained. Shoulders hunched, the final Initiate crossed her arms behind her back.

"It is time for the last of you," boomed the Moderator. "You know who you are. Come forward."

The girl nearly fell as she untangled her arms. Squeaking as she caught herself, all stared at her in silence. The Initiate brushed creases from her tunic and marched up the steps to the apse. Whether because the girl was the last or that she was the first Initiate the Moderator had not called by name, Dara found her curious. The light of the brazier illuminated her vibrant, olive-brown skin. Her face was soft-featured, with a rounded nose, full cheeks, and a high brow. Her shimmering hair ended in curls which bounced above her shoulders.

The Moderator folded his arms when she came to a stop. "Your name."

"My name? You said all the others' names," the girl said, her voice rich and smooth like warm honey. "I thought-"

"Your name."

"Wynne."

The Moderator laughed, a jarring reaction following his prior stoicism. "Why hide who you are, Llewelyn Pharadrax? Born to the Lord of Hantsburg, you are among her youngest, yet you are still the daughter of a Lord. You have no reason to shy from calling yourself by your proper name. How did the daughter of Brolwen Pharadrax come to study at the Academy of Ilsios, learning Flame Magic, the lowest of all?"

Wynne stood tall despite the trembling of her chin. "It was my choice."

"A choice, you say? I hope your presence here is not due to the influence of your mother. Although those who jaunt among Lords and Earls and even the Regent of Llendshold might be swayed by the words of your mother, only those truly worthy serve the Quinate through the Quinarium."

"I earned my place!"

The Moderator leaned close. "Then show me."

CHAPTER 4

Wynne's mind flew to a memory from a year prior. An unpleasant demand rang in her ears, as if she were reliving the moment again.

"Llewelyn Pharadrax, come here this instant!"

Wynne rushed down a long stone corridor. Guards stood at attention as she passed, while other servants bowed; more than one offered an encouraging nod or wink, all while her father's voice rang through the Citadel of Hantsburg. She burst into an expansive study. The sounds and smells of the ocean flowed in through tall, open windows lining the opposite wall. The deep blue stretched to the horizon, an entrancing sight that made Wynne pause and smile.

"What is this letter?"

Her father's voice reeled Wynne back. His brow furrowed, lines creased his forehead. His usually warm beige cheeks were puffed and cherry-red. He feverishly pulled at his waxed hair, leaving it a ruffled mess. As he paced back and forth, the tails of his long tunic flew up and down.

"Why am I holding a letter from the Quinarium, stating you are to train at the Academy of Ilsios? You are to learn *Flame* Magic? Tell me, Wynne, why does this say you are going to the lowest of the Academies? You are the daughter of a Lord!"

Wynne eyed the letter protruding from her father's clenched fist. "What is there to explain?"

"We can change this," he said, aggressively waving the letter. "It says the carriage won't be here for a few days. It's not too late, your mother has influence, connections in the Quinarium. Brolwen!"

"What if this is what I want?"

Wynne's father scowled. "What you want and what is right for you may not always be the same. You only think this is what you want—you are too foolish and young to know what you truly desire. Brolwen!"

Wynne scoffed. "Is it foolish that I want to help people? Going to the Academy of Ilsios is the best way for me to learn healing magic!"

"A Mage of Ilsios? The best way to help people?" Wynne's father snorted. "With your mother's influence, you could have become a Moderator. An Adjudicator, even! Helping others as a Mage of Ilsios... None from that accursed Academy have ever risen to a position of note. You may as well abandon thoughts of learning magic."

"You edge on blaspheming, Father! Ilsios is one of the Five. How can you call an Academy in his name accursed?"

"I decry the Academy, a construct of Humans, not the Gods themselves. And I am rightful in doing so. You aim to turn your back on the responsibilities of your birthright. In joining this Academy, you turn your back on the opportunity to rise to a higher station, to serve the Quinate in a greater way!"

Wynne gazed out to the white-capped waves surging across the ocean. "What if that isn't the future I want?"

"Now it is you who blaspheme with words against your family and for rejecting the highest form of service to the Five you might achieve. Your mother and I would have set you on a path to a position of respect, authority, power! You would squander the advantages of your birth, in pursuit of what?"

"I don't want power!"

Wynne's father breathed deeply. "You are the sixth of seven children. Your opportunities are limited, and a role within the clergy of the Quinarium would be far preferable to becoming a Mage, let alone one of Ilsios."

"I want to become my own person, born of my own efforts," Wynne said through grit teeth. "I want to earn my future. I don't want to hide beyond mother's position as Lord of Hantsburg and let her reputation carry me forever. She only became Lord because her parents were already Earls. Is it truly her accomplishment if her heritage did most of the work?"

"Don't you dare spit on the efforts of your mother!" Wynne's father raged. "She has done everything to create the life you enjoy. Her parents were the lowliest of Earls, yet she proved herself worthy of the title of Lord! You dare not speak ill of her without having accomplished anything yourself."

"That is what I am telling you I want to do! I want to achieve something on my own, without you!"

"Five above, this is what children are best at doing: lowering their parents into an early grave."

"Don't act so pained, Mother was the one who had to birth me."

"A petulant and reductive reply. I expect better from you."

The door to the study swung open.

"What is this commotion? What has caused two of my favorite people in all of Llendshold to sound as though they are ready to trade blows? Wynne? Mathrias?"

Wynne bowed her head with her arms crossed behind her back. Her father tapped his foot with his fists at his hips. Brolwen smiled at their flushed faces, raising her hands when they both began to speak. She snapped her fingers, and a servant hustled into the room.

"Bring us something to eat, please."

"Of course, my Lord."

Brolwen motioned to a table. "Shall we sit and talk, or should I call for weapons and armor, that you might settle this conflict another way?"

Wynne and her father plopped into chairs opposite each other and stared out the windows. Brolwen eased into a seat between the two. She placed her hands over Wynne's, drawing her daughter back into the room. A tear rolled down Wynne's cheek. Wrinkles formed at the corners of Brolwen's eyes as she smiled.

"Who would like to begin?" she asked, her voice reassuring.

Mathrias thrust the letter at Brolwen. "Read this."

After digesting the brief letter, Wynne's mother gently folded the paper, then placed it on the table. "Wynne?"

"I..." Faltering under the scrutiny of her parents, Wynne exhaled slowly, then restarted. "I sent a letter to the Confessor, requesting to partake in the Test of Mana. After, I asked if she might recommend that I attend the Academy of Ilsios. She agreed."

"Did you not speak with your father first?"

"No."

Mathrias shifted in his seat. "I told you. For years I have told you, Brol! We did not do enough to rein in Llewelyn's petty antics, her little explorations, avoidances of decorum. I told you there would be ramifications one day. I told her too!"

A servant arrived with a platter of soft and hard cheeses, glass dishes filled with honey and jams, fermented berries, and finely sliced bread.

"Thank you," Brolwen said as the servant bowed and departed. She neatly spread soft cheese on a piece of toast, then set a dollop of jam on top. "Wynne, your father has always been the one responsible for your care."

"Servants raised me as much as him!"

"We have taught you not to condemn those whose circumstances you do not fully understand, which includes your father," cut Wynne's mother. "He has devoted himself to you and your siblings, besides his extensive duties as partner to the Lord of our fine city. And you, dear. You still believe the storm, don't you?"

Mathrias squirmed in his seat. "Of course I do."

"I don't think we ever told you of this, Wynne."

Wynne's father sighed. "Llewelyn, I sincerely regret what you are about to hear."

"Don't be childish. She is more an adult now than we were on the day we married. Wynne, the night you were conceived, there was a storm the likes of which hadn't been seen in an age. The Confessor came to us that morning and told us not to conceive, that if we had a child born of the storm, it would be cursed."

"And of course you wouldn't listen to the Confessor, incorrigible woman. We should have called for a Mage of Seraeus."

Mathrias winked at Brolwen, who kissed in his direction.

"Mother! Father! Why are we talking about this!?"

"I speak of the storm that you might understand his superstition," Brolwen laughed. "Anyway, it's your father's fault for being an attractive man. What can I say but that it was an exciting time? Besides, he is the one who believes in a ridiculous curse, not me. The Moderator dismissed it as ridiculous as well."

"I trust the Confessor! His station may be lower than that of the Moderator, but can you deny where we are now? That curse which has led us precisely to this moment," Mathrias said. "A curse which has convinced Llewelyn to throw her life away to study *Ilsios*. Brolwen, you can change this. While the Moderator of Stellburg is responsible for the Academies, if you spoke with the Moderator here in Hantsburg, they both would have to consider the word of the Lord. You are their peer, equal in governance to their position in the Quinarium."

"Wynne, is this truly what you want?" Wynne's mother asked.

"Please tell me you aren't entertaining this? That you aren't allowing our daughter to throw her life away?"

"I asked her a question, not you."

A shiver ran down Wynne's spine at the icy response, while her father dug a spoon into a bowl of jam. Her mother took a bite of toast and leaned back in her chair.

"This is how I believe I can best serve the Five. It's what I want to do. It's the future I imagine for myself."

Brolwen nodded to Mathrias. "You can't catch a fish by squeezing your hands tightly around it—the fish will only slip away. If I followed my father's guidance, I would still be the lowest of Earls and not Lord. We would do well to remember how our own initiative served us."

Wynne's mouth dropped open. "Does this mean...?"

"Yes."

A few days later, Wynne strolled through the cobbled streets of Hantsburg with her mother. Four guards marched close behind, round shields on their backs and swords hanging from their hips. Residents of the city bowed as they passed; Wynne's mother spent as much time smiling, waving, and asking people how they were as she did speaking to her daughter. They reached the gate after nearly a half day of walking down from the Citadel; the Quinarium carriage waited outside. Brolwen stopped and embraced Wynne.

"I'm sorry about your father."

"It's alright," Wynne said, forcing a smile. "I expected him to be this way."

"You know he loves you. And not only that—keep this between us—he loves you more than any of your brothers and sisters. It's why he is bitter at your departure."

"I wish he would support me the same way he loves me. What is the point of loving someone so much if you never show it?"

Brolwen chuckled. "He will show you his love, in time. For now, be well."

A salty breeze swept through the city.

"Do you think I'm making a mistake?" Wynne asked.

"It doesn't matter what I think. You are of the age where your choices are your own." Brolwen placed a thin silver bracelet around Wynne's wrist. "Now is the time for you to do what you believe is right, my daughter. You have a wonderful mind, brimming with kindness and curiosity. Be yourself, and you will always make me proud, no matter whether or not I agree with your decisions."

After greeting the carriage driver, Wynne climbed in, carrying nothing more than a satchel slung across her shoulder. She waved farewell, her mother and the guards briefly returning the gesture before returning to the city, where a growing crowd waited to greet their Lord.

The road soon turned away from the coast. As the ocean faded from view, the rolling of the carriage wheels over cobbled roads replaced the crashing of waves. Though Wynne had traveled to other villages and cities before, it had only ever been for brief excursions. Knowing she would be away for months, if not years, she already longed to feel the sand beneath her feet and the wind against her face. Wynne's thoughts shifted to her father, hoping that perhaps she might one day make him proud.

The carriage pulled to an abrupt stop, jostling Wynne awake. The door opened, and the driver motioned for her to exit.

"Welcome to the Academy of Ilsios."

"Thank you!"

Wynne bounded from the carriage onto a grassy field a few dozen yards from the Academy. The word eclectic came to her mind, with a two-story, sandy stone structure that had clearly been expanded many times over the years. Spires of varying heights jut out from around the incoherent maze of extensions. The amber roof shingles matched the orange suns on white banners hanging from the walls.

Though foreign compared to the coast, Wynne found the surrounding landscape captivating. Tall mountains with snowy tops rose into the sky to the north and east. A large forest grew to the south, with a stream trickling out from it and into the vale to the west.

The carriage driver wasted no time; the snap of reins sent the horses into a trot. Wynne eagerly watched the other Initiates exit their carriages, though her joyful anticipation swiftly faded. She instinctively grabbed at her clothes on seeing her arriving peers; the hem of her tunic stretched down past her knees, further than any other. She wished she could have hidden the opulent stitching along its border, with gold threads woven among rich purples and warm reds.

The wide wooden doors of the Academy swung open, and a man stepped out. Wearing the tunic of an Instructor, with red and orange epaulets, he waved for the new arrivals to enter.

Wynne skipped ahead, but froze when she noticed her peers glaring at her. She smiled, but cold faces were the only response.

Hoping the reactions were driven by nerves, or perhaps that she was over-interpreting the expressions, Wynne tarried, entering the Academy last.

Once all were inside the octagonal foyer, the Instructor closed the door. Windows circled the room near the roof, with ample sunlight supplemented by candles and torches placed throughout the room. A statue of Ilsios was fixed to the wall overlooking the entrance; cast in bronze, the masculine face had a helm covering its eyes and ears, with flame-like extensions radiating out, each covered in white and yellow gems.

"Welcome!" said the Instructor cheerily, walking among the Initiates and squeezing their shoulders, his wispy gray hair flowing behind. "Welcome, Initiates of Ilsios. I hope your travels were pleasant. I am Harlen, one of your Instructors. I speak on behalf of my colleagues when I say we are overjoyed to have you with us. You all are here owing to the most beautiful gift, an attunement to mana. We are here to help you cultivate and grow that gift, that you might serve the Quinate through the Quinarium."

Harlen stood beneath the visage of Ilsios as he continued. "We have a few simple tenets to keep in mind. First, healing magic is central to the studies of Ilsios. You are strictly prohibited from intentionally harming each other to practice. Second, all Initiates here are equal as we are all equal in the eyes of the Five. We encourage you to bond with older Initiates, that you might learn from them and they might refine their skills in teaching you. Third, the word of the Instructors is final. We are here to encourage you and guide your learning, but we are also the authority within these walls.

"As this is your first day, it will be a day of leisure. Try on your new tunics, explore the grounds, take a bath and relax after your long travels, visit the library or take a horse out for a ride, whatever will help you settle in. You will be here for months, possibly years, before you are selected for your rite—we would like you to be comfortable. Dormitories are through the door to my left, and Instructors and Initiates alike will be glad to help you should you need direction. Welcome to the Academy of Ilsios!"

Most of the Initiates made for the dormitories, and Wynne followed. Wooden partitions lined either side of the residence hall. Nameplates displayed room assignments; Wynne pulled aside a privacy curtain hanging in front of her space. She smiled at the quaint alcove.

A double-bed topped with a plush mattress sat at one side of the room, with a chest of drawers on the opposite side. A table with chairs and a neatly arranged set of candles atop was positioned at the back wall. Wynne dropped her satchel and eagerly picked up the clothing, ready to blend in with her peers.

She emerged from her room and spied a nearby group of Initiates. Awkward pauses punctuated their conversation. Wynne stepped forward, hoping she might join them without judgement now that they all wore the same attire.

"Hello, I'm..."

Before she could finish her greeting, the Initiates turned and left.

Wynne shook her head, keenly aware of the sweat on her forehead and the tension building in her neck. She spied another group of Initiates and strolled over, but they all walked away at her arrival.

Standing with her arms crossed behind her back, Wynne blinked away tears. Being the daughter of a Lord had made it difficult to find friends in Hantsburg—worsened by parasitic Earls pushing their children to befriend Wynne in hopes of getting closer to her mother—but never had she been abandoned so brusquely.

Wynne sighed in relief when a boy walked over. "Hello, I'm Wy-"

The boy raised his hand. "I don't need your name. It's just that... I felt bad seeing you alone."

Wynne's brow furrowed. "I don't understand. Why are they fleeing as if I were an Ogre?"

"Are you serious, or are you playing me for a fool?"

"Of course not. I wish I knew what everyone else seems to know about me," she said, arms still behind her.

The boy sighed. "Everyone saw your tunic before. It doesn't matter that we're dressed the same now. Most of us are only modestly attuned to mana, and coming to the Academy of Ilsios is a dream that we can scarcely believe is real. For the daughter of a Lord to study here instead of at the Academy of Ramaia, or at least of Kosrya or Seraeus... they all think your family must be why you are here, if you're attuned to mana at all."

"That isn't what happened, I promise you. I chose-"

"Good luck," the boy said, leaving the dormitory.

Wynne stood alone, lost in the quiet.

"Brimming with kindness and curiosity," she murmured. "I could use a freshening up."

Wynne marched to the bathhouse.

The space was wide open, with ten raised stone baths spaced along one wall. Warm water poured in from spigots, trickling over the edge and into channels which disappeared into the floor. Used to privacy in the Citadel of Hantsburg, Wynne surveyed the space in search of solitude, grateful to see only a few others. Moving to the back corner, she slipped out of her uniform and into a bath.

The warm water was both refreshing and relaxing. Wynne sunk in until only her face floated above the surface, dulling all sounds. She inspected the cracks and mars in the ceiling, tracing each with her eyes as if she were getting to know the building as her friend. Unmoved until her hands and feet wrinkled like sun-dried tomatoes, she finally pulled herself from the water, grateful to find the bathhouse empty.

Roaming the halls, Wynne politely bowed to all she passed, though it was impossible to ignore when a group of new Initiates dropped their voices to hushed whispers and turned their backs to her. Faltering under their side-eyed stares, Wynne retreated to an empty room.

Once inside, a smile spread across her face. Rows of tables with benches were arranged in an arc facing the front of the study. Paintings and diagrams with ancient symbols adorned the walls. Books, pouches, bottles, gauntlets, and more crammed shelves. Though the room was disorderly, bordering on chaotic, Wynne found it calming. She drank in the smell, an intoxicating aroma which reminded her of kitchen stores stocked with dried herbs. Wynne sat at a desk, imagining the lessons she might learn in the coming days. Once her imagination had run its course, she made for the gardens.

Double-doors opened to an expansive outdoor space surrounded by columns topped with lintels, but no roof. Ten-foot-tall, manicured hedges sectioned off areas filled with themed plantings. Wynne passed one containing squat plants with long stems which ended in pink and white flowers the size of her palm. Another section brimmed with herbs, the smell leaving her curious as to what dinner might be.

Finding a space home to short trees sporting red blooms, Wynne lay on a bench. Her mind roamed as pleasant breezes flowed through the garden and the sun warmed her face.

Wynne had nearly dozed off when a ferret leapt onto her stomach. It spun in a circle, then sat beside her, its tail flitting about.

"Hello, nice to meet you," she said, sitting up and petting the ferret on its head. "I'm Wynne. Should we be friends? I'm going to be here for quite some time and I would appreciate your company."

As if her words were an invitation, the ferret ran up her arm, circled her neck, and ran down her other arm, its nails tickling her all the way. The ferret flopped to its back and patted its own belly. Wynne laughed and complied with the ferret's demand for attention.

"Are you alright?"

Wynne jumped at the voice, nearly launching the ferret from her lap.

A middle-aged woman with dusty tan hair eased into the secluded space. "My apologies, I didn't mean to startle you. I thought I heard you speaking to someone?"

"Oh! Erm..." Wynne stammered, attempting to wrangle the squirming ferret in her arms. "I am the only one here, well, not the only one. I found this lovely creature. Thank you for asking. I am alright though."

"I see you have found Reggie. If you ask around, everyone will call him a right nuisance, but secretly, we all love him." The Instructor held her hand out and Reggie ran up her arm then leapt into a nearby tree. "He can be quite selective about who he spends his time with. The picky boy has taken a liking to you. How are you settling in?"

"I am doing quite well, thank you."

The woman peered into Wynne's eyes. "I'm Sionan. I am the Instructor assigned to teach your first class tomorrow. You can be honest with me."

"Oh, my manners. I'm Wynne," she replied.

"I see. Llewelyn is a bit much of a name outside courts and lofty halls, isn't it? No need to be ashamed of where you come from or who you are. We are all equals under the gaze of the Quinate."

Wynne sighed. "The other Initiates are of a different opinion. It's not as though I chose to be born into that life."

"What I am about to say is not to excuse or justify such behavior. But you must recognize, no matter your intent, that those young people, they have envied everything you've had for the entirety of their lives. Unable to see what you've seen, not taking the time to understand who you are, they are allowing their insecurities, their anxieties, their fears to infect their behavior. You are the most different of the new arrivals and the easiest to rally against. Focus on your studies, be patient, and they will lessen their judgement in time."

"Thank you," Wynne said softly.

"No thanks required. I look forward to seeing you tomorrow."

Initiates sat in twos and threes at tables throughout the classroom. Sitting alone in the back corner, Wynne picked at a loose splinter of wood on the table where a ray of sunlight landed. Determined to free the sliver, she picked and dug and pried until the door swung open with a creak and Sionan strode in.

Wynne jumped to her feet. When the other Initiates broke into laughter, the Instructor raised her hand.

"Customs vary from place to place. I will remind you that the Quinate welcomes us all, as we must welcome each other no matter our differences." The Instructor gripped the sides of the podium while Wynne retreated into her seat. "I am Sionan, and it is my pleasure to welcome you to your first day of lessons. In the coming days, you will learn all manner of spells, though healing is a central focus.

"Mages of Ilsios, or more colloquially Flame Mages, serve in many roles within the Quinarium: some act as healers, whether in Sanctuaries or Temples or traveling to remote places; some act as officiants, sealing edicts and contracts of Lords and Merchants alike; still others join with Paladins, supporting them in protecting the Quinarium and the people of Llendshold. Whatever your destiny, we Instructors are here to ensure you are ready."

Sionan motioned to rows of gauntlets beside a neat stack of mana bottles on a nearby table.

"Come, take a bottle of mana and a gauntlet of your choosing. There are both right- and left-handed gauntlets, and a few different sizes and colors, if you have a preference between red, orange, or yellow. Oh, and you will have plenty of time to explore which hand you prefer for casting spells—some prefer to use their dominant hand, while others their off-hand. As They speak."

"So we listen."

Initiates eagerly pressed forward, but Wynne patiently waited until most had made their selection. On her way to the table, she locked eyes with Sionan, who gave her an encouraging nod. Though Wynne was the last to choose, a wide range of gauntlets remained. She took a pale orange gauntlet, then hurried back to her seat.

"Although many of you may already have some understanding of the fundamentals of magic, I will start with a brief primer, to ensure you all can begin with an equal footing. Casting a spell consists of four elements. First, drinking mana, the substance which carries the Gods' blessing and allows us to perform these miraculous acts. Second, the donning of the gauntlet. Prongs inside will pierce your fingertips, allowing mana to flow from your body as you cast spells. Third, the words of the spell. The incantation is a call to the Gods, and your words are crucial to drawing forth mana. Fourth, the motion of your gauntleted hand. Your movements, in concert with the words you say, dictate how the spell takes life. When done properly, you wield the very blessing of the Quinate."

Sionan inspected each face in the room.

"Despite the grandeur of magic, don't be intimidated. Today we will start simply. As I am sure you have noticed, there are candles on every table. Bringing flame to a candle is the first step in learning to harness the power of Ilsios's light. A side note, it is markedly easier to cast spells of flame when you are in the sun's light, drawing on Ilsios's domain. Enough talking from me! On with your gauntlets, please. I recommend a gentle touch until your fingers line up with the points, then a swift pull."

Sionan donned her gauntlet in a smooth motion; as the Initiates followed suit, they cried out in a chorus of gasps and groans. Wynne quietly observed, noting those who followed the Instructor's guidance were in markedly less pain than those who hesitated at the final stretch. Wynne exhaled, and slipped her hand into her gauntlet, then pulled tightly. A squeak broke from her lips as the cold points pierced her skin, staining the tips of the gauntlet red.

"After this session, I will distribute ointment to ease the pain. In time, you will hardly notice the discomfort. And you need not worry about cleaning the gauntlet; of mana's many wondrous properties, it will cleanse any blood which stains the fabric." Sionan raised a bottle of mana and took out its stopper. "Next, a sip of mana. And please, take one sip only. Mana is a precious resource, and a sip should be enough for a morning of practice. We need not overindulge—the quantity of mana consumed matches the intensity of the spell, and for lighting candles, a modest amount is sufficient. Drinking in excess is not only wasteful, but it will leave you jittery for hours."

Wynne took hold of the bottle and loosed the stopper. An intoxicating smell oozed out, like the door of a bakery filled with freshly iced sweet rolls had swung open, like stepping out of a carriage and into a field of flowers on a warm spring afternoon. Wynne took a sip and closed her eyes. Heat flooded her body. The invigorating sensation spread from her mouth to her chest, then through her arms and legs. Even the blood pooling in the tips of her gauntlets enrobed her fingers in warmth.

Sionan smiled at the expression of wonderment painted on the Initiates' faces. "Such is the blessing of the Five. If you all are ready, we shall continue. Putting on your gauntlets and drinking mana have no particular requirement for dexterity or timing. Casting a spell, however, requires precision. You must speak the words and complete the hand motions properly, together, or else your spell will fail. The words of this spell are simple: *Ilsios, grant me your light.* The motions for this spell are as follows: five fingers pointed upwards, close your hand and bring your fist to your chest, then point two fingers to the candle."

Sionan performed the spell, and a candle on her podium came to life.

"The morning is for you to practice. I am here to provide guidance and answer questions."

Needing no further invitation, the Initiates set about lighting their candles. Sionan roamed between tables to provide critiques and suggestions on everything from pacing of words to the positioning of arms. Wynne was initially content to watch, but as Sionan neared, she breathed deeply and readied to mimic the instruction. As she cast the spell, sparks crackled along the wick of the candle. Wynne held her breath until a flame billowed to life.

"Well done," said Sionan. "However, as with all things, practice is the path to mastery. Please put out your candle and continue. You may notice the spell becoming more difficult as you exhaust the mana you consumed. In which case, you are welcome to take another sip."

Wynne gleefully extinguished the candle with a small metal cap, ready to light it anew as the last curls of smoke faded.

Though Wynne did not become fast friends with any of her fellow Initiates, over the months she at least found herself accepted as a peer. She still longed to hear the oceans of Hantsburg, but days spent practicing magic gave her purpose and brought her joy.

One sunny day, Reggie leapt into Wynne's lap while she lay on a bench in the gardens. She adjusted her book that she might read while rubbing his belly.

"A rather complicated spell," came a woman's voice.

"Sionan," Wynne said, sitting up and setting her book aside. "I know such spells are beyond my ability, though I enjoy reading about them."

The Instructor swirled her finger around Reggie's nose until the ferret pounced onto her hand and ran up her arm, coming to a rest about her neck. "You shouldn't limit yourself to reading."

Wynne looked down to her feet. "Are these spells not too difficult for an Initiate?"

"I believe I described the spell as complicated, not impossible. Your hesitance has surprised me, Wynne. I see such potential in you, such desire for more. Yet, you hold yourself back. You still carry doubts. If you forever limit yourself, you will never reach the height of your potential."

"Coming here hasn't been easy."

"Such changes are never easy. I can only guess what motivated you, but in dedicating yourself to your studies, you have made a place for yourself here. See, Reggie agrees." The ferret curled into Wynne's lap as the instructor stared at the mountains in the distance. "Though this place will soon be in your past."

Wynne froze. "What do you mean?"

"I recommended you and Ellis for the Rite of the Faithful some weeks ago, and a carriage is already on its way. You will go to Stellburg, where the Moderator will evaluate you and see if he agrees with my assessment."

Wynne nearly jumped from the bench. "The Rite of the Faithful? Do you truly believe I'm ready?"

Sionan grinned and nodded. "I wouldn't recommend you if I didn't have complete confidence that you are ready for your rite. It is unfortunate, but the Academy of Ilsios is under constant scrutiny, being perceived as the lowest of the five Academies."

"Is this because of my mother?"

"It would be a lie to say your lineage was not considered, but the scrutiny exists regardless of an Initiate's history. But that is not your worry to carry. It is time for you to pack."

"When am I to leave?"

"Today. The carriage should be here in a few hours. I understand this is sudden, but it is the way the Quinarium prefers to conduct this process."

"I can't possibly thank you enough for..." Wynne's voice trailed off.

"Words escaping Wynne. I am fortunate to have experienced this," Sionan laughed. "If you wish to thank me, shine the light of Ilsios upon all of Llendshold. That is all the thanks I will ever need."

Back in her quarters, Wynne mindfully placed her belongings into a plain bag, leaving behind the packs she had brought from Hantsburg. Putting on the silver bracelet her mother gave her, she stepped out from her alcove. She found Ellis looking around the dormitory, from floor to ceiling.

"Are you alright?" Wynne asked.

"No," Ellis replied. "I'm scared, Wynne. Not everyone had a happy life before coming here. I'm going to miss this place."

Wynne smiled as best as she was able. "Well, as Mages, we will have the power to change things for the better."

"You think anyone has that kind of power?"

"I do. It's why I became a Mage and learned Ilsios's way."

"Good for you."

Ellis left the dormitory, leaving Wynne alone.

CHAPTER 5

"Stand with the other Initiates."

Wynne hurried away from the Moderator, taking a position at the rear of the waiting crowd. The Initiates glanced about, avoiding eye contact, while the Moderator and the Mage spoke in hushed whispers. Wynne closed her eyes and recited rules of etiquette in her mind. She had no use for the old lessons while at the Academy, yet she still found comfort in the memories of learning them in Hantsburg.

The brazier crackled and spat as a log disintegrated inside. The Moderator finally nodded to the Mage then drifted back to the lectern.

"Twelve came to us today. Eight will move on to their rites. Those who are not called, remember there is no shame in returning to your Academies. Train well, and I will see you again in due time. Those fortunate eight, you will be called in pairs to receive further instruction from one of my Aides. As They speak!"

"So we listen."

The Moderator left as four Aides arrived. They wore simple clothing—cream-colored tunics absent any decoration, with a hood covering the upper half of their faces and draped over their shoulders. The first Aide, a tall woman with rosy lips, approached the lectern.

"Dara. Wynne. Follow me."

Beaming at being paired with the sole Blood Mage, Wynne scurried up the stairs to the apse. On the way, she peeked over out of the corner of her eye. Dara was half a head taller than Wynne, her face stoic. Wynne thought her profile bold, and ogled at Dara's curiously pale skin, a shade rarely seen in Hantsburg where residents spent their days in the warm coastal sun. A bold jaw and pronounced eyebrow ridge framed round cheeks. Dara looked over, catching Wynne staring at her. Wynne's face blushed cherry-red, and she snapped her head forward.

The two followed the Aide through a simple wooden door at the back of the apse. They walked down a long hall until the Aide entered a room. As the Aide took her place at a desk opposite the two Mages, Dara surveyed the space. A few scattered candles cast a dim light over the bare walls. Aside from the desk, there was only a single table and no chairs. Two large packs, belts with mana bottles, a sword, hooded cloaks, and a few other items were arranged neatly on top. The Aide spread a map on the table, mindfully pressing the corners flat. Most curious was the smell of spring flowers, which Dara soon realized came from Wynne.

"If I may," Wynne said, leaning over the table, "might I ask how the Moderator selected us? What was the Moderator assessing? And will we find out who of the other Initiates are continuing on their rite?"

The Aide sighed. "You have no need for the answers to any of those questions. It is time to focus on your rite. If you are successful, you will be ordained as members of the Quinate's Faithful, the most dedicated of servants in the Quinarium. You two have been selected for a unique rite, one which is sure to challenge you. As Initiates of the highest and lowest Academies, and of disparate origins, the Moderator is most curious to see how you progress. Mages must work together as one in the Quinarium—it is essential that you complete the Rite of the Faithful together, or it is not complete at all."

The Aide planted a finger on the map over the Nomridian Forest, to the north of Llendshold.

"As for your rite... what do you know of Imreia?"

Dara looked at Wynne before responding. "Nothing."

The airy gentleness of Dara's voice took Wynne aback. When the Aide faced her, she spoke.

"A specter. A shadow. A horror and defiler of the Five. A tyrant who leads a secretive crusade against the Quinarium, and all who worship the Quinate."

The Aide grinned. "You speak of the embellished rumors which have spread far. I assure you, Imreia is as real as you and I. The daughter of an ousted, heretical family, she is a powerful mage capable of performing all five types of magic. She uses her substantial ability to upheave our peaceful way of life."

"Is our rite to face Imreia?" Dara asked.

"That would be a death sentence, not a rite," the Aide replied. "Imreia has been sighted in the Nomridian Forest, lands which the Fae live on by the generosity of the Llendshold Regency. Meanwhile, strange beasts have attacked the neighboring village of Cauldhill, purportedly at her behest. The power and behavior of these shadowy creatures fuel rumors that they feed from a mana source: a preposterous notion that mana flows freely from the ground."

"Mana source?" Wynne's face scrunched. "I thought mana can only be crafted through the Harvest Ceremony, from those who gift the last moments of their lives to the Quinarium? How could something like this mana source exist?"

"It does not," said the Aide. "As you say, only Agents of the Quinarium, as blessed by the Quinate, can harvest mana. As such, your task is twofold: first, destroy whatever beast or beasts are harassing Cauldhill, and second, investigate the source of the rumors and find out what has led to the spread of these baseless lies, as I assure you Imreia's involvement is an impossibility."

Wynne's mouth fell open. "Are you certain this is our rite? I can hardly believe such a task... this is monumental."

The Aide exhaled slowly. "This is your Rite of the Faithful, as assigned by the Moderator himself."

"Where are we to begin?" Dara asked.

"In Cauldhill. Maren, the Elder, and Uldrik, the Confessor, have sent many a panicked message to the Moderator. Their fears are fueling the rumors of this mana source. Stop the attacks on the village, uncover the origin of these rumors, and end this mindless worry about a ridiculous, nonexistent source. Once you have successfully completed both tasks, you are to return to Stellburg and report directly to the Moderator."

"When are we to depart?" chimed Wynne, eyeing the readied packs.

"A carriage waits; you are to leave without delay. It will take a few days to reach Cauldhill. There should be a sufficient supply of mana, clothing, and other supplies you might need, and the carriage is stocked with food and water. Each bag contains a pouch of Guilders as well, should you desire to purchase other supplies in Cauldhill. Any other questions you have will be answered by Maren and Uldrik. Travel well. As They speak."

"So we listen."

The carriage came to an abrupt stop, rousing Wynne. Rays of morning sun pierced the drapes covering the windows. Wynne blinked sleep away to find Dara awake, hand on the door. She pressed it open and stepped out in a single motion, leaving Wynne alone, yawning in the carriage.

A forest greeted Dara. Despite the bright sun, a dense fog darkened the understory. A pungent odor emanated from within, assaulting Dara's nose despite being some fifty yards away. The dry, aged mustiness reminded her of the mines, but with an overtone of dirt and decaying leaves. Though the trees towered higher than the spires of the Academy of Ramaia, they were all dead. Vines covered them, crisscrossing between the stout trunks like spiderwebs. All throughout, mushrooms, ferns, moss, and wiry shrubs grew on standing and fallen trees alike.

Dara inspected the road they had traveled on: behind, it wove between foothills of mountains on one side and hilly fields on the other; ahead, it continued along the forest's edge as far as she could see.

Wynne emerged from the carriage as the driver hopped down.

"Why have we stopped?" Dara asked.

The carriage driver rubbed his thick mustache and stretched his mouth, then spat. "Breakfast."

Wynne expected Dara to react poorly to the rude driver, but she walked back to the carriage without comment.

"We should change into our new tunics," Dara said softly.

"Right!" Wynne chirped. "They felt heavy. I haven't seen tunics like them before."

"They have armored padding woven in. We trained in similar ones at the Academy of Ramaia," Dara replied. "Flexible and light, but quite protective."

Dara unclasped her belt and tossed it into the fluffy grass beside the road. She undid the wooden toggles, which ran halfway down the front of her tunic, then took hold of the hem. Dara readied to pull the garment over her head when she noticed Wynne staring.

Wynne flinched. "Oh, you can use the carriage and change first, if you prefer."

"Why? It's cramped in there. We're only changing tunics—you can keep your undergarments on. I don't think he cares, either."

They looked over to the carriage driver, whose back was to the Mages. He already had a fire crackling in a shallow pit. Whistling off-tune, he dumped crudely chopped vegetables into an iron pan.

"Or would you prefer not to change in the presence of a lowborn? I know little of the customs of Lords," Dara said flatly.

Wynne's cheeks flushed. "I am not a Lord! And my family is in my past. And... you should stop calling yourself lowborn. No one is better or worse because of who their parents are. Have you forgotten that you're a Blood Mage? In the eyes of the Quinarium, you are my superior!"

Dara scoffed. "It's not like I chose to study at the Academy of Ramaia. I was just happy to become a Mage."

Before Wynne could protest further, Dara took off her tunic and knelt to fold it on the grass. Wynne stormed to the other side of the carriage and quickly changed, mumbling under her breath all the while. Her fury waned as she stretched in the new tunic. Despite the heft of the quilted fabric, it flexed with ease around her shoulders and waist. It curiously had no markings of the Quinarium; Wynne wondered if decorated tunics might wait until after they completed their rite. She cinched her belt and eased back around the carriage.

Wynne had hardly rounded the vehicle when Dara snatched Wynne's folded tunic and tossed it into the carriage. Wynne huffed in protest, but Dara ignored her and went to the carriage driver.

He had overloaded the pan, and his stirring sent beans and grains and crudely chopped vegetables tumbling into the fire. The sickly sour odor burned their noses, but the food looked passable, if not enticing.

"Food's ready," the man grumbled, setting the pan on a rock beside three bowls with spoons sticking out. "Get your fill but leave me a portion. I'm off for a shit."

The carriage driver hurried into the woods, quickly disappearing in the underbrush.

"Charming man," Wynne said.

"At least he's gone far enough to not offend our noses any further. Sloppy, knocking half the veg into the fire."

Dara warily inspected the gruel as she scooped it into a bowl. Though he was careless in cooking, the carriage driver had taken care to mix in spices, herbs, nuts, and berries. Dara took a large bite.

"Seems he's a fair cook at least," she said, a myriad of flavors melding pleasantly across her tongue.

Wynne plopped on a soft patch of grass. "What do you think of our rite?"

"It's a rite."

"Oh, I mean of our task," Wynne chuckled. "The way the Aide said that we are sure to be challenged... I thought our rite would involve performing some task in service of the Quinarium to show our dedication. Maybe helping repair a Sanctuary, or culling some aggressive animals to help protect a hamlet, but what we've been tasked with..."

"I try not to worry myself with what is or isn't supposed to be," Dara said between mouthfuls. "A rite is a rite. We're meant to complete it, no matter the details."

Wynne poked at her bowl. She pushed the beans into a neat pile, then began eating the rest.

"Something wrong with the beans?" Dara asked.

"I've never been fond of them," Wynne replied.

"I'll take them."

Wynne recoiled when Dara thrust her bowl out, waiting for the beans to be transferred. She hastily scooped them over and watched as Dara mixed them into her gruel, then resumed eating.

"I didn't think anyone actually enjoyed beans."

"They're filling. From time to time, the Quinarium would send shipments to my hamlet. There were days when we didn't have money for enough food, and they were all we would eat." Dara slid a bean across the top of her gruel. "I don't particularly like them, but I'm no stranger to the feeling of hunger and I would rather it remain a distant memory."

Wynne attempted to respond, whether with apology or sorrow, but words escaped her. She aggressively swallowed a few mouthfuls in silence, beans included, when she noticed the sword hanging from Dara's waist.

"Why don't Blood Mages carry a shield? All the guards and soldiers of Hantsburg carry shields, and the Quinarium Paladins carry large ones as well. I would think if you are to go into battle, you would want a shield."

Dara swallowed. "We were taught that shields are for those hoping to survive. Blood Mages don't fight to survive, we enter battle to deliver the righteous blow of the Quinate, or so the Instructors said. Shields are an unnecessary hindrance when we fight with Blood Magic."

"Or so the Instructors said? You seem a bit... distant from what otherwise sounds like fanaticism to me. I thought everyone should want to survive a battle."

"You asked a question, and I answered," Dara said.

"I merely thought an Initiate from the Academy of Ramaia would have a stronger conviction. I expected more belief and less recitation."

"What?" Dara said, her face scrunching. "And because you went to the Academy of Ilsios, should I expect you to be lazy, poor at magic, and uninterested in the Quinarium?"

"That's not what I meant," Wynne stammered.

"Daughter of the Lord of Hantsburg, adherent of Ilsios, please tell me then—what did you mean? You might have to speak plainly, as I am a simpleton born of a low family."

Wynne's cheeks burned. "It was a curiosity. I meant no offense! And why must you bring up my family? And since you did, does it not speak better of me that I didn't use my family's influence to further myself unfairly? Why does no one believe I chose to go to the Academy of Ilsios!?"

"Did you think it was an act of charity, a highborn studying among those called the lowest?" Dara snorted. "Or perhaps you enjoyed the idea of superiority? What with your lineage, I expect you enjoyed a great deal of power and influence there."

"That is a *perverse* misrepresentation of the truth!" Wynne snapped as she jumped to her feet. "We have only known each other for a day! Well then, since you know all about me despite the shortness of our time together, what do you suppose I should have done?"

Dara remained sitting on the grass. "You should have enjoyed your cushy life. Sit in a Citadel, eat whatever you like, do whatever you fancy. Maybe dance or draw or read, from dawn to dusk while your servants wait on you."

"As if that was what my life was like. Being the child of a Lord... there are expectations, procedures, rules, eyes, eyes always watching. A constant observation, criticism flying on the tails of every little thing you do. My family followed me everywhere. I was never just Wynne. It was always Llewelyn Pharadrax, daughter of Brolwen, Lord of Hantsburg."

Dara stifled a chuckle and slowly stood. "Do you think that pressure is unique to the children of Lords? Trust me when I say I also know about expectations. I've lived countless days working until my hands are raw and bleeding, only to be left with my belly aching, churning with hunger because we didn't meet our quota."

Wynne blinked rapidly, her head drooping. "Then what would you have done, were you in my place?"

"I would have used the luck of my birth to get everything I could."

"I thought you condemned that?"

"I envy it," Dara whispered.

"Envy it? All those words, and-"

A scream came from the forest.

Flocks of birds flew out over the canopy. Wynne set her bowl down and pulled on her gauntlet. By the time she uncorked a mana bottle, Dara had drawn her sword and held a bottle to her lips.

A terrifying quiet settled in. Then, a rhythmic thundering sounded from the forest, like the beating of giant drums. The carriage driver burst out, screaming.

"Help! Help me!"

Dara downed a mouthful of mana and strode out to meet the terrified man. Wynne's hands trembled as she attempted to cork her bottle, sending a few drops falling. She scarcely believed what she saw as blades of grass curled and twisted and grew when touched by mana.

A crash from the forest yanked Wynne back to reality. Tree-tops shook violently and tremors rumbled through the ground. The carriage driver stumbled and fell, a puff of dirt curling around his body. Dara rushed forward. She was a mere twenty paces from the fallen man when an Ogre stormed out of the forest.

Over ten feet tall, its arms and legs were as thick as tree trunks with feet like those of an elephant. Warts covered the beast's gnarly skin. Shaggy hair topped its head, which was small relative to its body. Bulbous facial features eclipsed tiny eyes. A loose robe of tattered animal hides covered its torso.

With speed and deftness counter to its size, the Ogre surged after the carriage driver. It snatched the crying, pleading man by a leg and dragged him back towards the forest.

Dara raised two fingers and traced a large circle in the air. Bringing her hand to her chest, she roared. "Ramaia, grant me your strength!"

The Blood Mage struck ferociously. Darting ahead of the Ogre, she slit its wrist, forcing the creature to let go of the carriage driver. Dara then sliced a thigh and stabbed its belly before retreating out of striking distance, blood dripping from her sword.

Groaning, the Ogre rubbed its wounds. The skin rapidly sealed as if a skilled Flame Mage had cast a multitude of healing spells. The Ogre grabbed the carriage driver again and stomped back to the forest, nearing the edge.

"Help, please!" the man screeched, clawing at the ground until his fingers bled.

Dara ran forth again, unleashing a flurry of blows at the Ogre's hands until bone protruded through the gashes. The enraged Ogre swung at Dara, forcing her to dive away. Meanwhile, the carriage driver crawled towards Wynne, drooling, his body quivering in fear. Wynne stood paralyzed as the Ogre stepped on the man's back, knocking him unconscious and pinning him in place.

Before the beast grabbed hold of the carriage driver again, Dara appeared. She whispered a spell, then drove her sword into the Ogre's thigh. The Mage twisted and pried the blade back and forth, sending blood spurting onto the ground. The howling Ogre limped to the edge of the forest, dragging Dara on the way. It ripped a tree nearly twice its own height from the ground, slamming it down.

Dara evaded the impromptu weapon, but was thrown off balance. The Ogre readied to swing again when Wynne broke from her stupor.

"Ilsios, unleash your fury!" she screamed, tracing a circle, then thrusting her hand into the center.

White flames billowed in a rapidly spinning ring. The circle seared through the air and slammed into the Ogre's side, charring its robe and singeing its hair. The beast was hardly affected, instead raising the branch to swing at Dara.

Not prepared to evade the incoming blow, Dara braced the flat of her sword against her shoulder and grit her teeth.

The force sent Dara flying. The Ogre readied to follow her when another ring of flame struck it, this time embroiling its head in white flames. It bellowed in agony as burns bubbled and blood oozed from its face. Wynne rushed over to Dara, when the Ogre growled again.

The tree trunk flew, headed squarely for where they knelt. Dara and Wynne dashed away, watching as the log tumbled down a hill. Turning back to their foe, they watched as the Ogre marched back into the forest, carriage driver slung over its shoulder.

Dara staggered to the forest's edge, but the Ogre was already out of sight, without a sign of its presence save a few broken branches and vines. The thudding of its feet faded, then ceased. Dara dropped to her knees, staring into the dark of the forest.

Wynne knelt and gently touched Dara's shoulder with a shaking hand. "Are... are you alright?"

Dara shrugged Wynne away. "You should have gone after the carriage driver, not me."

"I couldn't fight the Ogre on my own, I thought, maybe if I helped you..." Wynne's voice cracked as tears welled in her eyes.

"Sorry," Dara whispered. "I'm angry is all—it's not your fault."

Wynne sniffled back her tears, but forgot her sorrow on seeing a gash on Dara's arm through a tear in her tunic.

"You're wounded."

"I'll be fine," Dara said as Wynne reached for her bottle of mana.

The Blood Mage stretched out her hands to steady herself as she rose to her feet. Wynne grabbed Dara's arm and held tight.

"We are supposed to be partners. Healing your arm is the least I can do, and I assure you I am quite good at healing magic. Better than I am with offensive spells, anyhow. Or perhaps you have potions you'd rather use instead?"

Dara pulled her arm free. "We were taught that potions sacrifice too much potency for convenience. A waste of mana, according to my Instructors. Anyway, there's no need to waste mana on such a minor wound."

"Right," Wynne said, clasping her hands together. "I never particularly liked potions, either. There's something odd about them. Drinking a liquid made with mana instead of mana itself, a healing not designed for the ailment it seeks to treat, nor considering the person being treated."

Wynne's rambling fell on deaf ears as Dara stared at the edge of the forest.

"It's as if the Ogre was never here."

Wynne inched over to Dara's side. "Should we go after them?"

"I don't know about your Academy, but we studied various creatures at great length. Ogres may be dull, but they are able to run for longer and faster than we can, and their strength... you saw. Even if we were to track it down, I doubt we could stop the Ogre in its natural element of the forest."

Wynne's stoicism broke, and she openly sobbed. "Then we are abandoning our carriage driver to his fate."

A distant memory overwhelmed Dara. She was a young girl, but dust filled her lungs. A scream pierced the stone tunnels, followed by cries of a monster in the depths. Miners threw pickaxes aside, their rhythmic clinking replaced by stampeding feet. Dara ran with the mob, sobbing as she exited the mine. The bright midday sun blinded her. A shoulder knocked her to the ground and feet stomped past. Dara half-crawled, half-ran to her home. She yanked the door, but it would not budge. Pounding on the door, the windows, the walls, she pleaded for her parents to let her in. Silence was the only response.

Dara remembered climbing into an empty barrel and pulling the lid over her head. She didn't dare peek as sounds of horror ripped through the hamlet. The next day, she climbed out of the barrel to see blood smeared across buildings. A guard ordered her back to the mines, where her parents acted as if nothing had happened at all.

Dara coughed away the urge to cry. "We aren't leaving him. The Ogre took him, and there is nothing we can do."

"We should send word," Wynne said through her tears. "Did you see any dragonflies in our packs?"

"No. I inventoried mine during the night and I expect yours has the same contents. We're most of the way to Cauldhill, anyway; I think only another day or so of travel remains."

"I just want to do something, anything," Wynne said, eyes shut.

Dara looked around, uncomfortable next to her crying partner. "Do you know how to drive a carriage?"

CHAPTER 6

Red-eyed in the morning after a night with little sleep, they paused at a low wooden bridge crossing a stream. Dara eagerly cupped the brisk water and splashed her face. She scrubbed away sweat and dirt before moving on to her neck and arms. Meanwhile, across the stream, Wynne traced ripples with her finger.

"Are you alright going a few days without a bath? You can wash up if you'd like. I'll keep watch a proper distance away."

Wynne smiled wistfully. "It's no trouble going a few days without washing. There's something about running water, it always reminds me of home. The oceans of Hantsburg would swallow up this entire forest, but it's all I can think of when I touch a stream. I haven't felt this way in a long time... Do you miss your home?"

"No."

"Oh! I'm sorry, I shouldn't have asked, I-"

"It's fine," Dara interjected. "I've long made peace with the fact that there's nothing I miss from home and no one who misses me. The hamlet was hardly worth considering a home at all. We should get moving. We might reach Cauldhill by midday."

"Right, to Cauldhill! Without our driver."

Dara breathed deeply. "There is nothing we could have done."

The village of Cauldhill came into view in the midafternoon. Dara had read about it before, and expected the home of more than a thousand residents to be grander, cleaner, brighter. However, the village left her unimpressed.

Sprawling farms surrounded two-story stone walls, which were topped with reddish-tan clay shingled roofs. Inside, buildings were primarily one story and constructed from wood, with roofs matching those of the walls. The only notable building was the stone Sanctuary, home of the Quinarium, standing high above the rest of Cauldhill with enormous columns lining the exterior. Outside the walls, snow-capped mountains towered in the distance. Fishers on boats speckled a pond which fed a stream flowing into the Nomridian Forest.

As they neared the gates, a guard atop the gatehouse blew a horn. Two guards emerged and intercepted the carriage, motioning for them to stop.

Wynne happily complied, though Dara glared at the guards. Steel plates covered their tunics, which ended at the knee. Smooth domed helmets protected their heads, flared out by the neck and with a large T-shaped opening for their face. Simple swords hung from their belts and round shields bounced on their backs as they sidled over.

"Who are you, then?" growled the first guard.

Wynne bowed her head politely. "This is Dara, Mage of Ramaia, and I am Wynne, Mage of Ilsios. We are here on our Rite of the Faithful, as Initiates of the Quinarium. We were instructed to meet with Maren and Uldrik."

"Quinarium carriages always have a driver. Where's your driver?"

"Dead," Dara said flatly. "An Ogre took him into the forest."

"An Ogre, you say? And it let you two, and the horses, dance away?"

"A likely story," chimed the second guard. "What're the odds these two are scavengers, come across the carriage after the Ogre did its business and are pretending to be Mages?"

"Or maybe there was no Ogre at all," said the first. "Maybe these two killed a carriage driver traveling on his own, took the tunics from inside and are now pretending to be mages."

"Prove it to us," said the second guard. "Show us some magic."

Wynne shrank in her seat, but Dara sat tall in defiance. "We do not answer to you. Guards or not, you have no right to make such demands. We have orders to speak with the Confessor and the Elder. If they have doubts about the veracity of our story or our identity, then it is their responsibility to deal with us, not yours."

"The safety of Cauldhill is our responsibility," sneered the first guard.

"You are shitting in a cup and calling it pie," Dara said.

The second guard nodded to the first. "You two hop down. I'll take the carriage to the guards' stable, my compatriot here can take you to the Elder."

The guard took hold of the yoke between the horses. Wynne tied off the reins and hopped down, ready to follow into Cauldhill, when Dara pulled her back to the carriage. She ducked inside, then swiftly returned, shoving Wynne's pack into her chest.

"Do we really need to carry these? We can always come back after we speak with the Elder and Confessor," Wynne offered.

"The guards may know better than to touch our mana, but they wouldn't hesitate to dig through everything else and take whatever they fancy."

"What? Not everyone is out to take advantage of you. They are a bit coarse in behavior, but they aren't wrong that it's their duty to protect the village."

Dara sighed. "You think that because the guards of Hantsburg wouldn't dare steal from the Lord who pays them. The guards here were bold despite you identifying us as part of the Quinarium, and in my experience, even the outwardly kind ones will happily steal from whoever they consider an easy target. Please trust me, and take your pack with you."

"What a cynical perspective," Wynne grumbled as she followed Dara and the guard into Cauldhill.

Marching along, they passed inns and stores, stables and smithies, all coated in a layer of dust from the dirt roads. Wynne found the village curious and endearing, attempting to take in every detail. Meanwhile, Dara kept her eyes squarely focused on the guard. Despite her apprehension, the guard took them straight to a two-story building with a bell tower at the heart of a busy plaza.

"In there," she ordered.

"Thank you for escorting us," Wynne replied.

Dara's lip curled as she entered the building, the guard laughing all the while. Wynne bowed and slipped inside.

The room was poorly lit despite rows of windows on either side; walls of the too-close neighboring buildings overshadowed the glass panes. The only notable feature in the entire room was a large round table at the back end. A group of petitioners, wearing tunics ending around the knee and embellished with detailed trim, crowded around a seated woman. They all spoke over each other in a cacophonous garble, while the woman held her head in her hands.

Dara cleared her throat and coughed, but no one noticed. She folded her arms to wait.

Wynne shook her head and strode to the center of the room.

"Good people, excuse me! Please, pardon my interruption, but we are here on behalf of the Quinarium." Wynne spoke warmly yet with command, and swiftly received the attention she demanded. "My name is Wynne, and this is my partner, Dara. Our audience with Maren, your Elder, is expected."

The petitioners raised their voices to complain, but Maren rose from her seat. "Please, you heard Wynne! They are on Quinarium business—your troubles can wait until tomorrow. Yes, even you, Elivan. Please trust I won't forget the troubles with the shipments from Kivernswall."

"Dorslet!"

"Right, Dorslet! Let us speak more tomorrow. For now, I must attend to this matter of the utmost importance." Maren pushed and prodded the complaining petitioners out the door, then hurried back to her seat. "Come, come closer, please."

Dara and Wynne approached the table, which was covered in documents, books, maps, and a plate of half-eaten bread and cheese. Maren grinned. She had a pleasant face with wide, impish eyes framed by frazzled almond-colored hair. A wide collar with gold embroidery rest over her otherwise plain tunic. With no other seats in the room, Dara and Wynne stood uncomfortably across the table from the seated Elder.

"Much better without all that racket," she said with a wink. "I am glad to have two Mages with us, though it is odd indeed that the resolving of this most troubling situation has been handed to Initiates as their rite. I suppose I should tell you what I know. Or perhaps you should begin with what *you* know? I hardly know how to begin."

"We heard only of the attacks on your town," Wynne replied. "That there are rumors of strange beasts, and of a mana source."

"Yes." Maren clung to the word, slowly tracing a knot in a board of the table. "As with all oddities of this nature, rumors spin and billow and grow like storm clouds."

"Is there anything more?" Dara asked.

"Of course. I am the Elder of Cauldhill, after all! The attacks started some weeks ago. Always on the outskirts, beyond the reach of our brave guards..."

Dara scoffed. "Of course, the guards have done nothing."

"But how could they? The beasts swoop in, howling like demons, tearing through fences and gates, snatching up sheep and horses and any other animals they can grab. Before the guards can be called, they have disappeared, like smoke in the wind."

"Which direction do the attacks come from?" Dara pressed. "And how frequently do they happen?"

"Always from the forest," Maren said. "Reliable though the direction may be, the cadence is terribly inconsistent. Sometimes a few days pass between attacks, sometimes a week or more, sometimes no days at all. The most recent was last night."

"Have you not posted guards at the farms? Or placed more on night watch?"

Maren grinned. "You must be the Blood Mage. I thought I was to provide you information, rather it seems I have entered an interrogation."

Dara remained stoic. "Then what have you done?"

"You mistake an Elder for the Captain of the Guard. I make suggestions, recommendations... between the Quinarium, the Guards, the merchants, the tradespeople, and the farmers—to name a few of the many groups who petition me—I must balance all requests, most of which are unbalanceable. As for the guards, they are reluctant to station themselves so far from the protection of our walls. As long as the attacks remain on the fringe of the farmlands, I'm reluctant to request they risk their most valuable lives chasing whatever is attacking us, whether monsters or Fae."

"Bowing to the guard to ensure they'll stay loyal to you, is it?" Dara paced back and forth. "Besides, it sounds as though you hold the guards in high esteem. What makes you think whatever 'monster' is attacking would defeat them so easily? Or perhaps you believe it to be the Fae?"

"Yes, why mention the Fae?" Wynne asked. "I thought they kept to themselves, isolated in the Nomridian Forest, allowed to remain at the grace of the Llendshold Regent?"

"The relationship between Cauldhill and the Fae is perhaps more amiable than most are aware. The occasional Fae merchant comes to the outskirts for trade, and we host the occasional trader stopping on their way to visit the Fae. While the Fae are a convenient scapegoat, I wouldn't think it to be them. A slip of the tongue to bring those fine people into this un-fine matter."

The Elder looked up when the door burst open. In strode a short man with a wrinkled face, stout nose, thick brows, and long, flowing brown hair. His tunic, cut below the knee, was unkempt and stained. Over it, he wore an open-front black vest and a long purple stole.

"The people have strayed from the Quinate!" the man shouted in a nasal voice. "They have lost their faith in the Gods, our Five! They turn from the Quinarium, which seeks only to guide them to the truth! The lack of fealty of the people has caused these attacks! You, Maren, how can you sit there when it is the people of *your* village who are the cause? My Sanctuary seats three hundred, yet it is a rare day indeed that I see more than fifty!"

"Welcome, Confessor Uldrik," Maren droned. "Might I introduce you to Dara and Wynne? Young Mages on their rite, here to see us, as you remember. Dear Mages, meet Confessor Uldrik, my peer; as I obsess over the everyday needs of Cauldhill, so our Confessor guides our praise to the Quinate from the Sanctuary."

"There is little difference in our work, as the Quinate see all." The Confessor wagged a finger as his eyes darted back and forth between the two Mages. "As for you two, the guards said your carriage driver was missing."

Sensing Wynne faltering, Dara stepped towards the Confessor. "An Ogre attacked us."

"An Ogre!?" Uldrik asked, his voice rising in pitch. He ran his hands through his hair, his many rings clinking against each other.

Dara frowned defiantly despite the accusing glare of the Confessor. "Yes. Our carriage driver went into the woods to clear his bowels, then came running back with an Ogre right behind him."

Maren waltzed around the table. "We should send a missive to Stellburg. Rare for an Ogre to be roaming near the edge of the forest, let alone to be bold enough to leave it. Further odd the driver took the path along the Nomridian Forest instead of cutting across the plains. That route shortens neither the distance nor the time."

"We have neither the authority nor the responsibility to judge the driver's decisions. Rather, it is these two who have earned condemnation. Mages allowing their escort to be killed by an *Ogre* of all creatures," Uldrik said, pointing alternately between Dara and Wynne.

"How... You..." Wynne held her breath to catch her thoughts. "The Ogre nearly killed Dara! We tried to save the driver, we-"

"The Academies are too soft these days. In years past, it would be unconscionable to think of a Blood Mage bested by a mindless beast," Uldrik jeered.

Dara remained silent, unmoved by the jab.

"You speak of not passing judgement, yet how easily you judge us, when you weren't there!" Wynne shouted. "You speak of the Ogre as if it were as mild as a fox. It was near ten feet tall, with-"

"You don't need to defend me," Dara said coolly. "I feel no discomfort when slandered by a simple man living inside a walled village, hiding from the dangers of the world. His accusations are those of a man who, were he there in our place, would have fled with piss running down his legs."

The Confessor burned red as ripe tomatoes. "Need I remind you, *girl*, that you are here by the grace of the Quinarium, and I am the Confessor of Cauldhill!"

"Excuse me," Maren said, stepping between the Mages and the Confessor. "Might I suggest we return our attention to the reason for Dara's and Wynne's presence? The attacks?"

Uldrik pursed his lips. "Precisely the reason I came here, before I necessarily addressed their insolence, my dear Elder—which I will include in my report to the Moderator of Stellburg. Solving our *issue* is likely beyond their skill, but we must trust the Moderator's judgement that it is appropriate for a rite. There is a specimen from last night's attack in the Sanctuary. A Paladin and her Trainee were passing through and offered Maren and I their assistance, and they wait for us there. Follow me."

The Confessor marched out, allowing the door to swing shut. Maren held the door for Dara and Wynne, then cheerily strolled after.

A few minutes later, they stood in the shadow of the imposing Sanctuary. The only decoration was the symbol of the Quinarium, engraved in bronze above the double-doors. The lower floors had no windows, while small square windows lined the exterior near the roof. Uldrik waited in the doorway, feverishly ushering them in.

The interior was cold and bland. Rays of sun crisscrossed through the windows high above, leaving them all feeling small, hidden in the dark beneath the light. Rows of solid stone benches with no backs faced a dais with a single lectern at the center.

At the back were ten-foot-tall statues of the five Gods' faces. Two people waited by a stone table in front of the dais with only a few slender candles providing light.

Dara squinted to see the Paladin and her Trainee. Plate armor, painted white and bearing the symbol of the Quinarium, covered their torsos. Overlapping steel scales covered their tunics, with sleeves cuffed halfway down their forearms and a hem extending to the mid-thigh. Plated greaves and gloves protected hands and lower legs. Short spears, swords, round shields, and simple domed helmets sat in a neat pile at the edge of the dais.

On the stone table lay a bloody, putrid carcass, barely identifiable as that of a sheep.

The Paladins bowed in greeting.

"Dear friends," said Maren, "thank you again for lending us your aid. These are the Mages we told you of—Dara, of Ramaia, and Wynne, of Ilsios."

The Paladin bowed again. "I am Scireth. This is my Trainee, Caudro. Though I believe the Quinarium should have sent members of the Quinate's Faithful as opposed to Initiates, we are nevertheless most grateful to partner with Mages. A fitting rite, to be sure."

"A fitting rite?" Uldrik spewed. "A travesty has befallen this once fine village! I expected a contingent of Paladins and a complement of Mages! Not Initiates as likely to fail as they are to succeed."

Scireth chortled. "Unless I am mistaken, no physical harm has befallen any of the villagers of Cauldhill. There is no need for dramatics. Allow us to focus on the issue at hand, and all will be resolved."

"I am the Confessor of Cauldhill! I am the direct voice of the Five in this village, and you will not dismiss my determination of the severity of the situation. It is livestock for now, but look at the marks on these animals! What if a child was caught in the fields!?"

They all crowded around the table. Scireth tilted a candle close to the gaping slashes across the sheep's body; they came in threes, with black stains mixed in the dried blood. The attacker had sheared multiple ribs in half and removed most of the sheep's entrails.

"I am of a mind that the Fae are involved," Uldrik proclaimed.

Scireth took off her glove. Wynne spied the symbol of the Quinarium branded on the Paladin's wrist as the woman plunged her hand into the corpse. Squelching echoed through the Sanctuary as she pried inside, finally tearing free a piece of tattered flesh.

"What is it, Master?" asked Caudro, peering over Scireth's shoulder. The scant light cut across his gaunt cheeks, leaving his deep-set eyes in shadow.

Scireth spread the tissue on the table. "The most desirable cut of meat, according to accounts of those who trade with the Fae. Were they to have been responsible, I doubt they would mangle the most choice prize."

"The attacks have all come from the Nomridian Forest!" cried the Confessor. "What other people inhabit those cursed woods? These acts match the uncultured barbarism that is their society."

"Many creatures live in the forest," said Scireth. "Ogres, Jackals, Serpents. It would take a day or more to recount them all. Perhaps we should ask the opinion of our expert Mages? Dara, Wynne, would you care to inspect the carcass?"

The Paladin wiped her hands on a cloth as she stepped back. Seeing Wynne grimace, Dara approached the table. Choking back the urge to gag, she leaned close to the carcass. A shimmer by a gash at the animal's neck caught her eye; pulling back curls of fur, she traced a black ooze sticking to the flesh. She recoiled when a tingling sensation crept into her fingertips.

"There is a residue... it's mana," Dara said, accepting a rag from Scireth to clean her hands.

"Quinate save us!" shouted Uldrik. "This will only fuel the rumors of a mana source! This must be Fae trickery. Those demons of the forest have caused this, this monstrosity. They have devised some perverse method to infuse woodland creatures with mana, the precious gift of the Quinate, which should only be cradled in the loving hands of the Agents of the Quinarium. If they have gone this far, then it is only a matter of time until they will march upon Cauldhill! Stellburg! All of Llendshold!"

"I swear to you it is mana, same as what fills the bottles we carry," said Dara.

"Has anyone witnessed the attacks?" Wynne asked.

"None," said Maren, stepping towards the table only to retreat seconds later. "We have questioned all the farmers and everyone else who live nearby, though most have fled. As the attacks continued, the majority made arrangements with farms to the south to move their flocks and share pasture. The remaining few rightfully hide when they hear the howling."

"Could it be wolves?" Caudro asked. He pulled at his tousled, dark blonde hair.

"We would recognize wolves, and they are rather disinterested in Human settlements," replied Maren. "These howls are..."

"Evil," hissed Uldrik.

"No matter the cause, we must find out what is responsible for this," Dara said.

Scireth blinked thoughtfully. "Dara and Wynne, might I make a request of you? It is one that I believe to be in your favor, especially given the apparent challenge of your rite. As a Trainee on the verge of becoming a Paladin, Caudro is at a similar place in his journey as you two Initiates are. One task remains for him. A Trainee must be tested in battle and prove themselves honorable before becoming a Paladin. I would offer him to you, to face whatever has been attacking Cauldhill."

"Is this allowed?" Dara asked, looking at Wynne. "We were told to complete this rite together."

"There was no mention of us not accepting additional help, and this is hardly a normal rite," chimed Wynne. "The Moderator's Aide said we could acquire further supplies in Cauldhill. I think a Paladin would be a valuable resource. Confessor?"

"It would be unusual, but it is not explicitly prohibited. If you are to receive assistance, it seems reasonable to come from a Paladin."

Caudro dropped to his knees and bowed deeply. "I swear to serve you in the name of the Quinate, to follow your every command."

Scireth grinned pridefully. "While I assure you that there will be no issue with Caudro joining you, I will send word to the Moderator of Stellburg on your behalf. That is unless you prefer I not message your superior, Uldrik."

The Confessor shook his head.

Maren clapped loudly, the sound reverberating through the Sanctuary. "We are decided then! Our three young and eminently capable friends will set out to uncover the cause of the attacks."

"This rotting carcass has disgraced my Sanctuary for too long," grumbled Uldrik. "I support this partnership between Mages and Paladins, but find another place to do whatever you need to do, and let us remove this filth."

Wynne noticed a vein bulging in Dara's neck and moved for the door. "We should speak with any farmers who remain, while there is still daylight."

"AHEM!" shouted the Confessor. "As. They. Speak!"

"So we listen," Dara, Wynne, and Caudro replied in unison.

Outside the walls, unease filled the air. The farmlands, normally noisy as farmers tended their crops and flocks, were quiet and still. A breeze rustled through a field of wheat, sending overripe and unharvested grains falling. The forest of vines stretched into a sprawling vale, framed by tall mountains on either side. Rocky grey crags with sheer faces protruded throughout.

"I do not like the look of the forest," said Caudro. "How can it be called a forest if all the trees are dead?"

"I'm more worried about beasts like an Ogre than I am of the trees," Dara said as they made for the lone inhabited farm.

The pasture jutted out from the surrounding farms, running a mere fifty yards from the forest's edge; a field of shoulder-height grass stretched between. The two-story barn and a quaint house, not unlike the one Dara grew up in, were all there was to see. A flock of some twenty sheep bleated nervously, as if they knew what the night might bring. The three approached the farmhouse when Wynne noticed a farmer slouching against the walls. The man's eyebrows were as bushy as caterpillars, speckled grey like his wavy, dry hair. His simple tunic was draped loosely over his wiry frame. His face, though hawkish and sharp, exuded a relaxed kindness.

"Excuse me, good sir," she called from outside the fence. "Might we speak with you for a moment?"

"And who might 'we' be?" asked the farmer.

Caudro bowed so deeply his shield threatened to slide over his head. "I am Caudro, Paladin Trainee. I join the Mages Dara and Wynne. We are here on Quinarium business."

The man deftly hopped over the fence, then leaned against a post. "Two Mages and a Paladin, all shiny and fresh, come to old Evin's farm? Not Maren, not Uldrik, not a single guard could be convinced to stand here if it were Ramaia herself ordering it, yet now I have three Agents of the Quinarium visiting my humble little farm. I presume you are here to protect my lovely, dwindling, tiny herd?"

Wynne bowed graciously. "We are here in service of the Quinarium, and as such, we hope to aid you. We aim to uncover the source of these attacks. Have you perhaps seen anything at all?"

"I have!" Evin said cheerfully. "Every one of these attacks, it's been the same. Howls come from the woods, I get my herd situated, then I see exactly nothing more than the inside of my house for the rest of the night. No sane person is going to stay outside with such a racket, not to mention what happens during the attacks. Have you seen the sheep? We Humans have thinner skin than them. Whatever is doing this can rip them apart as if they were made of butter. I have no intention of loitering around to watch, waiting to be split open like an overripe bean."

"Have you heard anything other than the howling?" Wynne asked.

Evin kicked at a rock in the dirt, deep in thought. "Rustling in the trees. It's like there's a strong wind, but in a single spot of the forest. Then comes a deep growl, followed by the howling, at which point I flee. Soon after, screeching sheep, splattering of blood, then it's over near as quick as it all began."

"Why are you still here?" Dara asked, surveying the surrounding vacant farms. "A scant few farmers remain, and the others crowd by the village walls."

"I would as soon lose my flock in the night as pay those profiteering bastards on the southern side of the village." Evin spat into the field. "Those heartless scum demand such a sum, it's no better than losing the sheep here."

"The Confessor seems to believe the Fae might be responsible," said Caudro.

"The Confessor also has his head so far up his ass that he could wear his belt as a crown," laughed Evin. "Why would they do this? You would be hard pressed to find a farmer in these parts who doesn't trade with the Fae. Usually we send off sheep too old to provide good wool. They walk the animals away with kindness as if they had raised them since they were lambs. Besides, do you think the Fae would mangle the meat if they were stealing the sheep for food? Not likely, and they are as smart as you and I. Or at least smart as you, I'm a bit of a sad specimen, as far as intelligence goes."

"Selling animals for eating? Barbaric," Caudro muttered.

"Well, if a sheep's wool has declined, who is to pay for their food and care when they provide nothing in return? I see your faces, judge all you wish, but no day is an easy day for a farmer."

"I think we had best look around, see if there are tracks," said Dara.

"You're welcome to go where you please, but it's been days since the last rain. Ground is hard and dry as a rock, I found not a single track myself."

"Then perhaps we should stay and wait for the attacks," Wynne said.

"I agree. Waiting is our best option, that we might catch whatever it is as they arrive," followed Caudro.

Evin chuckled. "Might be some days of waiting. Attacks sometimes happen many days in a row, sometimes many days between them."

Wynne looked to Dara, who nodded in agreement. "As long as it isn't trouble for you, we need to see this resolved. Can we watch from your barn? It offers a good view of the fields, and I can't help but think your farm will be attacked next, as close as it is to the forest."

"Why not," said the farmer. "Be warned, there are no doors on the barn and not many places to hide. I'd be among the last to advise anyone to sleep outside the walls."

Caudro puffed up his chest. "We don't mean to sleep."

CHAPTER 7

Thin clouds passed over the moon, softening its glow. Caudro's armor shone in the night as he paced in front of the barn, attention fixed on the forest. Evin's flock lounged in a pen on the opposite side of the barn. The farmer had been unexpectedly open to using his remaining sheep as bait, trusting the three would do all they could to protect his livestock and that ending the attacks would be well worth whatever losses he might incur.

Dara stood in a wide, open doorway on the second level of the barn, surveying the fields. Owls hooted, crickets chirped, and lightning bugs bounded over the moonlit grass. A pleasant breeze rustled vines in the forest. Despite the serenity of the night, Dara couldn't shake her unease. She glanced over to see if her partner was similarly apprehensive.

Wynne sat on the floor, her legs dangling over the edge. A breeze carried the clouds away and moonlight illuminated Wynne's face. Long eyelashes blinked with a punctual regularity. Hair tucked behind her ears, Wynne's cheeks looked impossibly soft. Dara's eyes traced from Wynne's neck to her collarbone, then to her back. Wynne's impeccable posture made Dara wonder what her upbringing had been like: waited on by servants, decadent meals all day, tunics cut from the finest cloth, a life of luxury and ease. And yet, Wynne had described it as less than a fantasy. Was it possible that life as the daughter of a Lord was anything but perfect?

Dara stared with curiosity. Though they had only traveled together for a few days, Wynne was unquestionably different from the other progeny of Lords and Earls that Dara had the misfortune of meeting at the Academy of Ramaia. She pulled at her neck, torn between resentment for Wynne's upbringing and a fascination with how she acted, the sound of her voice, the way the moon shone on her face...

Wynne turned and Dara jerked, averting her gaze to the forest.

"What's on your mind?" Wynne asked.

Dara coughed and sputtered. "What's on my mind? Oh, well, whether or not there will be an attack tonight. It's so calm, it somehow feels both more and less likely that something will happen. I wish there were some Blood spell to improve my eyesight at night—shame it's the dominion of Almoya and the Mind. What about you?"

"I've never cast a spell this late at night."

"Something wrong about nighttime?" Dara asked, thinking of her evenings spent training with Okter.

"The sun makes spells of Ilsios stronger and easier to cast. I'm unsure how I'll fare with only moonlight."

"Your magic was fine when we fought the Ogre. I'm sure it's nothing to worry about."

"There's that too," Wynne said, running her fingers through her hair. "What if it's not something as mindless as an Ogre? I don't want to harm something intelligent."

"Whatever things are behind these attacks, they are the ones harming innocent people through their theft and carnage. They have to be stopped."

Wynne bit her lower lip at Dara's stark tone. She looked back over the fields and sighed. "I can't help but think about the Fae, too."

Dara chuckled. "You have a lot on your mind. What makes you think of the Fae?"

Wynne's face scrunched. "Of course there's a lot on my mind—a lot has happened the last few days. As for the Fae, don't you think it's curious how little we know of them? At least in Hantsburg, they're only ever a whisper. Then we meet Evin and he all but considers them friends. I can't imagine being friends with people who eat meat."

"Maybe they don't have a choice. I doubt the forest makes for good farming."

"Then why are they not a part of the Quinarium? The Quinarium always provides—if they joined hands with the rest of Llendshold, they would have plenty of food and wouldn't have to eat meat."

Dara's stomach churned as she remembered frequently going hungry after days of grueling work. As clear as the moon in the sky, she could see Agents of the Quinarium tossing cloth sacks bulging with dried beans from carriages, dust roiling as the donated rations struck the ground. The hamlet always buzzed with joy at their arrival, but the humble portions were barely enough to stymie hunger.

"I would not call the portion we were given *plenty*."

"Oh."

Wynne shrank at the condemnation of the Quinarium, which only amplified her discomfort at the quiet of the night.

"What was the Academy of Ramaia like?"

"Harsh," Dara whispered. "Constant training. Instructors who demanded perfection at every moment. Lessons learned with blood and tears. Relentless schedules with hardly a moment of pause. When I traveled to Stellburg, it was a strange, foreign sensation, sitting idly in the carriage. Even now, waiting here, it's the same. What about your Academy?"

Wynne blushed, hoping the darkness hid her cheeks. "Not so intense. We trained hard, of course, but from the sound of it, not like you. Much of our time was in classrooms, where we focused on building our connection with mana, and understanding the various ways Ilsios's light can be called upon using that connection. There was this beautiful garden... I loved taking books there and reading alone. Well, almost alone, there was always Reggie."

"Reggie?"

"A ferret, and my dearest friend at the Academy," Wynne said with a chuckle.

"Strange how most children of Lords and Earls train under Ramaia. Your Academy sounds a more fitting place."

Wynne squinted at Dara. "Are you making light of the Academy of Ilsios, or perhaps that was a condemnation of my parentage?"

"Nothing more than an observation," Dara said casually.

Wynne jumped to her feet. "Well then, are you willing to share of your childhood if mine was such a detestable plague?"

Dara squared up with Wynne. "I woke every morning, ate coarse gruel, with beans if we were lucky, then went straight to the mines. My first memories are of hauling food, water, tools, and candles for the miners. When I turned twelve, I was given a pickaxe. Work began at sunrise and ended at sunset, and I rarely felt the sun's warmth on my skin. All that to pray to the Five every day that the Quinarium carriages would come, that we might receive a meager portion of beans to supplement our food, which never seemed to be enough. And there you have it, my childhood."

Wynne's shoulders slumped. "I'm sorry. I didn't mean any offense."

"Then why ask?"

"Is it wrong to want to know my partner? I recognize that my life was easier than most, and I didn't ask to be rude. It's just that

I...I don't appreciate being treated as if everything was always perfect. My problems may not have been so severe, but it isn't as if they didn't exist."

"Such as?"

"What?"

"Tell me, what problems does the daughter of a Lord have?"

"Constantly being monitored, criticism at every turn, pointless formalities..." Wynne trailed off, leaning into the frame of the door and staring at the moon. "There was this endless expectation to be more, every day, because of my mother. Worse still was that I couldn't trust anyone. Workers in the Citadel were duty-bound to care for us. Then Earls and merchants alike would send their children to befriend me, in hopes our friendship would allow them an audience with my mother. Some would go so far as to propose marriages, to forge alliances.

"Being the sixth of seven children, my father planned my entire future, with my sole purpose being to support my eldest sibling's ascension to my mother's throne. The first time I made a choice for myself was when I went to the Academy of Ilsios. And as a reward for my defiance, I don't think my father even considers me his child anymore. I'm sorry, I know it all sounds silly compared to working in mines."

"You're rather trusting, sharing all this with me. I thought you would say that sometimes servants were late in serving you lunch."

"Oh, well, I mean... perhaps they weren't so trifling, but my issues were rather petty compared to yours." Wynne looked into Dara's eyes. "I guess you telling me of your childhood put me at ease. There's something trustworthy about you."

Dara smirked and rested her shoulder against the door frame opposite Wynne. "You are the first person to say that about me."

"Maybe you haven't spent time around the right people, then," Wynne retorted.

"Maybe it's because we were nearly squashed by an Ogre, together," Dara said.

They broke into laughter. Wynne lost herself in the creases of joy at the corners of Dara's mouth and the subtle dimples in her cheeks. The prior morning, any expression of joy seemed an impossibility, and despair had filled Wynne. Now, despite knowing they might soon face a monstrous foe, she felt a touch of lightness in her heart.

Dara suddenly leaned out the doorway.

"There, at the edge of the woods."

A breeze sent the entire forest rustling, but as the winds eased, vines and shrubs continued to tremor in one small area. Wynne's heart sank, and she shivered as chills ran up her spine.

"Caudro," Dara called out. "Movement. In the forest."

The Paladin crouched behind a barrel, his shield and spear at the ready. Over twenty lines rippled through the tall grass like fish in a stream. Dara and Wynne pulled on their gauntlets and took a drink of mana. Sweat dripped from Wynne's brow. She looked at her partner; sword drawn, Dara knelt at the edge of the doorway, ready to leap.

Growls and howls pierced the night as the lines reached the edge of the field. The creatures slipped out, shrouded in darkness, as they broke into a run.

"Wynne, now!"

Spurred on by Dara's command, Wynne called on Ilsios. A streak of white flame flew like an arrow and struck a vat of oil in the field. Fires erupted in a line between the three defenders and the charging attackers. They burst through the flames, revealed by the light.

Running alternately on two legs and all fours, the creatures were between four and five feet tall when upright. Covered in wiry brown fur, their paws had clawed fingers and thumbs.

Their heads were wolf-like, with narrow snouts. Black ooze dripped from long, bared fangs.

"Jackals!" Caudro cried.

Dara also recognized them from her studies—smarter than most wild creatures yet far less intelligent than Humans, they were nevertheless strong and hunted in fearsome packs. However, Jackals supposedly avoided large settlements, instead seeking easier prey. Dara shook her head. No matter what she had read, an enormous pack was rapidly closing in.

The first few Jackals reached the fence nearest the barn. They flew over and charged down the path.

"Wynne, again!" Dara shouted.

Moments later a second vat of oil burst into flames, coating the leading Jackals in burning pitch. They yelped and squealed, clawing at their fur, but the following Jackals ran by undeterred. When the Jackal in the lead neared the barn, Caudro roared out from behind the barrel and thrust his spear into its chest.

Dara whispered a spell and jumped from the barn, silent as an owl, landing atop a Jackal in the middle of the pack and slitting its throat before her feet touched the ground.

"Come, you brutes, meet the fury of a Paladin!" Caudro shouted, banging his spear on his shield.

The Jackals ignored the challenge, attempting to skirt around Caudro and reach the flock. While Dara cut down one after another on the open path, Caudro moved to intercept those that made it past her. He tripped a Jackal with his spear and slammed his shield into a second. A few slipped by, evading a lance of white flame hurled by Wynne.

Caudro yelled as he impaled a Jackal with his spear. When he tried to pull his weapon free, the Jackal grabbed hold and jumped forward, knocking his shield aside and forcing the Paladin into the wall of the barn. He punched and kicked as the mortally wounded Jackal clawed at his armor, blood pouring from its chest. Caudro drew his shortsword and jabbed it into the creature's throat, then shoved the corpse aside.

Before he could step free, three more Jackals grabbed hold of Caudro's armor, slamming him into the wall again, out of Wynne's view.

"Dara! Help!"

At the sound of Wynne's voice, Dara ran back to the barn; a shower of sparks and flames slowed the Jackals in the field. Dara arrived to see Caudro on the ground, wildly swinging and kicking at the Jackals. Dara swiftly dispatched the three attackers.

"Are you alright?" Dara asked, pulling Caudro to his feet.

"Yes, thankfully they don't know to look for gaps in armor—watch out!"

Dara grimaced as a Jackal slashed her back. She spun about, severing an outstretched hand. She kicked the Jackal's legs out from beneath it, then thrust her sword clean through its chest until the tip struck dirt.

Caudro threw his shortsword, killing another Jackal as more arrived from the field. A ribbon of flame lashed out from the smoldering remains of the vat, catching Jackals' legs and sending them tumbling.

"I'm fine," Dara said before he could ask about her. "Worry about the Jackals—I'll slow them in the fields, get to the pen!"

As Dara sped away, Caudro took hold of his shield and drew his dagger. Rushing into the pens, he found eight Jackals, some clawing at sheep while others hoisted the bleating livestock under their arms. White flaming darts flew down from the barn above, piercing two and killing them instantly.

Caudro leapt in, slamming his shield into a Jackal, knocking it to the ground. The Paladin raised his shield and rammed it down, crushing the beast's chest with a splattering crunch of bone and flesh. He threw his dagger, striking the leg of a Jackal.

Another dart flew down, and the Jackal crumpled. The remaining Jackals leapt out of the pen, fleeing from Wynne and Caudro.

Dara ran to intercept the would-be thieves, cutting down two more while the surviving Jackals sprinted into the darkness with sheep in their arms.

Wynne hurried down, lighting a torch on her way. She joined Dara and Caudro in front of the barn, staring at the mess of Jackal corpses littering the farm.

"Should we pursue?" Caudro asked.

"No," Dara said firmly. "They are far too fast, and the forest is their home. Who knows how near or far their den is, and how many more might be in wait? I'm also out of mana. I cleared two bottles."

"Me as well," Wynne said, shaking a bottle upside down. She spied red stains on Dara's tunic by her shoulder. "Dara, you're wounded. Let me look."

"I'm fine."

Caudro bowed. "I would not be, had you not saved me, Dara. I owe you my life."

"Dara," Wynne pressed, ignoring the Paladin, "let me see. That much blood means it is certainly more than a scratch, if you'll let me-"

"We need to head back to Cauldhill," Dara interjected. "Maren and Uldrik will be-"

"They must have been watching. I think they're already on their way," Caudro said.

Torches wavered on the path outside the gates of Cauldhill. Meanwhile, the door to Evin's home creaked open and the farmer emerged, his eyes bulging at the carnage littering his farm. He stood in silence beside the Mages and Paladin, waiting for the procession to arrive.

A few minutes later, Maren, Uldrik, Scireth, and a complement of guards rolled up to the farm.

"Strange-looking Fae, wouldn't you say, Uldrik?" laughed the farmer, recovered from his shock.

"I have not seen you in the Sanctuary for months, Evin!" bellowed the Confessor. "These monsters attacking your farm is no doubt due to your lack of faith, your lack of devotion to the Five!"

"You sure it was faith? My farm is nearest the forest, all but a miracle it wasn't attacked in full until tonight. Maybe it was the Five watching over me, knowing these three would come to protect my humble farm. Shame I didn't have any help from the Quinarium to relocate before this awful, awful raid."

"The true good fortune," said Maren with a sideward glance at Uldrik, "was the bravery of these Mages and this Paladin. They have slain a horde, and from the bleating I hear, they protected much of the farm."

"Maren, my dear Elder, may I be so bold as to ask why it took these young ones protecting my farm and not our guard?" asked Evin, his voice honey-sweet.

"You're the farmer. Aren't you responsible for your own flock?" grumbled a guard.

"The guard have neither Mages nor Paladins among their ranks," said Maren, turning to Uldrik. "Perhaps the Quinarium will one day station forces here, in Cauldhill."

"You both have no right to make demands of the Quinarium!" shouted the Confessor. "Mages and Paladins serve the entirety of Llendshold, and you, all of you, should be grateful for their presence tonight. Service tomorrow will be on the ills of waning devotion to the Quinate. The residents of Cauldhill have all but abandoned the Five, and this, this monstrosity, is the result! Maren, I beseech you, make attending my sermons mandatory for all in Cauldhill!"

"Yes, yes, as you say, my dear Confessor. I will do what I can to encourage attendance."

Scireth knelt by a dead Jackal, inspecting its wounds. "Clean kills. Well done."

Caudro's head hung low. "Master, many still escaped."

"Is it possible they will return?" Wynne asked.

"Unlikely," said Scireth. "These are simple beasts. In thoroughly reducing their numbers, you have shown them the error of their ways, and that Cauldhill is a poor target. Strange that they were ever so bold."

Dara knelt beside the Paladin. She stuck a finger into a wound, then smeared the blood in her palm. Hand by her nose, she inhaled deeply.

"There's a scent... Wynne, what do you smell?" Dara asked, hand thrust out towards Wynne.

Though Dara's bloodstained fingers repulsed her, Wynne sniffed hesitantly. Her eyes widened. "It's mana!"

"Impossible!" Uldrik shouted. "The Quinarium maintains all mana. There is no way these monsters could have accessed any. I refuse to believe the scent of the purity of the Gods has been found in such craven beasts! There must be another explanation!"

"They moved with such speed. No leader, yet they acted in unison, with purpose. It is counter to all I have read about Jackals," Dara said as she wiped her hand with a rag.

"Then our job is not yet finished," Caudro said grimly.

"I could send word to my seniors," said Scireth. "I am sure they would dispatch a larger force if need be."

"No!" Uldrik squeaked. He brushed his tunic smooth and puffed his chest. "I mean to say, these two Mages are on their Rite of the Faithful. The Quinarium has deemed this matter appropriate for them to resolve. No need to bring further attention to Cauldhill."

"Attention?" Wynne squinted at the Confessor. "I thought the Quinarium operated on the premise of openly sharing, never hiding. I wonder if our progress would please the Moderator of Stellburg, or if he would instead find fault in your declining attendance, Uldrik?"

The Confessor's face scrunched and he inhaled, ready to break into a fresh tirade, when Dara cleared her throat. "This is our rite. We were to stop the attacks, of which we can only be certain if we clear the den. Further, this scent of mana must have some relation to the rumors of a mana source. We must find the den, find out what led these Jackals to carry the scent, and end the threat."

"The Blood Mage is right," said Uldrik. "No need for Paladins or anyone else to be involved."

"It was merely a suggestion," said Scireth.

"That means going into the Nomridian Forest, the Fae woods," said Maren.

"Accursed forest!" shouted Uldrik. "The Quinarium does not exist there. Faith does not exist there. It is no wonder the Jackals live in such a place."

"The Fae believe in the Five as much as you and me," laughed Evin. "Might use different names, but the Five are the Five, no matter what you call them."

"Those meat eaters are not to be trusted," Uldrik seethed.

Caudro marched before Scireth and bowed. "Master, I should join the Mages."

"Oh? And why is that?"

"Dara saved my life," Caudro answered, shoulders sagging. "In doing so, she was wounded. I can't consider this my trial; it was not honorable combat, being overrun by mindless Jackals, laying on my back, kicking and fighting for my life. I may have faced battle, but it was not to the standards of the Paladins. Please, allow me to join the Mages, to redeem myself in service of their rite."

Scireth paced before her Trainee. "Your candor is appreciated, Caudro. Though you fought not as you expect of yourself, others in your place would happily be honored for facing battle at all. I will, however, accept your assessment of yourself. So long as Dara and Wynne accept your offer, I assent. Join them. See their rite completed."

"Of course we accept," Wynne blurted.

"Agreed," Dara said. "Though Caudro speaks too harshly of himself—he killed many a Jackal."

"I will repay my debt to you, Dara. I will regain my honor."

Maren clapped. "Ah, this matter is all but resolved! Your success will thrill the entirety of Cauldhill. You have done a wondrous deed for our village, and I look forward to seeing you when you return."

"Nothing is resolved!" screeched Uldrik. "Not until the faith of the people has been reinvigorated! Not until the Sanctuary teems with supplicants, their hearts filled with devotion to the Quinate, through the Quinarium!"

"Resolved? For once I agree with Uldrik," said Evin. "Do you not see my farm!?"

"He did offer his flock as bait, and many of his sheep were taken," Wynne said.

Maren waltzed over to the farmer and pat his back. "Worry not, my good citizen! I will have workers sent to assist you in the morning, and I will personally see your flock restored in recognition of your sacrifice. As for you three—Dara, Wynne, Caudro—you are most welcome to stay at any inn in Cauldhill. Might I recommend *The Badger and the Hare?* I will send word to the innkeeper."

Scireth turned back towards the village. "Caudro, come with me. I'll help you prepare, and you can meet Dara and Wynne at the inn."

"Well, that's enough excitement for me," said Evin. "Thank you, young masters, for doing what both the Quinarium and the Guards of Cauldhill could not. You lot will always be welcome at my farm."

"As They speak!" Uldrik shouted at the farmer.

The man laughed and waved his hand as he slipped inside his home, slamming the door shut. Maren pulled the Confessor away as veins in his neck threatened to burst with rage, telling him of all the people sure to crowd the Sanctuary come morning. With no alternatives in mind, Dara and Wynne made for *The Badger and the Hare.*

The innkeeper had stared at Dara and Wynne on their arrival. Though Wynne was largely clean, dirt and blood—both her own and that of the Jackals—covered Dara. The man nevertheless offered them the finest lodging at the request of Maren. After cheerfully showing them to their room, a prized suite on the second floor, the innkeeper brought a tray with a few bowls and a small pot of soup for their dinner.

By themselves again, they surveyed the room. Though modest to Wynne, Dara could hardly believe where she would spend the night. Four spacious beds with canopies and curtains lined one wall. A long table split the room, with a roaring fire in a hearth on the opposite wall. Steam rose from a hulking pot of water, and linen cloths were draped over a metal rack. Soft white moonlight flooded in through two broad windows, melding with the orange glow of flickering candles and the fire.

Dara set two packs with shared supplies on the table, then threw her pack on the bed furthest from the door and plopped beside it. Wynne set her pack on the table by the platter and peered inside the pot. Still bubbling, diced vegetables floated alongside oblong dumplings in a thick, creamy broth. The smell was enticing, promising a delectable blend of herbs.

"The stew looks good," Wynne said.

Dara pulled a fresh set of clothes from her pack. "I should have counted mana bottles and inventoried our supplies before we left anything with the guards."

Wynne rolled her eyes. "I thought you said they wouldn't dare steal mana."

"After seeing how they dealt with—or should I say didn't deal with—the Jackals, I'm having doubts about my assessment."

Dara dragged a chair over to the fire, then grabbed the hem of her tunic. When she lifted it over her head, Wynne blushed and scrambled to busy herself, nearly knocking a pack off the table.

"Am I so hideous that you have to turn away?" Dara snickered.

"Sorry, I wanted to give you some privacy."

"If I wanted privacy, I would have said something." Dara dipped a cloth into the pot of warm water. "Have you never taken a communal bath before?"

"They were communal at the Academy."

Dara wiped her arm; a sideward glance caught Wynne peeking. "Before then? If I were to guess, I would think a private bath in the Citadel, all for you."

"Yes."

"I envy you for that," Dara said, wiping her face.

"It was lonely," Wynne said, sliding into a chair by the table. She stirred the soup, staring into its murky contents. "I understand the appeal of privacy, of having space. The appeal fades quickly when your choice is either to be alone, to be with people who are there because it is their duty, or to be with people who are there because they want something. It felt like I was always on my own."

Dara paused her scrubbing. "That sounds familiar. Like we were both living in a prison, with no freedom, stuck in a never-ending circle, with no choice of what to do each day. Ouch!"

Dara grimaced when the cloth touched the top of her shoulder.

"You're still bleeding! And that wound looks far worse than I thought. No wonder you wouldn't let me see," Wynne scolded as she charged over. "I'll heal you."

"I'll be fine."

Wynne peered over Dara's shoulder, recoiling at the deep gashes running from her shoulder blade to the middle of her back.

"I'm not asking. Take off your undergarments and lie on the bed. If you aren't healthy, we can't complete our rite, and given how this rite has gone so far, I do *not* intend to repeat the experience."

Dara complied wordlessly, while Wynne rummaged in her pack and gathered a few items. She set a chair by the bed and inspected Dara's back. The Jackal's claws had torn clean through the padded tunic, slicing nearly to the bone. Such a wound would impair a regular person for days; Wynne knew her magic would be necessary for them to even consider traveling in the morning.

Wynne took a drink of mana, then touched her thumb and middle finger together, her palm steady in front of her mouth as she spoke. "Ilsios, grant me your healing light."

She blew and a white glow pulsed between her fingers, as if she held a hundred fireflies. She lowered her hand and pressed it against Dara's shoulder. The light surged across the wound, as if rays of morning sun were shining from inside. Dara squirmed and groaned, prompting Wynne to press down on her back.

The glow faded, and Wynne leaned close, tracing the edge of the wounds with a fingertip. A thin layer of skin sealed the gashes, as if days had passed with mindful tending. Grinning, Wynne scooped a heap of ointment from a tub and spread it over Dara's back; she was remarkably still despite Wynne knowing the injury was painful, regardless of her spell. Wynne then unrolled a fresh cloth, cutting it to shape with a small knife and setting it in place.

As Wynne adjusted the edges of the bandage, she rested her forearm against Dara's back. The warmth reeled her in. Wynne found her hands lingering, electrified from the touch. She traced the outline of a muscle with her fingertip, sending her heart racing. Dara shivered from the delicate sensation, but neither said a word.

Wynne jerked away as the door creaked open. Caudro stood in the entrance, eyes wider than when he had faced the Jackals in battle.

"I apologize for the rudeness of my abrupt entry. I should have knocked!" Spinning on his heels, the young Paladin readied to leave. "There is no need to rush your... activities on my behalf. I will wait outside."

"You can come in," Dara said, grabbing hold of the ends of the bandages as she sat up. "Wynne was helping me with my back, nothing more."

Wynne fled to the table, where she stuffed unused supplies into her pack.

Caudro turned his back to the room and spoke over his shoulder. "The innkeeper was kind enough to offer me a room of my own. I came by to inquire as to what our next steps will be. And to see how you are, Dara. Thank you, Wynne, for mending the result of my inadequacy."

"I'll be fine. Now come inside, you are being ridiculous," Dara replied, tying the bandages off across her chest.

Caudro entered the room as Dara pulled on her tunic. He slammed his gaze to the ground and coughed loudly.

"We should start early," Wynne said as she ladled soup into bowls. "I see no reason to delay."

"We will enter the Nomridian Forest, land of the Fae," Caudro said solemnly.

"Have you been spending too much time with the Confessor?" Wynne jabbed. "Evin thought positively of the Fae, and he lives on the edge of the forest."

"From my reading, the relationship is complex," said Dara, taking her bowl of soup. "They are not governed as part of Llendshold, but exist within its lands. There is no open conflict, rather a separation of preference, or at least that's what Okter said."

"Okter?" Caudro asked.

"One of my Instructors. As for the Fae, I don't think we will have any trouble with them. Perhaps they have been suffering from Jackals as well, and can tell us more."

Wynne rolled a map out on the table. "We should requisition a boat in the morning—I wager it'll be the fastest way to Keldarna. Hopefully, the Fae will help us find the Jackal den."

CHAPTER 8

The shallow fishing boat cruised along the few meters wide river; hardly a ripple disturbed the slow and gentle waters. The hours passed with little of note, save the occasional trout leaping to catch a fly and a herd of deer foraging near the riverbank.

By mid-morning, they reached the edge of the forest. Wynne shivered as their boat eased beneath the branches which arched over the river. Everywhere she looked, it was the same: vines hanging between dead trees, their bark shrouded by a thick layer of ferns, moss, lichens, and mushrooms. Shrubs with twisted branches and curly leaves spread throughout the understory. Bugs and birds flit about, their chirps doing little to calm the three travelers.

Caudro rummaged through his pack, checking the contents for the hundredth time. Lifting an oiled cloth flap, he revealed a loop of rope strung through slices of dried bread.

"What are those?" Dara asked.

"Paladin's provisions," Caudro replied. "We take a large supply whenever we travel. As long as they stay dry, they last for months. Filling, though a touch bland and hard on the teeth. We try to supplement them with other food whenever possible, and cooking them in a stew for a few hours greatly improves the texture."

"Hours?" Wynne gulped as Caudro repositioned the bread, the hard disks clacking against each other. "Hopefully we'll reach Keldarna before we have to resort to eating those."

Caudro scanned their surroundings, his head jerking back and forth. "Evin might be friendly with the Fae, but I feel uneasy in their lands. A forest of dead trees..."

"...it's like a graveyard, except with trees for headstones," Wynne followed. "We were told stories about the Fae as children. If we didn't finish our dinners, meat-eating Fae would climb through our windows and gobble us up. Or, if we didn't obey the commands of our parents, the Fae would snatch us from the streets and hang us upside down by our toes. Nonsense, all of it, but quite effective on imaginative children."

"I never heard such stories," Caudro said. "We Paladins begin our training as children and speak only the truths of the Quinarium. Dedication is our motivator. As the Fae are not a part of the Quinarium, we rarely heard mention of them at all."

Wynne looked to Dara, who slouched by the steering oar. "How are you doing? Are you in pain?"

Dara's gaze settled on Wynne's hands. Memories of their soft touch, of Wynne's fingers tracing over her back sent shivers through Dara. She adjusted her posture to hide her body's response. "I'm fine... the pain has eased to little more than mild numbness. Thank you."

"Think nothing of it," Wynne murmured.

"What do you think of the Fae, Dara?" Caudro asked.

"I don't," Dara said flatly. "We never spoke of them when I was a child, and everything I've read of them since leads me to believe we're in no danger in the Nomridian Forest. At least not from the Fae. We all heard Evin. He seemed more comfortable with the Fae than with the people of Cauldhill. I'll take his testimony before that of the Confessor."

Over the ensuing hours, the river narrowed and rocky outcroppings formed a wall to one side. The waters churned and their fishing boat rocked and swayed as the flow accelerated. Then, the bow of the boat abruptly rose a few feet into the air and came to a halt. Wynne clambered forward to see the cause: a log bound with ropes on either end.

"A trap!" she cried.

Dara drew her sword while Caudro readied his spear and Wynne pulled on her gauntlet. Stuck in the middle of the river, boulders rising above them to one side, they were caught in a precarious position.

When laughter echoed over the stream, they scoured their surroundings for the source. The boisterous sound blended with the churning river and bounced off the rocks, seeming to come from everywhere at once.

"We are Agents of the Quinarium! Show yourself!" Caudro shouted.

The laughing ceased, swiftly replaced by a wry, feminine voice.

"What's this then? Is that three wayward travelers I see? Oh dear, they have gotten themselves a bit stuck in the river."

A figure stepped out onto a nearby boulder. Billowy tan pants, pulled tight around the calves with leather laces, were tucked into leather boots. An oiled hide poncho, dyed a light shade of sage green and with a rounded hem, covered her upper body. A broad hood shrouded her face. Peeking out from beneath the garment at her waist were three oblong gourds, each the size of a small flask: one with a stubby spike at the large end, one with a stopper protruding from the narrow end, and one hollowed with a few small holes. The figure held a composite bow made of horn and wood, and a stack of arrows protruded from behind her back by her hip.

The figure pulled back her hood. A young Fae woman, not far in age from the three, gazed down at the trapped boat. Though similar in appearance to Humans, her eyes were noticeably larger. Her ears, rounded at the top, had lobes which connected to her jaw and tapered down to the base of her neck; bone earrings of various shapes and sizes decorated the entire length. Short black hair framed her tawny face, with low cheekbones, a narrow nose, and a sharp jaw.

"Big man, I suppose you're the leader? Protecting the two fair maidens as you delve into the wild Fae lands, is it?" The Fae guffawed, nearly doubling over.

"I take offense!" Caudro roared back, wobbling to his feet as he leaned against his spear to steady himself. "I am here in service of these two Mages of the Quinarium. You will show them the respect they are owed."

The Fae howled and cackled as she pantomimed the Paladin.

Wynne nodded to Dara, prompting her to sheathe her sword.

"We have no ill intentions, coming to your lands," said Wynne. "In fact, we hope our mission might be in service of your people, too."

Standing tall, the Fae took on a grim expression. "Three warriors of Llendshold, claiming to come into the domain of the Fae peacefully? I think not. Good for us, yet not for you, that a company of our finest archers are at the ready in the trees, ready to rain arrows upon you."

Caudro slammed his spear against his shield, then raised his weapon high. "Then let their arrows fly! Let them come, and they shall witness the fury of the Quinarium!"

Dara sighed. "Caudro, put your spear away."

"Please, let us talk, preferably on land. Let us tell you of our purpose, and I'm sure we can reach an agreeable accord," Wynne said.

"I may be young, but I know there is no reasoning with fanatics from the Quinarium."

Wynne pulled off her gauntlet and tucked it into her belt. "We are not fanatics. Last night, we killed nearly twenty Jackals outside of the village of Cauldhill. The surviving beasts fled into the Nomridian Forest. We intend to cleanse their den, to ensure there are no more attacks on our people."

"I see through your poisonous words. You call our people Jackals, claim we attack your people, and now seek retribution!"

Wynne squinted at the Fae, breathing deeply to control her rising passion. "Please, do not twist my meaning. I promise you, I speak plainly."

Dara stood at the edge of the boat. "Stop playing the fool and let us through, that we might speak with someone with authority."

The Fae grinned. "You all are quite the serious lot, aren't you? Oh come now, I see the disapproving look on your faces. I'm only having a bit of fun."

Wynne's face burned. "A bit of fun? You said there were archers waiting to loose arrows upon us! How did you expect us to react!? Offer to bake you pies? Five above, are all Fae like this?"

"Ah, I see. Poor luck that I stumbled upon three Humans, none of whom have the slightest touch of humor in their bodies. As for my people, I assure you I am one of a kind." The Fae bowed mockingly.

Caudro pointed his spear at the Fae. "You assume much about people you have only met this moment! How are you to know whether or not I am the cause of raucous laughter wherever I go?"

"I suppose that's a fair statement, given you've brought me plenty of humor today," the Fae chortled. "Well then, big *and* funny man, allow me to be serious for a moment, as your companions have requested. You three say you are here to find a

Jackal den, and you're on Quinarium business. You look about my age and are traveling alone, meaning you must be on some sort of trial. How curious!"

"Why hold us here? What are your intentions?" Wynne inquired.

"Perhaps I would like a ride to Keldarna. Your boat is a tad humble, but floating along the river sounds nicer than walking."

"And why would we allow a Fae trickster to share our ride?" Caudro demanded.

"Oh, ho!" The Fae threw her hands into the air. "You wound me, and here I thought you a righteous man of the Quinarium. Calling me a trickster, and saying 'Fae' as if the very word is filthy. You're lucky I find your armor attractive, if not the *boy* wearing it. Fine then. I will take you to Keldarna and introduce you to the right people, that you might find your Jackal den."

Dara stared at the Fae. "And if we decline?"

"I'll be disinclined to free your boat. I hope you don't mind walking. Oh! And swimming. You will undoubtedly need to swim to the shore before you can walk the rest of the way to Keldarna."

"You mean to blackmail us?" Wynne exclaimed.

"Encourage you! I told you I don't want to walk."

"Which people do you mean to take us to?" Dara asked.

The Fae grinned. "None other than the Elder of Keldarna. If anyone can help you, it's him."

Wynne's eyebrows raised. "You have Elders, too?"

"You sound surprised. Who else would lead our villages?"

"My apologies. I mean nothing more than I find it curious that your form of governance is similar to that of Llendshold."

"Ah. I see you," the Fae said, tapping her forehead. "What you meant to say is that you are surprised a lesser species such as the Fae, barely more intelligent than worms in the dirt, have a governance of any kind. You will be quite happy to know we have an entire social system! It all begins with-”

“Fine then,” Dara said, cutting in. “Take us to Keldarna.”

“Are you sure this is a good idea?” Caudro whispered.

“We’ll keep an eye on her.”

“Stay put then, lovelies! I’ll be down in a moment. I’m Ami, by the way.”

The three anxiously waited for the new arrival. The log abruptly sank, freeing their boat. As it regained speed, Ami leapt aboard from a nearby boulder. She comfortably plopped in the center of the boat, sending Caudro scurrying to the bow, while Dara and Wynne sat beside each other at the aft.

“I’m not diseased,” Ami said, opening her leather satchel. She retrieved a strip of jerky and began chewing at the end. On seeing the others’ faces, she broke into laughter. “If you tried it, you might not be so disgusted. I promise you, it is delicious.”

Caudro suppressed a dry heave. “Must you consume... animal flesh... in front of us?”

Ami gripped the meat between her molars and ripped off a piece, then lay on her back. “Yes, I must. This is all I have for food at the moment, and I’m hungry. Foraging is rather difficult from a boat.”

“I seem to have lost my appetite,” Wynne said.

Dara munched on a palmful of dried berries. “You’re shorter than I expected. Is your height common for the Fae?”

Ami rolled over to her stomach and propped her chin on her hands, the jerky hanging from the corner of her mouth. “I am precisely the right height for me, neither short nor tall. I suppose I am rather average among the Fae. Now, if you all are situated, I’m going to take a nap.”

Caudro scowled at Ami as she pulled her hood over her face. “It is the middle of the day.”

"Thank you for your observation, your declaration, of something I already know."

"It is odd to sleep now though, is it not?" Wynne followed.

Ami sighed. "Though not essential, when given the opportunity, all Fae will sleep through the middle of the day. As nothing is likely to happen between here and Keldarna, I will gladly nap."

Dara grinned. "Sleep well then."

Though none trusted Ami to actually be asleep, within a few minutes she began gently snoring. For hours, all was calm. As the sun climbed, trees parted around the widening river. Birds sang and insects chirped, while breezes rustled leaves and the waters gently lapped against the boat. Even Ami's snoring added to the growing sense of ease.

In the late afternoon, a strange whistle sounded over the canopy of the forest, not far from the river. Ami popped up, grumbling. She took the hollowed gourd from her belt. Spinning it by a rope attached to its end, she produced a bright whistle. Ami adjusted the length of rope at varying intervals, modulating the gourd's pitch. After a few minutes, she wrapped up the gourd and rope and plopped back down. Soon after, a whistle responded from deep in the forest.

"What was that?" Caudro asked.

Ami wiped sleep from her eyes and yawned, mouth wide open and uncovered. "That was me communicating with scouts. They'll send word to the guards, who will inform the Elder of our arrival. And these people are real. No joking this time."

"And what did you tell them?" Dara pressed.

"Curious, aren't we all?" Ami said jovially. "Don't fret. All I told them was that I am bringing guests, and that you three are in my charge and not the other way around. I am ensuring your safety."

"A curious way of communicating," Wynne said. "Spinning gourds. I doubt many back home would believe me, even if I showed them a gourd."

"Don't you all send bugs flying around to carry your messages?" Ami retorted.

"Dragonflies, though we use ones made of metal and powered with magic. They carry scrolls," Wynne replied. "Only used for the most important of messages, as inscribed and read by Mages of Ilsios."

"Liable to be eaten by a bird, or a frog, or maybe an ill-intentioned person might catch one," Ami said, tilting her head back to face the sky. "A rather... *curious* way of communicating, I would say."

Wynne blushed. "Well, anyone could overhear your whistling gourd."

"That would be a problem if the *people* the Fae are concerned about could actually decipher our messages. Even with training and practice, I'm not sure you would be able to catch the nuance of our ways. Though you might think our gourds crude, I promise you we aren't some base, mindless creatures."

"I didn't mean to offend," Wynne mumbled.

"Ignorance isn't a defense, as my grandfather always said. Still, consider it already forgotten. We'll be to Keldarna soon anyhow, and then you'll be rid of me," Ami said, winking at Caudro.

Not a quarter of an hour later and the river nearly doubled in width. The forest opened around a broad field with a village at the heart. Mostly two and three stories tall, the village was of a similar size to Cauldhill. Every building in sight was made of wood, with green domed roofs coming to a point at the center.

"There are no walls," Wynne observed.

"Should there be?" Ami said, slinging her satchel over her shoulder and picking up her bow.

"I thought the forest was dangerous."

"Maybe for you, Wynne," laughed Ami.

"Need I remind you, we are here in pursuit of Jackals?" Caudro interjected.

"Sure, sure," Ami said, waving her hand dismissively. "And there are Ogres, too. And many other creatures. But what of your lands? I've heard of Boars, with giant tusks and plates of bone growing like armor, and Wyverns descending in flocks in the night, and other ugly beasts. The creatures of the forest leave our villages alone, for the most part. Though, some smaller settlements are more vulnerable."

"Interesting that the Jackals traveled all the way to Cauldhill to attack," Dara said, steering the boat towards a row of piers jutting out over the river.

"We keep active watch over the forest, day and night. There are dedicated scouts, but most all our people take part. Our community makes our villages less than enticing targets for wild creatures."

"Explains the attacks on Cauldhill," Dara said with a snort. "The walls did more harm than good, giving the guards a place to hide while farmers were left in the open."

As they neared the pier, Ami tapped Caudro on the shoulder as if she were an Instructor getting the attention of a distracted Initiate. Motioning him away, she hopped onto the pier and pulled the boat to rest. Ignoring the stares of the Fae unloading fishing boats and small trade craft, Ami helped the others up then led towards Keldarna.

Fae abandoned fields of berries and grain and racks for tanning leather and drying meat to gawk as Ami and the Humans passed by. Whirling gourds sounded, increasingly loud as they neared the village. Before they entered the outskirts, a Fae strolled out to greet them. His dress was like Ami's, though his bright yellow poncho extended well below his knees, with pink and light orange patterns covering it. Two gourds dangled from his belt, and bright silver hoops wove along the length of his earlobes, forming a delicate lattice. His long silver hair was pulled back and tucked behind his ears.

Four guards flanked the Fae. Beneath earthy brown ponchos, they wore chain mail shirts, with plated armor over their elbows and knees. Steel helmets with a crest protected their heads. Splotchy black paint covered all the armor. They carried large round shields and swords with a sweeping curve at the tip.

"I am Hawel, Elder of Keldarna," the Fae announced, his voice rumbling and deep. "Who are you, and for what reason have you come to my village?"

"I thought Ami sent word?" Dara replied, stepping forward. She peered over her shoulder at Ami; she noticed the Fae was shorter than most of her people, who were similar in stature to Humans.

The Elder glared, his face wooden. "Ami, is it? So that is what she told you to call her?"

"It's easier than saying Aminantskeilara," Ami retorted. "Can't expect Humans to say something so delicate, so intricate, and... sooooo *looong.*"

"I'm sure that was your motivation, and not to hide from the purpose of your name being what it is." The Elder turned back to Dara. "If petulant children will cease interrupting, I would have the answer to my questions."

Wynne stepped forward and placed her right hand over her left shoulder. With her left hand out to the side, palm open, she bowed deeply. "Please, allow me to introduce myself and my companions. I am Wynne. Joining me are Dara and Caudro. Thank you for giving us an audience, Elder Hawel. We are here on behalf of the Quinarium, and-"

"Your formalities are appreciated but entirely unnecessary. Speak plainly of why you are here and what you want."

Wynne shrank, bringing her hands over her stomach. "Of course, my apologies. The farms surrounding Cauldhill have been harassed for some months, and last night we found the cause: Jackals. After slaying the majority of the raiding party, the survivors fled into the Nomridian Forest. We seek to cleanse their den to ensure the attacks are stopped for good."

Hawel broke into laughter, causing the Humans to share quizzical looks.

"I ask you to speak plainly, and you share a partial truth. How typical of Humans."

"It is the truth!" Caudro said, his lip curling.

"Wynne has spoken of a sapling which grows tall and slender, with branches, leaves, and buds. A compelling tale, and yet the most important elements are hidden: the roots beneath the ground." Hawel blinked. "You found mana in the Jackals, and are now investigating rumors of a source."

"How did you know?" Dara asked.

Hawel paced back and forth. "You three are young and may not yet be aware of this, but Humans, both members of the Llendshold armies and Agents of the Quinarium, spend countless hours spying on the Fae. We, in turn, spend countless hours spying on you. An equal exchange, if you will. We know your Quinarium is worried about rumors of a mana source. I admit, we are also curious about this particular mana source which vexes them so."

Wynne stepped forward. "You speak as if mana sources are real."

"Of course I do," Hawel said. "Because they are real."

"Impossible," Wynne muttered. "The Quinarium-"

"Lied. They lied. And they would have you believe many other things which are verifiably false. Humans, Fae, we are not so infallible as the Gods. Lies are a convenience to form narratives which lead to our desired outcomes. Do you truly believe the

Quinate would ordain a single organization to manage their ultimate gift, if that gift was for all who live in this world? If they had, then we Fae could not use magic, which, I assure you, we can. Mana sources were once found all over the land. Why they dried and faded—that is the more important question, for which we have no answer."

"If you no longer have sources providing mana, then where do you get your mana from?" Wynne asked, still uncertain of the Elder's words.

"We don't take it from Humans, if that is what you mean to imply," Hawel said. "We extract mana from animal sacrifices. The Quinarium would call it a lesser substance, but it is mana all the same, and is a suitable source, as our magic is centered on our connection to Mizaina."

Wynne's ears perked at the name. "Who is this Mizaina?"

"You would call her Kosrya. In the words of your Quinarium, the God of that which sustains us: earth, water, and the like." Hawel ceased his pacing and approached the Humans. "Enough chatter. We have indeed heard rumors of the source, and we know where it might be found. I suggest a trade."

"And what do you want in exchange for this information?" Dara asked.

"The same thing as you, conveniently enough. Jackals are usually not worth consideration, but this pack has become a nuisance of late. We will provide you with a map and a guide, and in turn you slay the Denmother. Should you succeed, I will send word to the Elder of Vouliona. She will tell you where to find the mana source, provided you agree to detail your findings with us before returning to your Quinarium."

Wynne wrung her hands. "May I speak with my companions for a moment?"

Hawel nodded, motioning for Ami to join him. Color drained from the young Fae's face as she trudged over to the

Elder. Meanwhile, Wynne retreated down the path until she was certain they were out of earshot.

"I think we should take him up on his offer. End the Jackal threat, then go to Vouliona."

"Our duty is to end the Jackal threat," Caudro grumbled.

Wynne crossed her arms. "Did you not hear Hawel speak of mana sources? If there is one still in existence, we must find it and inform the Quinarium! Its discovery would completely change our understanding of mana!"

"But our orders!" Caudro protested. "We were told to eradicate the Jackals, and see what caused them to have a trace of mana, not go gallivanting through the Nomridian Forest grasping after smoke. These Fae seem like tricksters. If they heard of a mana source, why have they not sought it? It could be a tale to rattle our faith. It could be a trap. It could be a lie entirely, but none of it rings true. And why should we tell them of what we find, if we go?"

Dara pat Caudro on the shoulder. "Wynne is right. The Jackals are undoubtedly a concern, but they are but one part of our rite. We are also to uncover the cause of the mana source rumors. Finding out if one is real or not is at the heart of our rite. Also, if the Fae scout and spy, as Hawel described, they'll likely learn of what we find, whether or not we tell them."

Caudro bowed his head. "I am here to follow your lead."

The three returned to find a Fae guard kneeling, his shield on his back. Hawel leaned over the impromptu table while Ami stood a few paces away, her cheeks red. Nearing the shield, they saw a map of the Nomridian Forest spread across it. The detail was astonishing, with tiny notes scattered everywhere like leaves on a forest floor.

"Did you gather anything from the Jackals?" Hawel asked.

Dara and Wynne pondered what anyone could possibly want to take from a Jackal corpse when Caudro dug into a small pouch on his belt. He held out a fang, which Hawel snatched away. The Elder placed it on the center of the map.

"I didn't take you for the sentimental type, big man," Ami chimed.

Caudro's lip shook. "It is *not* sentimentality!"

"Holding on to little trinkets from a battle? Sounds a lot like sentimentality to me, big man," Ami mused, her coy expression restored.

"Enough," Hawel cut.

The Elder uncorked a gourd and took a shallow sip. He then took hold of the second gourd and squeezed the spiked end tightly into his palm. Hawel chanted unintelligible words as he swirled his blood-stained hand over the map and the Jackal fang. A black mark burned as if an ember were dropped on its surface, west of Keldarna.

"If my reckoning is correct, it will take you a little more than a day to reach the den." Hawel slipped the Jackal fang into his pocket, then rolled up the map. "I recommend leaving tomorrow morning."

"Further from Cauldhill than I expected," Dara said.

"One of many oddities surrounding this pack of Jackals. Though the cowardice of your guards made your village a more appealing target than ours," noted Hawel. "I have business to attend to, but word will reach Vouliona before you reach the den."

"You seem certain we will make our way to Vouliona instead of returning to Llendshold," Wynne said.

"It's hardly a matter of agreeing. You already aim to cleanse the den, and I am well acquainted with Human curiosity. A modest detour and you might make a tremendous discovery for your Quinarium. Impossible for you not to investigate. Telling us of what you find is further a trifle. As for this map, the den is marked and once you arrive, a path will appear leading you safely to Vouliona." Hawel eyed Caudro from head to toe and back up again. "You, boy. You're a Paladin, are you not?"

"A Paladin?" Ami whispered.

"Yes—I am a Paladin Trainee," Caudro said proudly.

Hawel grinned. "Aminantskeilara will serve as your guide, as long as you are among the Fae."

"What!?" she exclaimed. "I'm... I'm not familiar with this part of the forest, Elder. Nor am I a scout or guard, I... Elder, are you..."

Hawel's humor vanished. "You are a Mage, Aminantskeilara. I have given you this duty, and this is how it will be. Take the Humans to an inn for the night and leave before dawn. I will provide deer and provisions."

Dara nodded. "We will see this den cleansed."

"Aminantskeilara is a capable guide, regardless of her complaint. May you be successful and find your answer in Vouliona. Be well, young Mages. Be well, young Paladin." The Elder lingered on the last word while smiling at Ami.

Ami trudged to the inn with the Humans in tow. The innkeeper hurried the group to a secluded room at the back, far from her regular patrons. The space was simple, with a rectangular table hosting six chairs near a small hearth, and a row of six tightly packed beds. Instead of cushions stuffed with hay or feathers or wool, the mattresses were formed with a lattice of tightly drawn vines.

They had barely set their bags down when the innkeeper returned with a platter. She hastily thrust it onto the table and retreated without a word. Ami sauntered over, taking the plate laden with roasted venison ribs and bread topped with a rough chopped mixture of marrow, root vegetables, and herbs. Three bowls contained a mix of raw greens, berries, and nuts, accompanied by crusts of bread.

"Kind of the innkeeper to not serve us meat," Wynne sighed.

Caudro untied the rope strung through his provisions. He cracked a slice of bread into his bowl, then took it to the fire, where a pot of water simmered. He ladled a spoonful over his bread, then mashed aggressively until the contents crumbled into a coarse porridge.

Ami grimaced at the sound of Caudro slurping. "I am happy to get a proper plate of food for each of you, should you desire!"

Wynne repressed a gag when Ami tore a sizeable chunk of meat off a bone. "Thank you for the kind offer, but the innkeeper provided well for us."

"As you say. Personally, I would rather eat a rabbit or a deer than eat as a rabbit or a deer," Ami laughed.

For a while, they ate wordlessly; Caudro loudly scraped his bowl in a futile effort to drown out Ami's noisy munching. When the Fae licked the last bone clean and tossed it onto her plate, Dara broke the quiet.

"Ami, why did the Elder make a fuss about your name? And why were you so disinclined to guide us to the Jackal den?"

Ami grinned mischievously, waltzing to the door. "Another tale, for another time. Rest well. I'm off to see a friend and will spend the night with them. Be ready to leave by first light!"

The Fae danced out of the room, letting the door swing shut by its own weight. Wynne grabbed a cloth and threw it over the bones littering Ami's plate.

"Can we trust her?" Caudro asked, pulling the edge of the cloth to hide a protruding bone.

"I think so?" Wynne said, pushing the last nut in her bowl in circles with her spoon.

Dara exhaled slowly. "Hawel had quite the hold over her. Regardless of how trustworthy she is, I think she will lead us to the Jackal den, and Vouliona, without trouble."

"But... her behavior, her demeanor, everything about her... it gives one pause," Caudro objected.

"We should not condemn others because we do not find their personality agreeable. Nor should we cast judgement because of their appearance. None of us choose how we look," Wynne countered.

Dara leaned away from the table and laughed. "Learn that trite lesson in the Citadel?"

"Citadel?" Caudro's brow furrowed. "Were you or your family servants to a Lord?"

"Not as such."

Caudro glanced at Dara, then back to Wynne. "The tone of your reply... are you... is it possible that you are the daughter of a Lord?"

"My mother," Wynne replied, staring at the fire. "She is the Lord of Hantsburg."

"I though the children of Lords were given positions high within the Quinarium, or would become Earls if not Lords themselves. If they were to study magic, then they surely would attend the Academy of Ramaia. Yet you-"

"I chose the Academy of Ilsios," Wynne said defiantly.

Dara noticed Wynne's face reddening as Caudro readied to question her further.

"We should rest," Dara said. "Tomorrow is sure to be a long day."

Retiring without further comment, the three tossed and turned, attempting to find comfort on the springy beds. With Jackals on their mind, sleep was a distant dream.

CHAPTER 9

Ami whistled the entire day, as carefree as a young child running through a field of wildflowers. It was as if the forest responded to her, with birds and insects singing louder than ever before. She had swiftly dismissed Caudro's worries about attracting unwanted attention, noting the distance to the den and that Hawel had marked a path meandering near Fae outposts and settlements. Despite Ami's assurances of safety, the Humans all jumped at the slightest disruption; at times they were certain Ami was tossing rocks or cracking branches to startle them.

At night, they sat around a campfire eating dried provisions. They had tied their six deer off to a stout tree, with packs of supplies resting nearby. Wynne stared at her boots; Ami demanded they put them on before leaving Keldarna, saying travel through the forest was entirely impractical without better footwear. The idea of wearing animal skins disgusted Wynne at first, but after a long day of travel, the comfort was undeniable compared to days spent wearing the traditional Llendshold cloth shoes.

Ami's laughter broke Wynne's concentration. "I promise you, though made of leather, the shoes won't magically come back to life and eat your feet."

Wynne grinned. "I appreciate these boots—they are excellent footwear. Yet I can't help but feel strange, wearing something made from animal skin."

"What is Humans' issue with using meat and hides from animals? You shear wool from sheep and make cheese from milk. Why not also make use of the skin and flesh?"

"Flesh," Caudro said with a shiver. "All living things are creations of the Quinate. We believe that to consume them is to claim that we have the same rights as the Five."

"Curious. We think of living things, whether plant or animal, as gifts from the Five for us to use. Tell me then, auspicious and dedicated followers of the Five, how did you come to find yourselves in the Nomridian Forest, pursuing Jackals of all things?"

"Wynne and I are on our Rite of the Faithful. Once completed, we will become a part of the Quinate's Faithful. Then our service to the Quinarium begins, as Mages."

"Sounds formal," Ami yawned. "And boring."

"There is no higher service than service to the Quinate," Wynne bristled.

"I don't disagree about the importance of the Gods, but I wonder whether or not your Quinarium is a necessary part of it all," Ami said, turning her attention to Caudro. "What about you, big man? If the Mages are on their rite, what is a *Paladin* doing with them?"

"I'm actually not yet a Paladin—I'm still a Trainee. Once I've proven my honor in battle, I will receive the title of Paladin. Then I, too, will be one of the Quinate's Faithful."

"Might be better if you stop where you are now," Ami blurted.

"We Paladins live to serve the Quinate. Is that so distasteful?"

Ami stared into the fire. "I don't need an institution to tell me how to serve or believe in the Five."

Dara's head tilted. "Interesting view for a Mage."

"We Fae say the same of your Quinarium. Every waking moment dictated by an organization claiming to be the sole interpreters of the Five, ignoring everyone living beyond the borders of Llendshold."

Wynne threw her hands into the air. "Why approach us in the first place if you carry such disdain for all we stand for?"

Ami rolled onto her side, propping her head up and grinning at Wynne. "I never said I dislike you! It's your institutions that are a problem. As for why I approached you... I was curious. A group of Humans, clearly not traders, floating towards Keldarna. It was a convenience that I was headed that way anyhow. What reason was there for me to *not* greet you?"

Dara scooted closer to the warmth of the fire. "Ami, perhaps I am mistaken, but I got the impression that Hawel doesn't exactly love you."

"He is entitled to his opinion of me, wrong though it may be."

"Then why did the Elder insist that you be the one to guide us?" Caudro asked.

Ami lay on her back, gazing at the night sky. "My grandfather once told me of a time when Humans and Fae lived in peace. He said it was not so long ago, when he was a child. That our peoples lived alongside each other as friends, and that in our kinship was a power stronger than that found in swords or spells."

"Your grandfather sounds like a wise man," Wynne said.

"If not a touch idealistic," Dara added.

"He was, on both counts."

"You speak of him as if he were in the past," Caudro said.

"Yes."

Caudro scratched at the dirt with a rock. "Did he pass of old age?"

"My grandfather would often leave our home to trade with Humans. One day, a knock came at our door. When I opened it, I saw Elder Hawel instead of my grandfather. He told me that my grandfather was trading with farmers outside Cauldhill when a group of Paladins accused him of stealing Quinarium goods. As punishment, they dragged him to the forest's edge, impaled him on a pike, and cut off his nose as a trophy. They left his body there as a warning."

"Five above, I am so sorry," Wynne whispered.

"Impossible," Caudro said. "Paladins would never do such a thing. We operate in service of the Quinarium, and act only to protect-"

"We made good ground today," Ami said, hopping to her feet. "The den is less than a half day's walk from here—we should keep watch through the night. I'll go first, then wake Dara. You all decide who is up next."

Ami strolled over to the deer, giving each a chunk of sweet potato. She slipped into the forest, her steps not making a sound.

A few minutes later, Caudro scanned the surroundings, then leaned close to the fire. "That story about her grandfather... could she be lying? Another one of her tricks?"

"She was on the verge of crying," Wynne replied. "And why would she lie about something like that?"

"But the Paladins..." Caudro's voice trailed off, his jaw tense. "Who knows what drives a Fae to think or act the way they do? But Paladins, we are sworn to protect all in the name of the Quinate. To kill senselessly, to commit such an act of barbarism, it goes against everything we stand for. Ami must be mistaken, or, or perhaps someone framed the Paladins."

"I'm inclined to believe Ami," Dara said. "Did you see her reaction to Hawel instructing her to guide a Paladin? Whatever his reasons for disliking her, he was smug when he demanded that she lead us."

Caudro scooted away. "I can hardly change who I am."

"We should rest," Wynne said. "I'll take watch after Dara."

Though the night passed without incident, all were tense in the morning. Dara and Wynne had donned their gauntlets, while

Caudro wore his helm and held his shield. Ami ceased singing, and it was as if the forest responded. Birds were a rare sight. Insects scurried beneath leaves and into burrows in rotting trees as the four passed by. When the sun reached its zenith, the deer pulled and brayed, reluctant to continue their journey.

Ami took a drink of mana and grasped her spiked gourd. Approaching the deer, she whispered soothingly. Green wisps flowed from her hands and into the creatures' ears; all six calmed, ready to resume the trek. Ami took the lead again when a guttural howl pierced their ears.

"Jackals!" Dara yelled, drawing her sword as she took a drink of mana.

Caudro raised his shield and readied his spear. "The howl was close! Any sign of them?"

"I don't see anything," said Wynne, ready to cast a spell.

Ami made a wide circle around her body as blood dripped from her fingertips. A thick fog shrouded the group, though they could see as if it were a mild haze. She took hold of her bow and nocked an arrow. "To the south, coming over the hill!"

Ami's bow twanged, and an arrow sailed through the air. A Jackal emerged from behind a tree not thirty feet away. The missile pierced the beast's neck. It yelped and gurgled, falling to the ground as five more Jackals charged over the hill. Ami's next arrow missed and struck a tree when a spear of white flame engulfed the Jackal.

Dara bounded forward, carving apart two Jackals with elegant and clean strikes. Caudro roared, knocking aside the burning Jackal with his shield and impaling another with his spear. The last of the Jackals grabbed hold of Caudro's shield when an arrow caught it in the shoulder. Dara severed its arm as a bolt of flame struck its chest, sending it writhing to the ground. Caudro plunged his spear into the Jackal, and all went quiet.

"A raiding party, or scouts?" he questioned.

"Neither, thieves!" Ami shouted, loosing an arrow.

The others turned to see Ami's arrow strike a Jackal in the eye. More than ten of the snarling beasts surrounded their deer. Dara and Caudro charged as Wynne sent a shower of sparks at the heads of the Jackals, but they powered through the assault and grappled with the deer. The animals, still docile from Ami's spell, made hardly a sound as Jackals tore away bags and hoisted the deer under their arms. Dara and Caudro dashed into the fray, striking down many of the Jackals and sending the rest fleeing into the woods.

"Cursed beasts!" Caudro yelled.

"Ever more curious and concerning," Wynne said. "They thought to distract us with a small group, that a larger force might steal the deer."

"They won't be a concern for much longer," Dara said.

Ami inspected the remaining deer, grateful to find no serious wounds and only two taken away. "For their barbarism, they at least caused little harm to these ones. I hope your legs are limber—we all have more to carry now."

After tossing aside unnecessary supplies to lighten their load, they shouldered the additional bags and carried on. Ami and Dara took the lead with Wynne and Caudro in the rear, ever watchful for Jackals.

They reached their destination at midday: a rocky butte with fifty-foot-tall sheer walls rose high above the canopy of the crawling vines of the forest. Live trees grew at the top, with curly branches and narrow leaves wavering in the wind. A dark, foreboding opening led into the side of the butte, with a tunnel leading upward inside.

Ami tied the deer's reins to a tree, then began unbuckling their packs.

"Is it wise to leave the deer close to the den?" Caudro asked. "The Jackals seem to have a taste for them."

"We're after the Denmother," Ami replied. "Although this brood is quite ahead of the others in their intelligence, I expect they will all come running when she is threatened. And we are going in the way they come out. Do your job, big man, and kill any that try to run by."

Wynne stared at the entrance. "I wonder how many are inside?"

"We killed more than twenty outside Cauldhill, then nine more today," Dara said, standing by Wynne.

"Thirty would be a sizable pack, though nothing is ordinary about this group. How many indeed... I know one way to find the answer to your question," Ami said with a wink.

The group prepared to enter the den, rummaging through packs and grabbing essential equipment. Ami took a thin leather strap and wrapped it under her armpits and over her shoulders, pulling her poncho snug to keep the garment clear of her bow. She then took a hooked stick with an iron lantern at the end and secured it to the wooden frame of her pack. After lighting the ball of tar and wood pulp inside the lantern, she pulled her pack on.

With mana bottles aplenty, gauntlets on, armor pulled tight, and weapons in hand, the four stared at the entrance. Wynne called on Ilsios's light, then touched Dara's sword. The metal shone with a soft white glow, as though the blade itself had become a candle. Dara nodded in appreciation, then entered the cavern.

Dara inched along at the lead, wary that at any moment Jackals might ambush them. As they crept forward, the rock around the entrance gave way to a crudely dug burrow. The tunnel was high enough for Ami to walk upright with her lantern dangling above her head, and two people could comfortably pass side by side. A few minutes later, leaves and branches began covering the walls. Arranged neatly, the lining pointed in a consistent direction, giving the appearance of flowing water.

"I've never seen an animal burrow like this," Ami marveled.

Wynne traced the outline of a broad leaf pressed neatly into the dirt. "Perhaps consuming mana... *inspired* them?"

Ami tilted her head. "What do you mean about mana?"

Dara paused. "The ones we killed outside of Cauldhill—their blood had the scent of mana."

"Jackals drinking mana? Strange, but if they found some, why couldn't it have 'inspired' them?"

"No matter the case, we must slay them all," Caudro said.

Ami tapped the top of the Paladin's helmet with the tip of her bow. "Right you are, big man!"

After nearly an hour of shuffling through the winding tunnel, they reached a large chamber with multiple branches radiating out. They were of a similar size, with no sign of which would lead to the heart of the den.

"Should we separate and explore them?" Caudro asked.

"No!" Wynne spewed. She inhaled deeply to gather herself. "I mean, no. We can't risk fighting alone. The Jackals know these tunnels better than we do."

"I agree," Dara said. "We are stronger together. Though the question remains: which path leads to the den? Not one of these is meaningfully different from the others."

Ami pushed Caudro aside, taking a sip of mana as she made for the center of the chamber. Palm pierced by her gourd, she slowly exhaled as she shook her hand in small circles over the ground. A dark green glow highlighted Jackal footprints. They spread down every branch, but a single tunnel shone brighter than the others.

"You still leading, Dara?" Ami said with a grin.

They carried on for what felt like hours in the upward-sloping tunnel, illuminated by the glow of Dara's sword and Ami's lantern. The path gradually widened, allowing them to advance side-by-side. A dim light appeared ahead, casting the tunnel in a pale orange glow.

Ami threw up a hand, prompting the Humans to freeze.

"I hear something."

Ami took off her pack and Dara sheathed her sword. Crawling forward, they arrived at an expansive cavern. A column of muted, early evening sunlight poured down from a hole in the ceiling. The tunnel split into two paths, winding down to an open area below. Wynne covered her mouth to suppress a gasp.

The Denmother towered over her snarling pack. Tatters of cloth hung over her pale fur in a crude approximation of clothing. Beneath her feet were the remnants of a carriage and countless bones. The bodies of the two stolen deer lay atop the pile.

The Denmother took a silver-wrapped bottle from a pack tucked inside the wreckage. She placed it in her mouth, the glass and metal shrieking as it rubbed against her fangs. She clenched, shattering the bottle and spilling the contents over the deer. The Jackals flew into a frenzy, climbing over each other and tearing into their meal.

Horrific sounds of chewing, ripping, and howling followed the four as they backed down the tunnel.

"That explains the mana in their blood," Dara whispered once the sounds were a distant echo.

"And their behavior," Wynne followed. "But how could they possibly have found or brought a Quinarium carriage this far in the Nomridian Forest?"

"Smugglers," Ami replied. "If not smugglers, then who else?"

"Impossible. Not a soul among the Quinarium would ever dare to steal, especially not mana," Caudro rebuffed.

Ami stifled a giggle. "Big man, you may be a looker beneath all that armor, but you are as naïve as a newborn babe."

Dara grabbed the Paladin's arm before he could condemn the Fae. "The question of how the carriage got here is not our concern, at least not at this moment. We need to kill the Denmother."

"It will be difficult to eradicate them all," Caudro grumbled. "I counted nearly thirty. We have slain as many, but not all at once and in not their home, with their leader. She looks a right monster."

"What if we kill just the Denmother?" Wynne posed. "Without her, would the pack fail?"

"Easy to say, hard to do," Ami said. "Even if we can kill the Denmother, and even if we gather up as much of the mana as we can, what if a new leader rises? Who knows how they found the carriage, and if they might find another? We might also simply enrage the pack if we kill her first."

"Then we have no choice but to fight them all," Caudro said.

"At least it isn't breeding season," Ami said.

Wynne's face twisted. "Why is that a good thing?"

"I don't like the Jackals any more than you all, but I also don't fancy the idea of killing a bunch of their young. *Especially* if they have some semblance of intelligence, thanks to the consumption of mana. I wonder, given how they've progressed so rapidly, would their young perhaps enjoy a nice biscuit and a chat over breakfast?" Ami snickered.

"Sh!" Dara cut. "It's gone quiet."

An oppressive silence filled the tunnel, as if the surrounding air was constricting them like a snake.

Then, a piercing howl flooded their ears.

Dara took a drink of mana and drew her sword. "I'll take the right path. Caudro, you take the left. Wynne, Ami, stay on the platform above. We'll have a better chance on the narrow ramps than if we face them in the open."

Wynne drank deeply as she ran, eyes fixed on Dara, who called on Ramaia for strength and speed. Nearing the cavern, Caudro cut to one side while Dara slipped around the opposite corner.

Ami lunged to the edge of the tunnel. She swiftly loosed an arrow, catching a Jackal in the chest as it lumbered up the left ramp. The beast growled and charged even as a second arrow pierced its hide. Caudro snarled in the face of howling Jackals lining the ramps, stabbing with his spear. A Jackal ran straight into his weapon, twisting it from his hands as it fell off the ramp and down to the ground below. As the horde of Jackals pressed onward, Caudro drew his sword and raised his shield. He charged to meet them, pushing down the ramp with all his might.

Dara, meanwhile, evaded Jackals' claws and fangs, swaying like a blade of grass in the wind. She struck with precision, but the mana-empowered Jackals fought until they were nearly hacked into pieces. Clamoring over blood-soaked corpses, the wave of Jackals seemed endless; it was all Dara could do to keep the beasts from reaching the top of the ramp.

As Caudro's charge stalled, Wynne looked to the shaft of sunlight pouring in. Calling on Ilsios, she ignited the leaves and branches lining the walls on the left. A second spell sent flames bursting out in a torrent, charring the fur and skin of the Jackals. Caudro took the moment of pause to jam the edge of his shield into the cavern wall by a protruding boulder. He heaved, hoping to dislodge the boulder and slow the Jackals. Instead, the boulder rolled free, and the ground trembled. Caudro ran back as the earthen wall, weakened from Wynne's flames, collapsed and destroyed the path.

Heading to the right, Wynne readied to cast a spell when flames dissipated in a spark around her fingers. She hastily uncorked a mana bottle as Jackals closed in on Dara. When a Jackal leaped at the unsteady Blood Mage, an arrow found its mark, piercing its neck. Caudro ran in full tilt, colliding with the nearest Jackal as a bolt of white flame struck the middle of the pack, giving Dara time to regain her footing.

"Dara, wait!"

Caudro's words fell on deaf ears as Dara leapt off the ramp and into the center of the chamber where the Denmother waited alone. Caudro desperately wanted to follow, but with Ami and Wynne at the top of the ramp, he planted his feet amidst the corpse-littered floor. Raising his shield to his shoulder, Caudro shoved back a Jackal then stabbed with his sword before pulling his shield in close, repeating the strikes again and again as arrows and flames flew over.

Wynne paused her flurry of spells and looked to the heart of the chamber. Dara and the Denmother fought in a blur of steel, fur, and fangs; Wynne could hardly tell Human from Jackal. A cry from Caudro drew Wynne's attention. The Paladin had tripped over corpses and was on his knees, stabbing wildly as Jackals attempted to rip his shield away. Arrows pierced flesh as Wynne hurled a bolt of white flame, giving Caudro time to rise to his feet again.

Wynne turned back to the heart of the cavern. Dara and the Denmother faced each other, both heaving. Blood coated both Dara's sword and the Denmother's claws. The Denmother snarled when Dara uncorked a mana bottle.

The Denmother surged forward. Before Dara could raise her sword, the beast wrenched it from her hands and threw it aside. Dara shouted a spell and blood burst from the Denmother's wounds, but the enraged Jackal pounced, pinning Dara to the ground. The Denmother spread her claws, ready to strike.

Wynne screamed, her throat burning as if a fire billowed inside.

Dara held her arms out in a futile attempt to stop the Denmother, when the Jackal's body glowed white. Flames erupted from the beast's mouth, nose, eyes, and ears. Open wounds boiled, spraying blood across the cavern. The Denmother hissed, unable to howl as she burned from the inside out. Dara scrambled away as the charred corpse crumpled in a pile.

Gasping, Dara looked up to see Wynne, her hand outstretched and jaw quivering.

Their leader dead, the Jackals fell into disarray and in minutes the four dispatched the rest.

Caudro pulled his spear free from a Jackal while Dara flipped over the hem of her tunic to find a clean patch and wiped blood from her sword; Ami tiptoed down the ramp to join them. Wynne fell to her knees at the tunnel entrance, staring at the carnage below: mangled Jackal corpses were piled on top of each other, the scorched Denmother at the center.

A few hours later, the four emerged from the cavern to find the sun had nearly set. Exhausted, they resigned themselves to camp outside the Jackal den.

Caudro set down a pack by the deer, bottles of mana clinking loudly inside. "How is it possible to have hoarded this many bottles? For weeks they have harassed Cauldhill, and yet so many remained."

Dara unbuckled her sword belt, letting it drop to the ground as she slid off a second pack crammed full of mana bottles. "Between our three fights with the Jackals, we must have killed more than sixty. That doesn't even account for any the Fae took care of. I can't imagine even a well-guarded carriage surviving an attack by a pack of half that number, mana empowered or not."

Caudro shook his head. "I agree. They certainly had the numbers to overtake a carriage. But why was one near enough this den to attract their attention?"

"A matter for the Quinarium to deal with, not us," Wynne replied. "Dara, are you alright? I can't tell if it's Jackal blood or yours covering your tunic."

"I don't think the Denmother landed any serious blows, thanks in no small part to you."

"You are entirely unconvincing. Sit down and let me see."

Dara complied, plopping onto a fallen tree as Wynne helped her out of her torn and stained tunic. "When the Denmother burst into flames... how did you learn such a spell? I have never seen or heard of its like. It was as if you lit a hundred fires inside her, all at once."

Wynne grimaced at the sight of scratches and punctures across Dara's arms and shoulder, though she had avoided any wounds as serious as the slash from the battle outside Evin's farm.

"I... I honestly don't know. I panicked when I saw her standing over you. I was terrified. I called for Ilsios and... well, the flames surprised me as much as you."

"I think I know."

Dara and Wynne jumped when Ami's voice came from inches away. She grinned at their reaction.

"It was undoubtedly the most powerful magic of all."

"I'm not trained in the ways of Ramaia."

"Ramaia? Ha!" Ami slapped Wynne on the shoulder. "The most powerful magic of all... is *love.*"

"Oh, come off it," Wynne said, scowling and playfully shoving the Fae. "We were taught that emotions have nothing to do with the magnitude of our spells, only our ability, earned through practice."

"How boring."

Dara wagged a finger at Ami. "I suppose you're the expert? Casting spells fueled by love, relishing in the enhanced effect?"

"Quite the opposite. I am yet to find someone worthy of my affection!"

Ami giggled as she climbed up a tree, more than one branch threatening to crack as she navigated the mess of vines. Reaching the canopy, she nocked an unusual arrow—a small gourd at the end had holes bored across its surface. She oriented herself with the sun, then loosed the arrow. It released a piercing whistle as it arced across the sky.

"What was that?" Caudro asked as Ami climbed down.

"Nothing serious, my serious man. Oh, if you must know, I was sending word to Hawel."

"Your arrows can travel far enough for him to hear?"

Ami hopped to the ground. "Of course not. If the winds help carry it, an arrow might travel a quarter of a mile, but the sound will carry for a few miles more. Hawel is certain to have sent scouts to monitor us, and they will hear my message."

"Then we should get moving," Dara said, rising from the log. "If Hawel has held to his word, then the Elder of Vouliona will be waiting for us."

"No." Wynne stood and pushed Dara back down. "It's nearly nightfall and you need rest. I haven't finished with you, and I haven't even started with Caudro. Untended wounds can fester and if either of you take ill, we will hardly be able to travel."

"I assure you, I am fine," Caudro said. "Thanks to you and Ami."

"Ha!" Ami exclaimed. "I finally receive a hint of appreciation from the big man. I'm inclined to rest as well, though we will need to leave at first light. While the Jackals likely cleared out any nearby threat, by midday tomorrow the stench of this much death will attract scavengers for miles around. Bears and Ogres alike will stop by for an easy meal."

Ami and Caudro prepared the camp while Wynne finished bandaging Dara's wounds and helped her into a fresh tunic. They soon had a warm fire crackling, with a pot of vegetable stew roiling inside. Ami reconstituted dried meat in her portion, but otherwise happily shared the meal.

When her bowl was empty, Ami picked up a mana bottle, tracing the silver wrapping with a finger. "Shame there was nothing else worth taking. These bottles will be a right pain to haul, seeing as we have fewer deer to carry them for us. The bottle must weigh as much as the contents; such a strange design."

"I always thought the bottles were rather light," Dara said.

"Strange design?" Caudro scoffed. "Mana is the gift of the Five, and these bottles were designed by the Quinarium in their name."

"Yes, clearly designed by Humans," Ami retorted. "If they are above reproach in the perfection of their design, and you hold such love for them, you can carry the bottles tomorrow. I took first watch last night, I'm off to bed. Wake me for last watch. Sleep well!"

CHAPTER 10

Three days after slaying the Denmother, the four stood at the edge of the forest atop a low hill which stretched down to the village of Vouliona. Positioned between the woods and an expansive river delta, the village was otherwise near identical to Keldarna in terms of architecture and size. Two docks crowded with ships neighbored the village: one jutted out into the ocean, while the other stretched into the largest branch of the delta.

Dara stared out at the endless blue, rippling with white-capped waves. "Is that roaring sound-"

"The ocean!" Wynne said with delight.

"Is that what we're smelling, too?"

"Yes," Wynne replied, breathing in deeply. "Nothing as refreshing as ocean winds—it's like I've come home."

Ami snorted. "I can think of a few things I would consider more refreshing."

"Like what?" Caudro asked.

"Fresh picked flowers from the forest. Fields of grass coated in morning dew, drying as the sun rises."

"How poetic," Wynne opined.

"Oh, I could go on! Bones burning after being left for too long over a fire. Deer shit festering in the heat of the summer. Rotting Jackal corpses. All delectable compared to the stench of the ocean."

"I take it you don't like the coast," Dara said.

"It reminds me of my grandfather. He loved it here."

Ami strode ahead of the others, her pace making clear she didn't want to talk further.

The grassy dirt trail met a stone-paved road packed with soft sand. Approaching from the forest, they encountered few Fae; the villagers instead flowed to and from the docks on the other side of Vouliona. As they neared the village, a squad of guards marched out. When they were a hundred yards away, the leader raised his hand and the guards halted.

"Ami, is it not odd that guards have blocked our way, and so far from Vouliona?" Dara asked.

"Stay here—I'll speak with them. We are deep in Fae lands, and though we sometimes trade with Humans by ocean, residents here are unaccustomed to seeing your kind near the village itself."

Ami walked over, hands behind her back and shoulders slumped. The three Humans watched as the lead guard crossed his arms and shook his head at Ami, though the ocean drowned out his words.

"It appears that Ami has a reputation," Dara said.

Wynne nodded. "I thought Hawel was an exception."

"I wonder what would cause someone—or everyone—to not like her," Caudro said.

"Sometimes the way people act or speak can be a cover. A protective barrier, if you will, hiding the truth of what they feel," Wynne said with a smirk.

"Whatever the cause, I hope the Elder honors Hawel's pledge," Dara said.

Ami returned after a few minutes; the guards lingered on the road.

"We aren't welcome in Vouliona," she said with a scowl. "They have directed us to stay at an unoccupied dwelling by the shore."

"We? I thought it would be only us Humans not welcome," Wynne said.

"I'm here with you three. That makes us 'we,' according to the Elder."

"We have done nothing wrong," Caudro fumed. "We eradicated the Jackals, as agreed upon! What crime have we committed? What is the cause for our exclusion?"

"They gave many reasons, which ranged from the ridiculous to the understandable. It's not worth repeating any of it, because no matter how unfair you believe it to be, we won't change their mind," Ami said. "You're welcome to head back to Cauldhill, my Paladin. You've faced the Jackals honorably like a good big man."

Caudro glared at Ami. "I pledged to follow Dara and Wynne until they complete their rite, which they have since asserted includes the uncovering of this mana source. And it would be entirely easier if those guards were reasonable."

Dara sighed. "Fae guards are rather similar to their Human counterparts. They're still waiting. Worried we might try to defy their refusal?"

"No," Ami said. "Although the Elder has entirely refused to see us and further barred us from staying in Vouliona, she honored the promise of Hawel. The guards told me the believed location of the source, and it explains why none of my people have gone in search of it. We are to sail deep into the Zanerian Archipelago."

Wynne smiled at the docks packed with ships. "I'm sure we will find a crew willing to take us."

Ami snickered. "I see tales of the archipelago have not reached your people. When the Elder spoke of Humans, in service of the

Quinarium, wanting to sail into the Zanerian Archipelago, only two captains entertained the idea. We are to meet them in the morning, and can decide then who we wish to sail with. Oh, and you'll need to give the guards the mana we recovered from the Jackal den."

"No," Caudro said through grit teeth.

"Then say goodbye to your little investigation."

"Why must we give them the mana?" Dara asked.

"Because if you don't, they won't allow you to sail," Ami said. "The mana is payment for the voyage. And trust me, even if you were to offer every Guilder, every piece of armor, every item of worth on you down to your tunics and your shoes, it wouldn't come close to covering the cost."

Caudro threw his hands in the air. "We *cannot* turn Quinarium property over to the Fae! How do they know of it!?"

Ami sighed. "Scouts roam the woods, and I'm doubly sure Hawel had some watching us since we left Keldarna. If they somehow missed Jackals hauling a Quinarium carriage, those following us would have seen the empty mana bottles in the den. Anyway, the how doesn't matter. They know you have a large quantity of mana, and they want it. Fine with me if you won't give it over; it would mean we're done and I get to stay on solid ground."

"We should give them the mana," Wynne said.

Caudro gripped the pack until his knuckles went white. "If we do, the Quinarium will not look favorably upon us. Or the Fae."

Ami laughed. "I don't think the Fae care much about the opinion of the Quinarium."

"None of that matters," Wynne said. "The Moderator's Aide and the Confessor alike said nothing of stolen mana. Our duty was in two parts: first, to end the attacks, which we have done, and second, end the rumors of the mana source. If this mana source exists, then finding it *is* ending the rumor by proving its truth. We cannot do that if we don't give them the mana we recovered."

"Dara, do you have nothing to say?" Caudro pleaded.

"I don't like it, but I agree with Wynne. We have to comply with their demand."

"What is it, big man?" Ami asked with a giggle as Caudro stared at her. "Say what you will about me, but it's the Elder and her guards making the demand. And it's your fellow Humans wanting to go along. I don't care what you all choose."

Caudro grumpily trudged to the deer and retrieved the second pack of mana. He stomped to the guards, ignoring their outstretched hands and dropping the bounty at their feet. He stormed back while the guards returned to the village, packs in tow.

"Good show there, big man. Truly showing your strength, your honor, your mettle, tossing those packs on the ground like a child giving up their favorite toy before suppertime," Ami said. She pointed to a small wooden shack built atop a rocky outcrop and surrounded by tall grasses. "I believe that is our home for the night. Take the packs and go get yourselves situated. I'm at least allowed to enter Vouliona—I'll gather the supplies we need for the voyage."

"What about the deer?" Wynne asked. "I don't see a place to stable them."

"They're for dinner," Ami said flatly. Her nose wrinkled as she broke into laughter. "Joking! You all need to lighten up. I'll trade them for provisions. I may be a while. Haggling and bartering are all but a sport for my people."

While the outside of the shack was humble and of questionable appearance—and the building swayed with the wind—the interior was pleasantly warm and dry. Eight beds, similar to those of the Keldarna inn, jutted out from the walls on either side.

There were no chairs, instead a knee-height table at the center of the room was situated within reach of the foot of each bed. A stash of logs rested on one side of the ash-stained fireplace, while a round tub with a simple wooden curtain waited on the other.

With a fire roaring in the hearth, the shack was all but homey. Caudro spread his armor on one bed while he sat on another, mindfully inspecting every inch. Wynne had taken it upon herself to repair everyone's tunics, and happily plunged her needle through fabric by the light of a few candles. Dara had filled a host of buckets with water and now hovered by a hulking black pot hanging over the fire.

When the pot bubbled heartily, Dara lifted it and stirred the boiling water into the bath. Checking the temperature with a finger, she grinned and set the pot aside. Dara disrobed and stepped into the bath, laughing when Caudro coughed and turned away.

"It's nothing more than a bath."

Caudro jumped to his feet. He grabbed a set of clothes and a spare cloth then made for the exit, ever keeping his back to Dara. "Bathing sounds appealing. I will go for a swim in the river."

"What about you?" Dara asked as the door swung shut.

"I'll wash later," Wynne replied, hunched over a tunic with needle in hand. "Why do you always rush to bathe?"

"I thought you would be one to appreciate me wanting to wash off the stink, whether from Ogres, Jackals, or days of travel."

"Oh, I didn't mean it in a poor way," Wynne stammered. "More that, it seems almost a ritual for you."

Dara swirled the warm water with a finger. "When I was a child, the one place I could properly wash up was at this little stream near our hamlet. It only flowed if it had rained in the last few days, and it was terribly cold. I remember scrubbing until my skin was raw, but I never felt like I was able to wash all the dust away. Any time I can take a proper bath, it's like I can put a bit more of that dirtiness in the past."

"Thank you."

"For what? Sharing with you the sadness that was my childhood?"

"For sharing with me at all. I appreciate it." Wynne dug at a split nail on her finger. "When I was a child, my father taught me that we should never tell another any truth of ourselves unless there was a purpose. That every word we shared was a tool, and if we didn't wield the tool ourselves, it would be used against us. I lived my life so guarded, so hidden, so scared of honesty that hearing your story feels... good?"

"Well then, I'm happy you have found joy in my past misery."

They both laughed for a while. When the sounds of their humor faded and the crackling fire was all that could be heard, Wynne turned to face Dara.

"What do you think we will find in the Zanerian Archipelago?"

Dara rested her head against the edge of the tub. "I honestly hadn't given it much thought. I find it hard to look away from what is right in front of me. A bit of a difference between us—you always have your eyes on what comes next."

"I'm sorry. I can't seem to pull my head out of the clouds. My father always said I lacked in attention for the present. He said it was entirely impractical to only dream."

"You don't have to apologize. If anything, our differences are a benefit. As for what we will find... Hm. Maybe the source will be a hole in a rock, with mana dribbling into an endless pit below. Or, perhaps, it's a little old man with a bald head and a three-foot-long beard, sitting on a rock at the top of an island, spitting mana out whenever he fancies."

Wynne giggled. "I can't deny that a part of me hopes we find such a strange man, though it might be difficult to convince the Moderator of what we found."

Dara chuckled, stretching her arms over the rim of the bath. "No need to convince anyone. We simply scoop the man up and bring him with us! The real question is if we fill bottles from his mouth as he spits, or if we must drink straight from the source."

"Maybe we could convince Uldrik to lock lips, and really *deepen* his connection to the Five as he tastes of the old man's mana," Wynne snickered.

"Oh Five above, that would be a sight! Just don't ask me to kiss the old mana source man."

Wynne followed a droplet of water as it rolled down from Dara's brow, across her cheek, under her chin, then lazed along her neck. "Me neither."

Wynne traced the path of the droplet back up until she met Dara's eyes. The two gazed at each other, lost in the moment, until the door to the shack swung open and Caudro stepped inside.

Dara lurched forward and resumed scrubbing while Wynne spun about, fumbling with her needle.

"How was the river?" Dara asked.

"Cold. Has Ami not yet returned?"

"No, but hopefully she arrives soon. I'm getting hungry and don't fancy another bowl of bread soup."

"It's not so bad," Caudro said, spreading his washed clothes by the fire, cautious to avoid glancing in Dara's direction.

"Oh come now, we all know the bread soup is horrible," Wynne jabbed.

The door kicked in, slamming against the wall and nearly swinging shut again. Ami bustled in, then tossed a few satchels onto the nearest bed.

"I called for you, big man! I saw you when I was on my way out of Vouliona. Big oaf must not have cleaned your ears properly in the river," she said with a chuckle. "Shame you three aren't allowed in town, I could have used a hand or three lugging all this back. I got as much veg as I could find, among other things. Hopefully, there's something suitable for you all in here. I want eggs—I trust you can sort yourselves."

Ami rummaged around by the hearth until she found a pan. She shoved it on a pile of hot coals, then slapped down a glob of lard. Wynne tucked away her needle, joining Caudro by the satchels.

Ami, waiting for her pan to get hot, shamelessly watched Dara step out from the bath and dry off with a coarse cloth. She laughed on seeing Caudro position himself with his back squarely towards Dara. "Maybe I've been calling the wrong person strong. Oh, if you all don't find anything to your liking, you are welcome to some eggs."

The lard sizzled as Ami cracked in three eggs. The smell sent the Humans' stomachs rumbling, though all politely declined her offer. In a fresh tunic, Dara joined Wynne and Caudro. They inspected the variety of root vegetables, dried greens, and cloth bags stuffed with coarse grains. Few of the ingredients were familiar, and since leaving Cauldhill they had consumed simple porridge and stews requiring little more than dumping provisions into a pot of hot water. The three looked at each other expectantly.

"Oh, I absolutely cannot cook, at all," Dara said, leaning away.

"I would not call my ability *cooking*, rather more of horrifying ineptitude."

"Fine!" Wynne reached for a few recognizable items. "I am far from a good cook, but given your recusal, I expect you both to not complain, no matter the result!"

Though it took the better part of an hour, Wynne sighed with satisfaction as a simple but hearty stew bubbled over the fire. Ami had long finished her meal and retired to her bed by the time the Humans ate. After a wordless meal, Dara and Caudro gave their thanks, then collapsed into their beds.

Wynne tucked the large black pot into the fire and filled it to the brim with water for a bath. She stared into the flickering flames, her mind retracing the steps that had taken her from the Academy of Ilsios to the tiny shack on the coast in the lands of the Fae, right up to the sight of the water droplet flowing across Dara's skin. Then, visions of the Denmother intruded, flames bursting from her mouth, as the pot began to boil. Wynne cast the memories aside and poured the bubbling water into the bath.

Slipping into the crude but comforting tub, Wynne pondered what her parents would think of her now. She expected her father to be judging her every move, but would her mother at least be proud? Thoughts of her siblings and life in Hantsburg weighed on her until the water grew cold.

The shack was lit as much by the moonlight as by the stubby remains of candles and the dwindling fire. Wynne stepped out of the bath, pausing by Dara on the way to her bed. A peaceful calm replaced the stern strength the Blood Mage exuded during the day. The memory of healing Dara's wounds sent shivers up Wynne's spine. Filled with desire to reach out and touch Dara, to feel the strength of her arms, Wynne tore herself away and hurried to bed.

A delectable smell crept into Dara's nose. She leapt up to see Ami tending a neat row of sausages in a pan; the Fae speared one with tongs and waved it in invitation. Dara politely declined, instead warming leftover stew for the Humans to share.

After breakfast, the three packed quickly and stepped out into the morning. A warm breeze blew in from the ocean, the sweet and salty air and rays of the rising sun bringing smiles to every face.

"Nothing like the smell of the ocean first thing in the morning," Wynne said, her arms outstretched and eyes closed.

"I've never felt anything quite like this," Dara marveled.

"I'd rather smell a pan full of roasting sausages, which I thankfully enjoyed this morning," Ami said. "Still... even I have to admit, this is quite the pleasant start. Let's hope the rest of the day is its equal. Oh, and the guards told me before I left Vouliona that you all aren't allowed on the docks. We are to meet the captains on the beach. How auspicious!"

Waves crashed against a coarse rock protruding over the beach, spraying the four with a pleasant mist as they walked along the shore. High hopes and cheer drove their steps, but the sight of a single rowboat dashed the mood.

A fierce-looking Fae stood on the beach, wearing Human-style trousers beneath her poncho. The overgarment had been modified as well, with sections cut out of the sleeves and the body tucked tight by her waist, leaving her arms free. Beneath the poncho, she wore a tunic similar to that of Humans, with cuffed sleeves. A sword and dagger hung from her belt, along with multiple pouches and bags. A broad, flat-brimmed hat pulled in her short hair.

The Fae rested her hands on her hips and smiled broadly. Her teeth had been carved with strange patterns then inlaid with silver. "Unless you all have seen another trio of Humans mucking about, I take it you're my passengers. Ami, Caudro, you two are the obvious ones. Now, which of you is Dara, and which is Wynne? I take it the scrawny one is Wynne, that leaves the tall one to be Dara. Come along, winds are lively and we have a long journey ahead."

"What of the second captain?" Dara inquired.

"I'm your captain. The second backed out when the reality of your destination settled into his thick head. The other captains are all neither as dumb nor as dull to life as I am, and not even the sum offered for your passage was enough to sway their proper sensibilities."

"A stirring endorsement of yourself," Wynne said.

"Indeed. Some claim they need no introduction. I prefer to instead introduce myself honestly. I'm Catarin, by the way."

Though the others readied to follow the captain, Wynne kept her feet planted in the sand. "Shouldn't you tell us of the dangers we might face? Ones serious enough to scare off *all* the other captains?"

Catarin grinned. "If I were to tell you about every possible dangerous creature we might encounter along the way, then we would sit here on this beach for a month or more. All you need to know is that my crew and I have been paid to see you to your destination and we'll keep you as safe as we're able. Likewise, if you see anything climbing aboard that isn't one of the crew, you're welcome to kill it, as you'll likely see us trying to do."

Ami faltered and scooted close to Wynne. "I thought the coast was safe? Droves of fishing boats sail from Vouliona, and as many return in the evening as set out in the morn."

"Ah, you see, most all stay on the landward side of the islands. They never venture into the archipelago. We, however, will weave between the islands. At least we will, if we are to get to where you want to go. The supposed oddities have been sighted on an island far to the north of the archipelago, where ships rarely sail."

"If there is so much to be afraid of when sailing around these islands, why would you accept this task?" Dara asked. "You must forgive me, but I don't fully believe that you being dumb and dull is enough reason to set out on such a voyage."

"I'm bored, as are my crew," Catarin said with an unquestionable seriousness. "We are all former soldiers, and ferrying passengers along the coast doesn't quite do it for us anymore. As unpleasant as this trip might be, we might at least also find a touch of entertainment along the way. Now then, enough loitering about. Let's get to it."

The captain strode to the rowboat, waiting at the bow for the passengers to board. A Fae sailor sat at the ready, oars in hand. Dara took up a second set of oars, while the others settled in at the aft. When all were situated, the captain heaved the boat out with the tide, leaping aboard gracefully.

Dara rowed choppily at first, though she mindfully observed the sailor's technique and soon matched his pace. She found the simple exertion a pleasant distraction as the rowboat skimmed swiftly over the choppy ocean waters.

"Oy, you're as strong as half my crew at less than half their age," Catarin called from the bow. "You'd be welcome to join us if you weren't preoccupied with your Quinarium."

Weaving past fishing and trading ships alike, they soon reached the cog, which would take them through the Zanerian Archipelago. The ship, fifty feet in length and twenty feet wide, had a single mast. Despite its modest size, it sported four large ballistae, two at the bow and two atop the quarterdeck at the aft, bolts stuffed inside barrels beside each. Seven sailors waited aboard, both Human and Fae. They dressed similarly to their captain, with a mishmash of clothing and armor.

The captain led the passengers aboard, welcoming them with a sweep of her arm.

"Welcome to the Andaira."

The crew grunted and nodded, echoing her sentiment as they raised the rowboat.

Dara eyed the ballistae, and noticed bows and arrows, axes, and maces stashed across the deck. "The ballistae are weapons of war. Curious to see them mounted on what might have once been a fishing ship. Doesn't Llendshold bar the Fae from sailing warships?"

Catarin waved off laughter from her crew. "This was once a trade vessel, in fact. Though in design, she's not terribly different from a fishing ship. Also, the *requests* of the Regency of Llendshold are precisely that: a request and not a prohibition. They ask why the Fae need warships, presuming the Llendshold navy will protect us from any foes. You are fortunate we have taken their request and properly tossed it overboard—the ballistae are a necessity given where we are sailing."

"You still have said nothing of the dangers we should be prepared to face," Caudro said.

"It won't help to trouble yourselves over the question of what might be. We'll do the looking, and you'll know if we see something that we shouldn't want to be seeing."

Wynne ran her hand along the railing. "The Andaira... you've modified her, haven't you? Her hull and mast resemble ships I've seen in Hantsburg, but the rest... She doesn't look like the Fae ships we saw docked at Vouliona."

"The Andaira is as much a curiosity as her crew," Catarin replied. "We fix her up as we need, whether that be near Human ports like Rushlet, here in Vouliona, or further north by Zanrena. We tend to stay offshore, though. It allows us a bit of, how should I say this, *flexibility* with the jobs we attract."

"Like ours," Dara said.

"Precisely. You all are welcome to make yourselves comfortable. There are beds below deck—you'll know which ones are vacant."

Meanwhile, the crew began singing a rhythmic but unintelligible song. They secured the rowboat, unfurled the sail, and raised the anchor while Catarin strolled up to the quarterdeck. She took hold of the tiller to steer, motioning for Wynne to join her.

"I hope you don't mind the singing. I reckon it'll be two or three days' sailing, winds depending, before we reach our destination. You mentioned Hantsburg—girl of the sea, are you?"

Wynne's head turned like a hunting owl's as she took in the ship.

"I grew up there. I'm no great sailor, but I always loved going out to sea."

"Any day with passengers who aren't scared of wet feet is a good day in my book."

Wynne examined the crew, noticing none had a gauntlet or carried mana. "Do you not have a Mage of Seraeus among you?"

"Seraeus? You mean a wielder of air?" Catarin chuckled. "I would love to see the ships you sailed on. A Mage is a fine addition to any crew, but you'll find those not sailing under the banner of the Quinarium lack such luxury. Your little keepers of the faith don't like letting their Mages loose, most certainly not to aid a questionable crew such as ours. Nor can we afford one of the strays who break free. The Fae aren't keen on sending their few Mages out on the waters, either."

"Break free?"

The Captain surveyed the archipelago ahead, adjusting the tiller to guide the Andaira between the isles. "You are young, but I see in you a curiosity that will serve you well. Allow me to offer you a bit of uninvited advice: people of all kinds will tell you all sorts of things, about what is right, what is wrong, what is yours, what is theirs. Especially when said in the name of the Five, remember that the words come from a creature of the world. Everyone speaks with motivations in service of themselves, no matter how honorable or selfless they aim to be. And some—including the occasional Mage—have decided that the

Quinarium has said and done too much based on the worldly desires of Humans, and not of the Five.

"Bah, here I am rambling. You shouldn't trouble yourself over the words of a grizzled, bitter sailor. Why don't you go get settled with your friends? The Andaira rocks, she sways, but she sails true. If you all relax your bodies, flow with the ship, and feel the ocean in your souls, you might just keep your breakfasts down."

CHAPTER 11

Carried by a strong tailwind, the Andaira wound between islands, her crew scurrying about as if they shared a single mind. At first, the sights excited Wynne: strange trees with ringed trunks and giant, fern-like leaves, unusual birds with long necks and tails soaring above, and colorful squid surging beneath the water. However, after passing countless islands, the scenery grew all but mundane.

As the last rays of sunlight faded, the sailors stored the sails and lowered the anchor. Ami joined them for a meal of cured fish, though the Humans politely declined, retiring to the lower deck for the night.

The next day, the four woke well before dawn to the rocking of the ship. Heading to the deck, they found the sail already full of wind. Dara and Caudro went to join a few sparring sailors, while Ami lounged on a pile of rope and netting. Wynne joined Catarin up on the quarterdeck.

"Idle seas getting the better of your wandering mind? Though you are from Hantsburg, anyone who spends too much time staring into the endless blue can easily lose their way," said the captain.

"How did you come to be a sailor? Were you born near the coast?"

"Quite the opposite. I'm from Stellburg, back when it was ruled by the Fae."

Wynne shook her head. "Impossible. Stellburg has always been one of the five cities of Llendshold."

Catarin laughed, her voice resonating with the splashing of waves. "Curious how quickly fact becomes fiction. To be taught that Stellburg was always a part of Llendshold... While I'm sure the Quinarium has always considered it a part of the Humans' lands, that doesn't change the fact that I walked the streets some forty years ago, and they were crowded with Fae. A few Humans were mixed in there, as well. If you can believe it, there was a time we got on well enough before the war. Five above, I was born a stone's throw from the city."

Wynne stared at a lone white cloud in the sky.

"Not quite what you expected to hear, I'm sure."

"I was taught that the Fae invaded from the Nomridian Forest. That it was the Fae who attempted to capture the city in the First Battle of Stellburg, and that led to the war."

Catarin's lip curled. "The books you learned from are as clean as a horse's stall not mucked for a month. No matter what your books say, my family fled from Stellburg, as sure as you and I live and breathe. It's how I ended up here, answering your question. We ran as far from the war as we could, all the way to Zanrena. When I saw the ocean, I fell in love."

Wynne offered a hesitant smile. "Maybe the truth lies somewhere between my lessons and your experience. I agree with you about the ocean, though. It's like I'm home again, being on the waters."

"Home... not sure I have one of those anymore. But I know this is where I belong."

Wynne watched as Dara grappled with a sailor. Even without magic, she was a fierce fighter, besting the man; he hopped up cheering and praised her skill to the other sailors.

"How did you happen upon such a crew? I can't recall ever seeing Humans and Fae sailing together. And the Humans… they eat fish."

"Of course they do. What else do you expect them to eat at sea? Five as my witness, you look at me the way my mother used to. Fine, fine, an answer to your question. I learned to sail on a trade cog hoping to avoid the war, but that proved an impossibility. Before long, the trade cog I served on was volunteered to fight."

Catarin rubbed her palm against the tiller, lost in memory.

"We hoped to do nothing more than run supplies, but within weeks we were caught in a battle. In the mess of ships, a storm rose, and we drifted away, tangled with a Human ship. After countless hours of fighting through rain and thunder, barely a dozen of us remained. We stared at each other, bloodied and disheveled, wondering why, and for what? Realizing how pointless it was, we decided then to leave it all. We nine are what remains of that day, officially lost in battle. Ghosts of the sea, if you will. So, even though we all turned our back on the war, it's still in our hearts. No matter how much we resent it, we all thirst for a good fight, and that thirst is never quenched. And it's why we are the only ones willing to take you out into the archipelago."

"Is this life not lonely?"

"It is, and terribly so. We all lost much, going to war. We lost more still, choosing this life. You never truly know what you have until it's gone and only the memory remains." Catarin grabbed Wynne's wrist and stared into her eyes. "Ask yourself, Wynne—ask yourself what is really important to you? Find your answer and hold fast. Hold fast, and never let go."

Wynne nodded, and the captain loosened her grip, taking hold of the tiller once again. Wynne's eyes drifted over the deck. Dara leaned against the mast, watching as the sailors scrambled to catch the shifting wind. As the ship rounded an island, a harsh headwind blew in, stalling the ship.

A horrifying screech pierced the air. Wynne slammed her hands over her ears to drown out the sound. Her mouth fell open at the sight of Catarin chortling as she stuffed cloth plugs into her ears.

"Blood in the waters, blood on the deck!" she roared.

"Sever them all, heads from their necks!" the sailors cheered, plugging their ears then arming themselves with axes, maces, and shields.

The captain waved over the four passengers and distributed cloth plugs from a pouch on her belt. "Keep these in your ears or you'll bleed from the cries. Listen too long and you might go deaf."

Ears plugged, they recoiled as the shrieks struck again. In the distance, Dara spied a patch of the ocean roiling and bubbling. In moments, the disturbances appeared in every direction as if a hundred boulders had been thrown into the ocean.

"What could cause the ocean to boil?" she shouted.

"Drink some mana and get ready for a fight, my dear," the captain replied. "The water isn't boiling; that'll be from the Sirens, singing beneath the surface."

"What is a Siren?"

"You'll see soon enough. Keep away from the heads and watch for the tentacles. And the claws!"

Sailors manned the ballistae as the bubbling condensed into narrow lines which raced towards the ship. One pulled ahead of the rest. When it was some fifty feet from the ship, the surrounding water suddenly went calm.

Seconds later, a Siren burst into the air.

Eight feet long, it had the head of a giant eel with rows of slender teeth, mouth gaping and screaming a horrible song. A long neck led to a body like that of a seal. Leathery wings with clawed hands halfway down their length spread wide. At the end of its body was a squirming mass of tentacles covered in black barbs. The Siren landed on the deck and reared back, snapping and swiping at the crew.

A nearby sailor leapt in, beheading the Siren with a swing of her axe. Bright green blood spewed out as the tentacles flailed wildly and wings flapped against the deck. The sailor kicked the still-gnashing head into the ocean, its body sliding after it as the ship listed from a wave. Sailors cheered as they aimed the ballistae and took up positions around the deck. Dara and Caudro split, ready on either side of the ship, while Ami joined Wynne on the quarterdeck.

The Sirens approached rapidly in an ever-tightening circle. A ballista fired, its heavy steel bolt slamming into the water. A puff of bright green stained the ocean. The sailors, smiling all the while, launched the bolts in a frenzy, but the Sirens swam ever faster.

A wave crashed over the starboard bow, followed by four of the Sirens. A sailor swung his ballista and launched a bolt clean through one, but the other three grabbed hold of him with their claws. Ami loosed an arrow and struck a Siren as the sailor hacked wildly, but the Sirens would not relinquish their grip. Dara rushed over and sliced through tentacles and wings alike, but the beasts held tight and threw their weight back, pulling the sailor overboard.

Dara clambered after, reaching for the sailor's hands, but his fingers slipped away.

The Sirens gave her not a moment of respite as tens more climbed the sides of the ship, grabbing hold with claws and tentacles. Dara slashed furiously, driving back as many as she was able.

Wynne murmured with her eyes closed, rhythmically waving her hand back and forth. Making a broad circle in the sky, she yanked her fist down. A cascade of flaming white orbs fell around the ship, scalding the Sirens. Ami cheered, but distress flooded Wynne; the Sirens still scaled the ship despite being covered in burns.

A screech sounded from behind as a Siren climbed over the quarterdeck. The sailor manning a ballista abandoned the heavy weapon and charged in with an axe. Wynne took over his place, cranking as fast as she was able to draw the string, then heaving a bolt into place. Wynne aimed the ballista at a Siren scrambling towards Caudro and pulled the release. The bolt flew true, spearing the creature to the deck of the ship.

While Wynne loaded another bolt, Ami climbed to the crow's nest at the top of the mast. From the perch, she rained down arrows, timing each release with the rocking of the ship.

The Sirens had been vulnerable while climbing up, but as they reached the deck, half on their winged arms and half on their undulating mass of tentacles, they threatened to overrun the crew. Caudro kept many at bay, battering with his shield and stabbing with his spear, while Dara dove into the mass of attacking beasts.

Struggling to find her mark with arrows, Ami drank a mouthful of mana, then took hold of the spiked gourd at her belt. She squeezed until blood seeped between her fingers. Pulling her fist tight to her chest, she exhaled slowly, extending her open palm.

A section of churning water went suddenly still, as if it were frozen in deep winter. A group of Sirens surged upwards, expecting to fly into the air but hit the solid surface, cracking their heads.

Aboard the ship, the situation grew dire as Sirens swarmed the deck. Caudro dove to block a Siren from grabbing hold of a sailor when his shield slipped from his hand. He stabbed one in the gut, but two more immediately arrived to take its place.

Unable to scratch through his armor, Sirens grabbed hold of his breastplate by his shoulder and wrapped their tentacles around his arms and legs. They pried and pulled until a crack rippled across the plate from his shoulder to his waist. Dara leapt in, slicing and hacking apart the Sirens alongside Catarin. No sooner had they pulled Caudro to his feet than a fresh horde of Sirens was upon them.

A Fae sailor dove into the charging mass. She knocked the horde to the deck, protecting Catarin, Dara, and Caudro from the outstretched claws, but the Sirens took hold of the sailor. Before any could save her, the Sirens dove overboard with the Fae wrapped inside their claws.

Slow with the ballista and her magic ineffective against the Sirens, desperation brewed in Wynne. Spying a cluster of towering rocks protruding from the ocean near the ship's path, she tied a sturdy rope to a bolt and loaded it into the ballista. She secured the rope to the base of the weapon, then took aim.

Wynne sent the bolt flying as they passed the rocks.

"Grab hold of something!" she screamed.

Catarin relayed the command, shouting until the sailors all acknowledged the orders and grabbed hold of whatever they could wrap their arms around.

As the rope pulled taut and the bow of the ship rose out of the water, Sirens flailed and slid off the ship. Dara sprinted to the quarterdeck, vaulting over sliding crates and slipping past flailing Sirens. She scampered up the stairs, then jumped with sword in hand, slicing through the rope.

The bow of the ship slammed back into the water, catapulting Sirens away.

The crew dispatched the few remaining beasts on the deck, then set about catching a crosswind. Dara and Wynne hurried to the main deck, rejoining Caudro as Ami climbed down from the crow's nest. They were relieved to see the waters calm as the ship gained speed.

Wynne expected the crew to be sad at the loss of two of their compatriots, but the sailors removed their earplugs and cheered, regaling each other with tales of the battle. They praised Wynne for her use of the ballista, though she pulled her arms tight across her chest and stared at the bright green stains covering the ship.

"How can you laugh? The Sirens took two of your crew."

A Human sailor came over and pat her on the back. "You sail with a crew who have no place among Humans and no place among Fae. Garrett and Orlin were not taken. They have gone home, to the depths of the ocean."

A Fae sailor nodded in agreement. "And how they fought! Many Sirens died today. A fitting end for soldiers to make their enemy bleed with their last breaths."

"A fitting end?" Caudro questioned. "They died fighting mindless beasts, protecting... us. Not in service of a higher order. Nothing more than us four. If you all seek such an end, why not sail around the islands until Sirens or some other creatures kill you all?"

"We aren't suicidal," said Catarin. "We relish the thrill of battle, and consider an end in a proper fight to be glorious. All the better that theirs came in service of a purposeful, dare I say honorable, task."

Dara's brow raised. "You consider ferrying Mages and a Paladin of the Quinarium, along with their Fae guide, to be honorable?"

Catarin and her crew laughed. "Close enough."

The sailors rebuffed any attempt of the passengers to tidy or scrub the ship, urging them instead to join the captain up on the quarterdeck. Wynne shifted her attention from the cheerful crew to her companions.

"Dara, Caudro, are you alright? Don't lie. You know I won't relent until I'm certain you're well."

"Of course you don't worry about the Fae, typical Human!" Ami exclaimed, crossing her arms and shaking her head. She recoiled at seeing Wynne's pursed lips. "I am joking, of course! I can keep myself safe. Though, there were moments while I was up in the crow's nest that I worried you all might be torn apart, and I would be stuck up there, waiting to be killed last."

Dara grinned at Wynne's revulsion. "I'm fine, Wynne. Nothing more than bruises and a few scrapes. Caudro, your armor…"

"It served its purpose, thankfully," he replied, inspecting the crack in his breastplate. "Though I am not looking forward to repairing it."

"Repair it? Might as well get a new piece when you're back with your Paladin friends," Ami said.

"A Paladin's armor is their lifeblood. When we reach adulthood, blacksmiths forge a set for us, and we are to maintain it. I've replaced scales and mended gauntlets, but this… I expect it will take many hours with the blacksmiths to learn how to fix it properly, if I'm not forced to reforge it entirely."

"Better to be dealt a tedious job than to lose your life," Dara said, patting his shoulder.

Wynne gave the bottle at her hip a gentle shake. "I'm running low on mana. Barely a sip left in this one, and the one in my pack is nearly empty as well. How are you faring, Dara?"

"Same as you. We should have kept some bottles from the Jackal den; I doubt the Elder in Vouliona would have realized a few were missing. At least we can refill our bottles at the mana source, if it exists."

"You're welcome to a portion of mine," Ami offered. "But wait—would consuming mana extracted from animals be considered eating meat? It shouldn't, should it? Your mana comes from Humans, and you all are animals of a sort. Though I don't have what I would describe as a generous supply, either. I used a fair portion stopping the Sirens from popping up through the water."

"I hear your ask for praise, and it's praise well deserved," said Catarin. "Nice trick, that."

"Thank you!"

"Should we expect more dangers on the way?" Dara asked the captain.

"Sirens are a noisy lot. While not the largest by a sizable margin, a swarm of them is enough to drive most everything away for miles. If you can believe it, they're rather weak out of the water compared to when they're beneath the surface. Only things that aren't scared of Sirens are things we shouldn't fear, as they'd end us before we had a chance to worry."

Wynne shivered away thoughts of creatures worse than the Sirens. "Shouldn't we be helping your crew? Will they be able to manage the ship with your numbers so reduced?"

Catarin snorted. "It'd take you more than the entirety of our voyage to learn the basics of handling this ship, not that your offer is unappreciated. We can get along well enough with six crew. I've run this ship with as few as four, and I'd wager three could manage in a pinch."

A green stain by the railing drew Caudro's attention. "We should perform rites for the two who were lost."

"Why? They're dead. Nothing to be done for them," the captain said.

"Sacrilege!" Caudro shouted. "Your behavior is an affront to the Five!"

"Worry yourself not, Agent of the Quinarium. Sure as the Five formed our world, they have left it. Perhaps if my crew and I are heretical enough, it'll draw them back and they can explain to us why they left." Catarin stared at the Paladin through half-closed eyes. "I see the anger brewing in you. You would do well to learn the world is not as simple as the righteous goodness of the Quinarium, opposing the evil of any who don't fall in line with your ways. You don't have to agree with who I am to make use of my services. Do what you need to make peace with who you are sailing with. We should arrive tomorrow morning."

CHAPTER 12

Ami's legs dangled from the crow's nest, wishing she were atop a tree in the Nomridian Forest instead of onboard the Andaira. She gazed at the countless islands, some little more than a large rock protruding from the ocean, while others sprawled for acres. She had long tired of looking for shapes in the passing clouds. When she thought she could stand the sight of the archipelago no longer, she noticed a plume of grey rising from a large island.

"On the horizon! Northwest!"

Catarin waved. "Hands on deck, you heard the boss!"

Dara and Wynne eagerly stood at the bow as the crew adjusted course. The island was larger than most, but aside from the smoke, it was otherwise unremarkable: trees covered rough hills and the occasional flock of birds flew above.

"It looks rather plain, and there are no signs of... anything, other than the smoke," Wynne said.

"Maybe that's how it's stayed hidden," Dara replied.

"I wonder if there will be some form of protection, whether a guardian or a magical enchantment."

"I already told you who I think we will find."

Wynne giggled. "If the mana source is a bearded old man like you think, I swear I will convince my mother to name you Lord of Hantsburg."

"Then I had better pray to the Five that the old man is waiting for us."

The Andaira anchored in the shallows near the island; Catarin joined the four in the rowboat. Dara and Caudro rowed steadily while the captain steered.

"What other sea monsters are there?" Wynne asked. "Perhaps you could share a few of your favorites?"

"Favorites? Fascinating choice of words," Catarin replied. "You're from Hantsburg. You sure you aren't the one who should regale me with tales of wild sea creatures?"

"Stories read from books are different than stories told by those who have lived to tell the tale."

The captain spoke rhythmically, matching the sloshing of the oars. "The idea of a monster is entirely a matter of perspective. To a minnow, a mackerel is a monster. To the mackerel, a Fae is a monster. Who is to say what is monstrous or delightful? But as I've been asked the question of what I consider my favorites, I would start with the humble Seahorse. Have you heard of them?"

"I have," chimed Ami. "I heard they are majestic creatures, with the head of a horse and body of a whale. They'll offer you a ride over the waters, but once you're out at sea, they pull you into the deep to drown and eat you."

Catarin chuckled. "I've seen many a seahorse. They aren't much more than three feet long. Good luck taking a ride on one—you're as likely to break the poor creature's back as to be dragged underwater by them. Pleasant little things. They swim alongside ships late at night, when it fancies them."

"I heard a similar description," Wynne said. "How does such a reputation exist if the creatures are small and harmless?"

"Fear and ignorance are the authors of mighty tales. While the Seahorse is misunderstood, a victim of sailors' stupidity, I will tell you of a creature which has more than earned its reputation. Perchance, have you heard of the Keeper of the Deep?"

Wynne shook her head. "Never."

Catarin paused, allowing the splashing of the oars to carry on for a minute. "Few have. As tall as twenty men, the Keeper has the head of an octopus. Its giant beak, large enough to swallow a sailor in a single bite, is hidden beneath hair of tentacles. Bone plates cover its body. Four fingered hands reach out from arms as thick as the Andaira is broad. Its body tapers down with a tail like that of the greatest of whales. The Keeper swims at a speed far exceeding the fastest of ships with a sheet full of wind. You might consider the Sirens dangerous, and rightfully so, but the Keeper... none compare. Precious few are lucky enough to have seen it and survived."

"Your description is rather extreme," Dara said. "Is it possible that fear and ignorance have exaggerated the description, as you said?"

"I might well think so, had I not been one of the fortunate ones to survive seeing it." The captain's cheer returned as they neared the shore. "Steady as you were, run the boat aground."

The rowboat skidded to a halt on the sandy shore. Catarin threw an anchor into the sand and walked to the tree line while the four readied themselves. Though the island appeared mundane from a distance, the trees were the tallest they had seen in the archipelago, and the dense underbrush was sure to make exploration tedious.

"Wynne, are you worried about monsters?" Dara asked, leaning close as they pulled on their packs.

"Not as such..."

"Don't worry!" Ami interjected. "Dara will protect you."

Wynne's cheeks flushed.

"That is obvious, is it not, Ami?" Caudro said. "They are Mages on their rite. They have to protect each other and complete the rite together, or it is not complete at all."

"You big, strong, baby of a man." Ami chuckled, pinching Caudro's cheek before walking to the forest.

"What!?" he called, stomping after.

Dara grabbed Wynne's shoulder before she could join the others. "I'm sure we will be fine."

When Dara relinquished her grip, Wynne paused, her shoulder cold despite the warm sun. She scurried after the others, joining them by the edge of the forest.

Catarin lay beneath an arching tree with her hat over her face.

"Good luck."

"I thought you would keep watch," Caudro said.

"A question as much as a condemnation of my supposed laziness. There is no need for me to keep watch, master Paladin."

"How can you say there is no need?" Caudro pressed. "We are on a foreign island, with neither a map nor knowledge of what might await in this forest! None of your sailors joined us—we rely on you for our return."

"Precisely. If there is something nefarious about, it will certainly assail the four traipsing invaders first. Please scream loudly, that I might have plenty of warning to flee."

"Calm your worried mind, big man. She won't be paid until we are safely back in Vouliona," Ami drolled. "Dara?"

Armed with a machete provided by Catarin, Dara took the lead, followed closely by Wynne, then Caudro, then Ami. It was a slog to cut through the underbrush. The air was hot and humid, and strange plants surrounded them. Pods of long stems grew up to their shoulders, hosting leaves broader than Caudro's shield. Trees grew high into the air, only to bend down and nearly touch the ground again. Tufts of long, slender leaves covered their branches. A teal bird with four wings flew overhead, snatching a whirring beetle with a glossy purple shell from the air.

Wynne wiped sweat from her temples and cheeks and rolled up her sleeves, the oppressive humidity drenching the group. Dara lifted a branch, then paused, grabbing Wynne's attention; she watched as a bead of sweat dripped down the Blood Mage's forearm, tracing the lines between her strained muscles. Wynne thought of the strength in Dara's arm, the power and elegance with which she wielded her sword. If she would instead take hold of Wynne, bring her close...

Dara released the branch and wiped the sweat from her brow. She peered back over her shoulder, and Wynne jumped, offering a meek smile. Dara turned her attention ahead and continued pushing through the forest, chasing the trail of smoke.

The sun arced over the sky, beginning its slow descent by the time they scaled the peak of the tallest hill on the island. Dara was certain they had found the source of the smoke when the forest abruptly ended.

Before them stretched the remains of a stone-paved road. Decrepit stone structures were scattered on either side, the remnants of a modest village. Though a few buildings were intact, the roofs and walls of most had caved in ages ago. Vines and plumes of grasses covered the ruins. The doorways of the few standing structures were over ten feet tall.

"No sign of the fire anymore," Dara said.

While the others explored the nearby structures, Wynne scrambled atop a partially collapsed building.

"Everyone, come here! You have to see this. It's... it's unbelievable."

After clambering up to join Wynne, the view shocked them all.

The island stretched for miles into the distance, much further than they had imagined. Abandoned buildings ran down a slope and up over another prominent hill. What had seemed a small village was instead a sprawling complex that was once home to thousands.

"We have to search all of this? It's going to be a long day," Ami said.

"The smoke came from this hill. Whoever started it must be nearby," Caudro said.

Dara knelt down, brushing aside a clump of vines and running her hands over the surface of the building.

"There are fine circular marks on these—I've never seen stone cut in such a way. The workmanship is impeccable. It's polished smooth, even after what must be countless years of neglect and exposure to the wind and rain."

A rumbling laughter boomed over the ruins. A tall creature appeared in the distance on the central avenue. It glided over the road on a tangle of tens of tentacle-legs. Shimmering, palm-sized scales covered its body. Wide shoulders led to two long, slender arms, with webs between the limbs and its torso. A craning neck led to a domed, hairless head with no nose and beak-like lips.

Wynne glanced back to see the others as stunned as her, staring at the approaching creature. She turned to find it a mere stone's throw away.

"Who are you?" Its voice resonated as if twenty people had spoken at once, the timbre beautifully rich and warm.

Wynne gulped. "I am Wynne, Mage of the Quinarium. I am accompanied by Dara, a fellow Mage; Caudro, Paladin of the Quinarium; and Ami, Fae Mage from the Nomridian Forest."

"Quinarium? What is this Quinarium you speak of?"

Wynne put on a practiced cordial smile. "It is our religious body. As the sole organization ordained by the Quinate, the Five Gods, the Quinarium guides our faith and shepherds us in our supplication."

"Ah, I see, I see." An undulating, twisting, swirling tongue emerged from the creature's mouth and flittered across its face. "Now that you have told me who you claim to be, tell me: why have you come here?"

"I assure you, I speak truthfully. We came in search of a mana source. I'm not sure what form it takes, but supposedly there is a place where mana flows freely from the ground. Mana being the gift of the Gods, used by Mages to empower our spells. Do you perhaps know of mana?"

The creature laughed, the sound like the churning of a hundred waves in tidal pools. "Of course I know of mana. A more interesting question is, how did you hear of a mana source on this island?"

"There were rumors, heard across Human lands of Llendshold and the Fae home of the Nomridian Forest. Unfortunately, I am uncertain as to the origin."

"Llendshold, Nomridian... strange names."

"I can show you a map," Wynne offered, moving to take off her pack.

"I have no use for your maps. I take it the notion of a mana source has spread far, given your description. Rumors, whispers, how could they have reached your lands from this island, which you believe holds this mystical, magical, mana-producing source? I see your face. Who, or what, could this creature be? Did it send word itself? Perhaps it was me, roaring into the winds, sending thoughts of a mana source, that sailors might hear it. As they found their way home, they would certainly regurgitate the whispers. Intrepid adventurers would then sail forth, one day reaching this island. And thus I would be rid of my loneliness, my longing to see another intelligent being."

Wynne squinted at the creature. "The mana source... it exists?"

"I prefer to call it the Fountain. And of course it does."

"What do you know of it?"

The creature took squelching steps until it was within arm's reach of Wynne. "What do I know of it? Juvenile questions you ask. I drink of it every day. It is the entirety of my sustenance. As you say, a gift of the Gods."

"To... to drink of it every day... You are blessed to have such a source," Wynne said, remembering the Instructors' cautions against the over-indulgence of mana.

"Blessed?" The creature stared at the horizon. "I am cursed. I hunger, yet food has no taste. I thirst, yet water does not satisfy. I long to roam, but my body always brings me back to the Fountain. Nothing else matters except drinking from it. That accursed thing has given me an endless life, alone. My kind were once wild and without thought, then through this *gift* we ascended, only to fall again. I am all that remains."

"Last of your kind?" Wynne squinted. "What are you?"

"I've heard the name your people used, carried over the winds by the storms. I am the last of the Sirens." It gurgled and chortled at Wynne's shock. "I told you that my kind had fallen. Slaves to mana, we drank too deeply. Greediness drove my people to madness, and the Gods called us *failure*. That is what you may call me, Failure. I am a forgotten memory, a wisp of cloud, too frail to turn into rain, doomed to drift across the sky, alone. You, however—Humans, Fae, Dwarves—they consider you the finest of their creations. The result of an age spent refining, tinkering, toying with life until they were satisfied."

"How is this possible?" Wynne asked. "We thought Humans, Fae, and Dwarves to be the only creations of the Five."

"Consider my kind a trial. A test from which the Gods learned: a race whose sentience depends entirely on mana is an unsustainable creation. Nor was it wise to create a creature that yearns for water when on land, and yearns for land when in the water. You can hardly believe my existence, despite me standing here. Have you not wondered why we can understand each other? We were all molded in the shape of the Five to speak in the way they wanted to hear. Though I digress—tell me, why do you seek the Fountain?"

"We are on our Rite of the Faithful, a test of Mages..." Wynne's voice cracked as she looked to her companions, only to see them all still as stone. She turned back to find the Siren's face inches away from hers. "What magic is this?"

A rumble resonated from Failure's throat. *"Mine.* It is the magic of a being who has consumed mana every day for days uncountable. You need not worry yourself about my spell. Tell me, young one, sent on behalf of this Quinarium, what will you do, should you see my Fountain?"

Wynne peered at Dara. Despite the heat, the humidity, and the tickle of sweat trickling over her skin, chills ran through Wynne's body. Turning her attention to the Siren, Wynne noticed liquid seeping out from between its scales. She wondered if it was water or mana or something else entirely.

"I think our leaders would want proof, perhaps a bottle filled from the Fountain."

Failure leaned away. "And what do you suppose they will do with the mana, certain of the Fountain's existence, of *my* existence?"

"I don't know."

"I wonder then, why should I allow you to fill your bottle?"

"You mentioned your loneliness. Surely we have brought you intrigue, a respite from being alone?"

"Intrigue, intrigue... But what if it is entertainment I crave? Something more than a simple satisfaction of curiosity. Ah, of course! I can think of some ways your friends might entertain me. For example!"

The Siren swept its hand and burst into laughter. The three danced a lively jig, their faces frozen and emotionless, horrifying

Wynne. Failure hooted and hollered, waving about like a puppeteer.

"Stop! Stop it, please!" Wynne screamed.

"Oh, should I? But what if I don't want to?"

"Tell me what you want," Wynne pleaded.

"You spoke as if you knew my desire, and my desire you claimed to be entertainment. I am presently entertained."

"All we want is a single bottle, a small amount. Please... we have caused you no harm."

Failure's mouth fell open and its tongue flailed about as it danced the three companions to the edge of the building. "You caused me no harm because you are unable to cause me harm. And no matter the quantity, why should I give you something if I am not to receive something in return?"

"What is it you want?" The veins in Wynne's neck bulged as she yelled in desperation. "Gold? Jewels? What can we offer that will satisfy you?"

The Siren oohed as it made the trio leap over a gap to a nearby building.

"Entertainment."

"Then tell me how to entertain you! Whatever you want, just let them go!"

Failure's arms relaxed, and the three slumped over like dolls set down by a child. It raised a webbed finger to the sky, then pointed at Wynne.

"I will ask questions of you, and you shall answer. If I am satisfied, I will take you to the Fountain and release your friends. If I am dissatisfied, there will be consequences."

"Answer questions? That is preposterously broad," Wynne said, crossing her arms behind her back. "There is no end, no conclusion, no measure of success or failure. How can I possibly satisfy you?"

"You simply must. Otherwise I will keep your friends here, and you can report back to your Quinarium alone. Walk with me," Failure said to the three, forcing them to march as it stepped along the stone-paved avenue. "Dearest Wynne, tell me, if you could only save one of the three, who would it be?"

Wynne's head pounded, the gravity of the question hitting her like a falling tree. Sweat drenched her clothes and her vision blurred as she pondered the question.

"Dara. She is my peer in the Quinarium, and we are partners on our rite."

"I don't believe you."

"It's the truth!" Wynne spewed. "I would choose Dara. We have traveled together the longest, our purposes are the most closely aligned, and we are to complete our rite together. Caudro would gladly sacrifice himself for our cause, and Ami-"

"Oh, my dear, I don't disbelieve your choice of Dara. Rather, I disbelieve your reasoning. Be honest with me."

Wynne's face burned. "What do you mean?"

The Siren chortled. "Ah, perhaps I have touched on an emotion not yet explored, not yet embraced. Are you certain your choice was purely professional?"

Failure halted and turned back to the three. The Siren leaned in, lifting Dara's limp head by her chin with a moist, scaly finger. It pored over Dara's face as it noisily licked its lips.

"Fine!" Wynne shouted desperately. "Fine. I care for her."

"Better," Failure said, drifting away from Dara.

"And what exactly makes it better? What does it prove, having me admit my attraction to Dara?"

"Nothing. But I enjoyed hearing the truth from your lips, seeing you squirm. One might say it was quite... *entertaining.*"

"What else would you ask of me?"

Failure resumed its lazy stroll. "Let us consider the reverse. If instead of saving one of your companions, imagine a sacrifice is demanded. Which one would you choose to die, that the rest of you might live?"

Wynne froze.

"I shouldn't think Dara, you already have your eyes set on her. Would her opinion of you change based on your choice of sacrifice? Perhaps it should be Ami. She is not a Human, nor is she a part of your Quinarium. But then there is Caudro. He's not a Mage, and he is Male. That's two differentiating factors each for the Fae and the Paladin. I'm sure we could find many more little details to consider. Oh, which one, which one, as one must be chosen?"

A thin silver bracelet slid down Wynne's wrist, and her thoughts turned to her mother. Echoes of lessons about leading, sacrifice, dignity, choice, and responsibility swirled in her mind. Did the Siren truly intend to keep one of them?

"Myself. I would sacrifice myself."

"Yawn." Failure dragged the word out, allowing the final consonant to linger. "Self-sacrifice, heroics, martyrdom, the way you carry yourself, your behavior—I would wager you the child of nobility. False martyrdom is little more than vanity and an inflation of your ego, placing such high worth on your own life. Offering yourself is both boring and does not answer my question. I asked you which of your companions you would choose, so choose."

Wynne faltered. The Siren pressed its hand against her back. It was a strange sensation, damp and cool, with jelly-like pressure spreading across her skin through her tunic. It spun her about until she faced the three.

"Which one?"

Wynne stared blankly, trying to imagine what each would say if she told them they were to be sacrificed. Ami was nebulous, with her irreverence and perpetual lack of seriousness, yet Wynne believed the Fae to be more sincere and caring than she wished to admit. Caudro would likely be angry, if not chosen as sacrifice. Dara... what would Dara say? Would she be as Caudro, stalwart and accepting? Would she demand to be the one?

"I tire of waiting."

Failure waved, sending Dara, Ami, and Caudro to the edge of a nearby cliff. The Siren flicked a finger, and all three stretched one foot out over the nothingness below.

Wynne's heart raced. Surely Caudro was the obvious answer, but would the obvious answer entertain the Siren?

"Dara."

Failure threw its head back and laughed boisterously. "Must you find a way of making yourself into a martyr? Why Dara?"

"Caudro would be enraged at not being chosen as sacrifice, but a sacrifice must have meaning. Dara is the strongest of us, a Mage of Ramaia, and the one I care for most. She also would not abide being a survivor in lieu of another."

"A high opinion of her. Your care for Dara runs deep."

"As does the Fountain of mana, I presume."

"Fear not, fret not," Failure said, striding along the road, summoning back the three. "I will take you to the Fountain. But why is it so important to you, I wonder?"

"Our rite."

"Oh, not that. I care not about some trivial test set for you by your institution. I care about the institution itself, the Quinarium. Why are they interested?"

"Is it not obvious? Because a free flowing source of mana would be unconscionably amazing. Mana pouring out of the ground..."

"Hm." Failure peered at Wynne. "Is this not how mana is always acquired?"

Wynne scoffed. "Of course not. The Quinarium manages the harvesting and storage of mana. When a person is near death, they can offer themselves in service of the Five. Agents of the

Quinarium collect mana from their body, shepherding their final moments from life to death. It is a beautiful ceremony."

"Crude."

"Crude? It is the process ordained by the Quinate, carried out with sacred respect by the Quinarium."

Failure grumbled. "Mana should seep back into the soil as the life of a creature ends. With death comes release naturally, regenerating the Fountains. Or should I say *Fountain,* as it seems your Quinarium's meddling has dried up the others. The Gods created mana for all. It should not be hoarded by Humans, Fae, or Dwarves."

"Hoarded?" Wynne fumed, staring at the pocked stones lining the road. "What a poor assessment. The Quinarium operates based on the decree of the Quinate. They manage the gift that is mana with reverence and care. What is this silliness you speak of, seeping back into the earth?"

"A decree, or so they tell you. You have much to learn, young one, but I trust you will discover the truth in time. For now, fill your bottles. I have much to consider."

"Is that it? You torment my companions, torment me, all for a few minutes of entertainment and...."

Wynne turned, ready to continue her tirade, yet Failure was gone. Instead, she stood before a waist-high mound of smooth rocks, positioned unassumingly amidst the ruins. A clear liquid bubbled over the top and trickled down, shimmering brightly in the sun. A breeze washed over the island and an intoxicating scent reached her nose.

"Mana. It's mana! Do you all see this?"

Dara, Ami, and Caudro remained still, their heads drooped like cut flowers set out in the heat of summer with no water. Wynne shook Dara's shoulders and touched her face. Her skin was warm, but after Wynne raised Dara's head, it immediately rolled down again.

Wynne dashed between all three, shouting, talking, pushing, prodding, begging that the Five might free them. She yanked on her gauntlet and tried a multitude of spells, shaking the last drops of mana from her bottles.

Clutching the neck of an empty bottle so tightly that her fingers went white, Wynne darted to the mana source. She slammed the bottle into a trickle, not caring that her knuckles bust and bled against the stones. When mana overflowed, she flew back. Grabbing hold of Dara's chin, Wynne tried to pry open her mouth to pour mana in, but she couldn't force her lips apart. Screaming and cursing the Siren, Wynne shook the bottle, sending mana sailing through the air.

Droplets cascaded over the frozen Mage, showering her in mana. Moments later, Dara fell to her knees, gasping and wheezing.

"Five above," she cried out, rubbing her neck and chest. "My body aches as if I've climbed a hundred mountains."

Wynne hurriedly splashed the others.

"What did that thing do to us?" Ami sputtered.

Caudro spat and knelt, shaking his head.

"Are you all right?" Wynne repeated herself over and over, scurrying between the three in a frenzy.

Dara grabbed Wynne by the shoulders and forced her to sit. "We've all had better days, but I think we will be fine. But you, your hand is bleeding."

"The source," Caudro whispered, staring at the flowing mana.

Wynne nodded, catching her breath. "Yes. We should fill our bottles and leave this place. I'll tell you everything on the way back, but I don't want to stay here any longer than we absolutely must."

INTERLUDE

Moonlight flowed in through the tall windows of Okter's office. Hunched over his desk, he lowered a candle to the page of an ancient tome, so close it threatened to singe the paper. Satisfied with his review of the contents, Okter delicately turned the page with a single fingernail.

The door flung open, banging as it struck the wall.

"I appreciate it when guests knock," Okter said, unmoved from his tome. "A closed door generally indicates that those inside have a preference for privacy."

"And what if your guest is an Adjudicator?"

Okter calmly set aside the candle and closed the tome. Rising to his feet, he examined his unexpected guest: an Adjudicator, one of the highest-ranking members of the Quinarium, above the Moderators and second only to the Voice of the Five.

Steel-capped wooden shoes clinked on the stone floor. Ornamental plate armor covered the Adjudicator's elbows, knees, and shoulders; gold trim with engraved patterns decorated the edges. Though the room was dim, her white tunic shone brightly, with ribbons of silver and gold woven throughout like waves. A wide silver collar covered the upper half of her chest with a broad golden stole over the top, the tails extending past her belt. Vibrant purple and red trim adorned every piece. A solid gold mask inlaid with gems shrouded her face.

Okter calmly kneeled and lowered his head. "Adjudicator, you grace me with your presence. I apologize for my informality."

"Sit."

Chin raised high, Okter sat at his desk. He stared at the Adjudicator, who halted at the center of the room.

"Adjudicator, if I may..."

"You have been busy, Okter Bosmun."

"Yes, Adjudicator. The Academy of Ramaia, is... the Academy... it's..."

Color drained from Okter's vision. His head pounded as if an Ogre had struck him. He held his hand in front of his face; his fingers blurred into a tangle of cloudy lines. Okter attempted to stand, but his legs buckled. He grabbed hold of his desk, his fingers trembling as he fought to maintain his hold.

Through the haze, Okter saw the Adjudicator, mask removed, smiling. Duplicates of her face spun in circles. A flash of light came from his side. Okter slipped and fell to the ground. He scrambled, attempting to grab his desk to pull himself back up, but his hand could not take hold. He raised his arm to see a bloody stump. Peering over the edge of the desk, he saw his severed right hand twitching.

Fighting the urge to scream, Okter pulled his bloodied arm tight against his chest. Sweat soaked his collar. He heaved himself up, leaning against his desk, groaning like a feral animal. Tremors overtook his body. Squinting through the pain and fog clouding his eyes, he made out a man wiping a sword blade clean. Bottles of mana surrounded the man's belt. He wore a simple brown tunic, lacking any decoration save the symbol of the Quinarium on his left shoulder, stitched in white. The clothing designated the man as an Enforcer, a deadly Mage with total dedication to his Adjudicator.

The Adjudicator sauntered over to Okter. "You stole mana. You consumed it for your own benefit. You explored magic outside the generous bounds afforded you by the Quinarium. You thought yourself of such power that you might learn more than the ways of Ramaia, did you not? As consequence, your blood has been spilled. Your hand has been taken because of your actions. Consider yourself fortunate you did not spread your evil ways, or else it would have been your tongue taken instead."

"My every action was in service of the Quinarium!" Okter barked. "I did everything in the name of the Quinate, for this Academy!"

"Lies! You were given everything, and yet you still sought more. And yet, the Quinate are not without their mercy. A horse is waiting for you. You are to leave for Draethhold. You, Okter Bosmun, are henceforth exiled, never to return to Llendshold. And before you call upon the name of your family, we have informed them of your actions and they have shunned you before both the Lord and the Moderator of Brewardsburg. Be gone, heretic! Live out your days with the heathens of the southern lands. Live on without your hand, that you might never forget your overreach!"

CHAPTER 13

"Seek me out, should you ever need a ship!" Catarin called from the bobbing rowboat.

"With our luck, if you sail with us again it might be your last voyage!" Dara called after.

"All the better then! Good luck with your rite, master Mages. And you too, master Paladin. Ami, be seeing you."

"Not if I can avoid the coast. Come visit me in the forest, where Fae belong!"

Catarin laughed. "You'll have to find better lodging than that rickety shack - it rocks more than the Andaira during a storm!"

"Safe travels!" Wynne said with a wave.

Ami grumbled as they made for the shack. "My head still aches, and I'm not sure if it's from that creature or from Wynne dumping mana on our heads or from too many days on the ocean. At least this will be our last night on the coast. A few days' walk to Nomridacai, then a few more to Keldarna, and we'll have you back to Cauldhill soon enough."

The sun hung low in the sky four days later when the Fae capital city of Nomridacai came into view. It rose to the height of the tallest trees, with buildings made of twisted branches held together with thick clay that was smoothed and painted bright tan. Domed roofs, painted in varying shades of green, swirled to sharp points. Decks filled the city, jutting out from every floor and coming in every imaginable shape and size. As with the villages, no walls or fortifications of any kind protected the city.

Wynne gasped in delight. "I never imagined the city would be so tall! It reminds me of Hantsburg, towering over the ocean. I would love to see the view from those upper decks."

"I don't see any rails," Dara said. "Not sure I'd fancy being that high without something keeping me in place."

"The discomfort is well worth the view, I promise you. I used to flee to the watchtowers in Hantsburg whenever my father's droning became too much to bear. I could have sat there for days, looking out over the world."

"I've never been to such a place," Dara said, averting her gaze.

Wynne blushed. "I'm sorry, I shouldn't have gone on gloating about my childhood, I-"

"Think nothing of it!" Ami chimed. "Because you will get to keep your feet on solid ground, Dara. Humans are welcome enough in Keldarna, and occasionally you'll see one in Nomridacai, but you all are Agents of the Quinarium. Not so welcome as merchants."

"Then where will we stay?" Wynne inquired.

"I have a place in mind."

Ami led onward until they reached the outskirts of the city. She kept to a long, winding path along the forest's edge, staying fifty paces or more away from Nomridacai. They crossed a stone bridge that arched over a wide and deep river, reaching the north side of the city. A cluster of a hundred buildings was nestled against a squat ridge of solid rock. Cut from reddish stone, they were only half above ground, with flat roofs and short chimneys. A single row of tiny square windows wrapped around each, shrouded by curtains.

"Is this a place for children?" Wynne asked. "The buildings are all strangely short."

"I would expect more noise with children," Dara said. "You can still hear Nomridacai, but it's quiet here."

"We will be staying with the Dwarves," Ami said.

"Dwarves!?" Wynne and Caudro screeched in unison.

"Something wrong with that?"

"Only that they were defeated in the Second Battle of Stellburg, decades ago, and since have disappeared," Caudro said.

"Many generations of Humans have never seen a Dwarf, and for the few still living who have seen one, Dwarves are little more than a foggy memory," Wynne followed.

"You Humans need to read more books that aren't written by Humans, and see more places that aren't ruled by Humans," Ami said. "How can you think they magically disappeared when they've been refugees under the protection of the Fae?"

"Refugees?" Wynne asked.

"Let me introduce you to my friend," Ami said, leading into the Dwarf district. "It will be much better for you to hear the story direct from the source."

Dara peered at a nearby building, appreciating the workmanship of the stone. "Are you sure he's here? This place is deserted."

Ami laughed. "Dwarves are not fond of sunlight. They respect Shidor—or should I say Ilsios—but from afar. They are most awake at nights, and I usually see them about in the mornings and evenings. Though my friend is always a gracious host, no matter the time of day."

"It would have been nice if you warned us we would be staying with the Dwarves," Wynne said.

"And how was I to be aware of your ignorance? If traveling with Humans has taught me anything, it is that your people know so little about so much!"

Ami scurried off before the others could protest her jab. She led them to an unassuming building and slipped down a narrow set of stairs.

"Hello, Vinzen, dearest innkeeper!" she called, brushing aside a curtain of dangling strips of cloth. "Sorry to wake you, but you have guests."

"Did I hear properly?" replied a sweet and bright voice. "You said *guests*? As in more than one? Are these voluntary accomplices, or have you coerced them into your company?"

"Would you believe me if I said that your guests are representatives of the Quinarium?" Ami snickered as the others followed her in. "Two Mages and a Paladin. Precisely the sort you'd expect to see with me."

Vinzen, who had been lounging across a few padded, backless chairs beside a stone table, rocketed to his feet. The Dwarf was a few inches shorter than Ami and of a lean build, with long arms. He had sizeable eyes, but his ears, nose and mouth were all small by Human standards. There was not a single hair on his head, but wrinkles and creases showed he was in the early part of his later years. He wore a trim shirt and pants, with an apron wrapped around his neck and tucked into a belt.

The Dwarf stood, mouth agape, lost in his own inn; the three Humans were similarly off-kilter.

"You haven't said hello!" Ami said with a smirk.

"Mages and a Paladin, Ami? What explanation could you possibly have for bringing such people into my inn? You're hardly a strange sight. Five above you spend as much time with us as your own people, but Humans from the Quinarium?"

"Worry not, my good friend. Have I not shown myself to be trustworthy through all the years?"

Vinzen chuckled. "You and I both know trustworthy, reliable, and dependable are rarely used in association with you."

"Well, if such traits are absent in me, I assure you they can be found in droves in these good souls. Or at least in Wynne. The other Mage, the tall one, is Dara." Ami puffed up her chest in mock formality. "They're on their Rite of the Faithful, seeking to become members of the Quinate's Faithful, in service of the Quinarium! The big man there is Caudro, a Paladin Trainee. Thanks to these Mages, he has faced battle honorably and is to be named a proper Paladin."

"Ami, the less I know of your friends, the better." The Dwarf turned to the three. "I'll try not to judge you, but Humans from Llendshold are unlikely to be friends of mine."

"Trust me, Vinzen! You speak with barbs, but tell me, when have I ever led you astray? Wait—don't answer that. But this time, I swear to you on my grandfather's grave, you can trust me."

Vinzen crossed his arms and grumbled. "Well, you've never *intentionally* led me astray, and they're already here as it were. You all can stay, but I ask that you stay in your rooms when my people come to eat and gather during the night. If they knew I had Mages and a Paladin under my stones, they might well banish me. Ami, take a candle, you can stay in the back room. You all stow your things and I'll get some breakfast going. And don't worry, Ami, I'll make some sausages just for you."

No one spoke a word until they passed through a curtain at the end of the hall, arriving in the designated room. Ami lit a few more candles, revealing a tidy but cramped space. Two pairs of beds with a small chest at the end of each flanked the room. A square table occupied the center, with an ewer, a basin, and a stack of towels.

"Are we sure staying here is a good idea?" Dara whispered. "Vinzen was far from pleased by our presence."

"If you want to spend another night camping in the woods, I will be the last to stop you," Ami said. "Vinzen is also an excellent cook, and much like you, Dwarves don't have much taste for meat. But sure, go traipsing back among the trees, enjoy some crusty bits of dried bread."

"I have never heard nor read good things about Dwarves," Caudro mumbled.

"I read precious little outside of the incident at Stellburg," Wynne said. "Though I don't see harm in staying here. I'm curious what Vinzen might have to say, if he will speak with us at all."

"I'm willing to listen," Dara said.

"Oh come off it, you three sound as if you're spending the night with the Siren," Ami chided. "There's three of you, battle-tested, and one old Dwarf. If anything, it's Vinzen who should be more worried about you than the other way around. I can smell the food—let's go eat."

Vinzen slid a platter onto the table where the companions sat expectantly; the smells had tempered their nervousness. The Dwarf had loaded four plates with charred vegetables tossed in a spiced oil and mixed with toasted barley, nuts ground into a cream, and fresh herbs. Ami's portion was much the same, with the addition of a few roast sausages.

"Eat up, then," Vinzen said, wiping his hands on his apron.

Dara munched happily, inspecting the stonework. "The workmanship of your inn... it's exceptional."

"A far cry from what Dwarves used to be capable of, but your compliment is appreciated, nonetheless. You might be the first to notice—how did a Mage come to know of the cutting of stone?"

"I all but grew up in a mine. I've never seen a Human produce stones like these."

"Oh! We should pay," Wynne interjected, reaching for her coin purse.

"I don't take Llendshold Guilders," Vinzen said. "Ami and I can settle up later."

"Food is great as always, Vinzen!" Ami exclaimed.

The Dwarf loaded a plate for himself, then pulled a chair up to the end of the table. He watched as Caudro and Wynne ate hesitantly. "Don't worry, I didn't poison the food. I suppose it's a shock for Humans to see a Dwarf, let alone eat a meal cooked by one. What brought you all to my humble inn, anyway?"

"Convenience," Ami said, mouth full of sausage. "We were passing Nomridacai, and I can't exactly take this lot into the city."

"You'll have to forgive my suspicions, but Ami, you and I both know that wasn't what I was asking about." Vinzen squinted at the Humans. "Why would the Quinarium send two young Mages and a Paladin into the Nomridian Forest?"

The three looked amongst themselves, shuffling in their seats.

"Rumors of a mana source in the archipelago, which turned out to be quite real," Ami said.

"Ami!" Wynne said, slapping the Fae on the shoulder. "I thought it was understood we should keep such a finding to ourselves!"

Vinzen laughed. "Worry not, master Mage. A mana source is hardly a surprising thing, though I'm not surprised it's a curiosity for the Quinarium."

Dara set her spoon down. "How could that be? I thought the responsibility of mana was given to the Quinarium by the Five?"

"You regurgitate that ridiculous message because your Quinarium speaks half-truths and lies in equal parts," Vinzen snarled. "Dwarves once had the auspicious responsibility of curating, tending, caring for the greatest mana source in all the land. Deep below the mountains, in the heart of Yuvsgrend, mana flowed like you couldn't imagine."

"We were told that the Dwarves stole all their mana," Caudro challenged. "That it may have been the motivation for the attack on Stellburg, to steal from the mana reserves."

Vinzen waved his spoon as if he were an Instructor chiding a pupil. "True as you saw a source out in the islands, there was one in Yuvsgrend. I saw it myself as a young boy. Many times! My father was a Priest, a part of the order responsible for tending the source. Our people had no need to steal mana. You speak of theft and Stellburg in the same sentence, when it was Stellburg stolen from the Fae by the Humans, not ten years before our flight."

"At the mana source in the Zanerian Archipelago, there was this strange creature. It claimed to be a Siren, one of the Five's first creations..." Wynne shuddered at the memories of Failure. "It said that mana sources were fueled by dead bodies returning to earth. Do you believe that to be true?"

"To a Dwarf, that is a rather mundane question. Of course, that is the truth of it, and one that is well understood. We buried our dead in tombs surrounding the source, and the mana flowed ever strong."

"Then why attack Stellburg?" Caudro pressed.

"Yes, a curiosity of mine as well," followed Wynne. "Why did the Dwarf army attack Stellburg?"

"Army?" Vinzen scoffed, rising from his seat. "I will tell you what happened, as seen with my own eyes, which you will also find confirmed in the writings of the Fae."

The Dwarf paced back and forth as he spoke.

"I'm sure you were taught that the Dwarves sealed themselves away for some unknown reason, abandoning all other civilization. That perhaps our failed theft led to our hiding from repercussions. The truth is simple: the Quinarium instigated a genocide of my people.

"Before you strike me, young Paladin, allow me to finish. And remember, I have no motivation, no purpose, no possible reason to lead you astray. It would be pointless to warp the minds of a few young Humans—my people are already without their home. As for the genocide, it was conducted by both the Quinarium and the armies of Llendshold. Over months, they took control of Yuvsgrend, and our lives became markedly worse. I was fortunate that through my father, I was a part of a convoy sent to Stellburg to beg for a reprieve. While we were gone, the genocide began.

"Word reached us that the Quinarium and Llendshold armies united and flooded Yuvsgrend, with everyone inside. Our city locked away, our people wiped out, we had nowhere to go. It was the grace of the Fae that saved us. The attack on Stellburg was little more than a diversion created by a few brave soldiers, willing to charge the armies of Llendshold to ensure the rest of us survived."

All went quiet, with only the sounds of Ami taking bites of sausage punctuating the silence. Vinzen plopped back into his chair.

Wynne shook her head. "Why would they teach us that the Dwarves attacked Stellburg to capture the city?"

Vinzen smiled wistfully. "History is told by the victors, and they rarely care to account for the whole of the truth. In fact, there were Dwarves who marched on Stellburg. It is the details—their motivation, their numbers—that were skewed to uphold the image of the Quinarium and your Lords. I see your faces. I care not whether or not I have convinced you. It's a futile effort anyhow, to undo the work of years of indoctrination and persuade those manipulated by the Quinarium's Mind Mages."

"Mind Mages? What manipulation?" Dara asked.

"As I understand it, unless things have changed, Mind Mages are ever attached to the leaders of the Quinarium and are seldom seen elsewhere. Moderators and Adjudicators keep them on a tight leash, always ready to pry into the heads of the unsuspecting.

"Dwarf Priests wore crowns infused with mana and sealed with powerful enchantments to keep their minds clear as they tended the source of Yuvsgrend. It was through the wearing of these crowns they realized your Mind Mages were influencing our people. If only they knew it was all a part of their preparation to *cleanse* the world of our people. You wear one of those crowns around your Quinarium and you'd quickly see the truth."

"But why deceive us?" Wynne asked. "The Quinarium has the mandate of the Quinate. Nothing else should come before or above it."

Caudro dropped his spoon onto his plate. "I don't doubt your experience, and I thank you for sharing your tale. Yet, I can't help but doubt the wholeness of what we are hearing."

Vinzen sighed. "As I said, I don't aim to convince you. It was as much for me as it was for you that I said all of this. Though, if you ever happen to find yourselves inside Yuvsgrend, grab yourself a crown. You'll eventually see the truth."

Voices sounded outside the inn. Vinzen frantically stacked the plates onto the platter and slid it behind the bar. "Off to your rooms then! Ami, you'll be alright to come grab dinner in the morn, the rest of you stay hidden until the sun has risen."

Retreating to their room, the four toppled into the beds, finding them plush and comfortable.

"We should go to Yuvsgrend," Ami declared.

"We?" asked Wynne.

"Yes! I bet we could find those crowns Vinzen was talking about, find out what the Quinarium really plans to do once they know about the source."

"You're serious?" Wynne propped herself up on one arm. "It's a long journey to Yuvsgrend, through Human lands. And, if we manage to get there, we have to find a way into a sealed and abandoned city. And, once we get into the city, we have to find the crowns. And, if we find the crowns, I don't think we can simply put on ancient Dwarven artifacts and walk around Sanctuaries and Temples, waiting for the truth to find us."

"Our rite is complete," Dara said. "We are to return to the Moderator in Stellburg, which is in the opposite direction from Yuvsgrend."

"We have fulfilled our duty, and so ends our journey," Caudro affirmed.

"Have you not been listening?" Ami seethed. "Hawel! Vinzen! Catarin! Even that disgusting Siren! They all agree, the Quinarium isn't being truthful, not to you, not to anyone! You found a mana source, something the Quinarium told you was an impossibility, despite them being quite real. Something is not right with all of this. Please, at least consider investigating Yuvsgrend before you go running back to your Moderator."

Ami blew out the last of the candles and curled up with a sigh.

Sleep refused to come for Dara. Beneath the ground and surrounded by stone, she felt equal parts at home and unsettled. The impending conclusion of their rite further weighed on her. Wynne and Caudro had such dedication to the divine right of the Quinarium. Okter had sensed a different motivation in Dara, one he said would not matter, but would the Moderator agree? Would Dara have had the same conviction as Wynne and Caudro, had she been raised as they were?

Then there was Ami's pleading. Dara knew it would be a lie to deny her curiosity about Yuvsgrend. An underground city, magical crowns... if they found a way in, what would they discover? Did Wynne hold the same curiosity?

Dara listened to her counterpart's gentle breathing. She would miss the sound of Wynne slumbering, a restful calm that made all seem right. She would miss the scent of flowers which always seemed to hang around Wynne, a freshness that lifted Dara's spirits. Did Wynne feel the same way? Did her heart also race when their eyes met? Did she ache with a longing to be touched, only to be held back by fear of trusting another?

"Dara, are you awake?" came a whisper.

"Wynne? I thought you were asleep."

"I've spent a shameful number of nights pretending to be asleep. Sometimes, it was to avoid evening appearances before

Earls or whoever else might be visiting. Sometimes, it was so I could sneak off to the library to read or climb the watch-towers and just stare at the dark of the ocean. Sorry, I'm rambling... how are you?"

Dara breathed deeply, staring at the smooth ceiling. "I can't stop thinking about what Vinzen said."

Wynne rolled to her side. The flickering of the last few candles illuminated Dara's profile. During the day, she was ever stoic; yet there, lying in bed, she was almost vulnerable.

"Do you think it's true?" Wynne asked.

"I'm not sure, but I would like to know."

"Seems to be your perpetual preference."

"What do you mean?"

"Dara, Mage of Ramaia, trusts her own eyes above all else."

"I've never had much of a choice other than to trust what I see myself. I spent my childhood barely scraping by, only to end up at the Academy of Ramaia. Most of the other Initiates came from wealthy families, and they tormented me every waking moment. All my efforts, my determination, only to go on my rite and find the Quinarium may have deceived us. Trust has been a stranger."

"Is that why you don't like me?" Wynne said.

"What do you mean?"

"You were cold when we first started. Do you think of me as the same as the others, the ones at the Academy?"

Dara frowned. "No. When we first started on our rite, I assumed too much. You've since proven me wrong."

"I can't help but feel a touch sad that it will be over soon."

"I thought service to the Quinarium was all you lived for."

"I'm overjoyed in that regard, but..." Wynne gulped as her heart raced. "I don't imagine we'll stay together after Stellburg. I... I think I'll miss you."

Dara froze, her body more tense than when she had faced the Denmother.

Minutes burned until a candle on a nearby shelf wavered, then extinguished in a puff of smoke. Dara shook her head and looked over. Uncertain if Wynne had already fallen asleep, her eyes traced the curls in Wynne's hair. Dara burned with a desire to say something, but her mind was a cloud. She was unused to any expression of care that she could not begin to form an idea of how to respond. She desperately wanted to reach out, to feel Wynne's hands against her skin again.

Dara shut her eyes as a tear fell onto her pillow.

They departed after a polite but drowsy farewell from Vinzen. Tensions rose in the ensuing days. Ami frequently shared her belief that delving into Yuvsgrend was a necessity, while Wynne and Caudro rebuffed her at every turn. Dara's quiet was infuriating to all three, who perceived her silence as a rejection of their stances.

When they reached Keldarna, Hawel came out to greet them.

"Elder," Ami said curtly.

Hawel ignored the greeting, instead addressing Dara and Wynne. "How did you fare on your rite, young Mages?"

Wynne stepped forward. "We found the source. A... creature protected it. It claimed to be an ancient Siren, but we were able to gather mana."

Hawel squinted. "The Quinarium must have records of sources from ages past. I wonder why they would send you on such a rite, under such a guise. Only the Five can know what they plan to do next. Why can't they be content with their stranglehold over the Human lands, I will never understand."

"The Quinarium owns no land," Caudro challenged. "Sanctuaries, Temples, even the Basilica in the capital city of Llendswarne, they are built at the invitation of the Elders and Lords and the Regents. There is no stranglehold."

"A reductive and childish view," Hawel chuckled. "The Quinarium owns no land in name, but they own your faith. Their influence is boundless. I fear that some day your Quinarium will lead a crusade into the Nomridian Forest, not stopping until all who live in the north either fall under their influence or flee. And then they will turn to Draethhold."

"Curious you would pose this future to us," Wynne said. "If you believe such a time is coming, what do you intend to do?"

"We are on the verge of desperation. Trade with Draethhold is limited, and must pass through Llendshold-controlled seas. Cauldhill becomes ever more distant. We allow Mages of the Quinarium to roam our lands. Our military strength is less than a quarter of what the Llendshold Regency could gather, perhaps even less than the forces of the Quinarium on its own. Despite this, there may be a time when we Fae can no longer hide in the forest."

"And what happens then?" Dara asked.

"As I said, only the Five can know."

"Elder!" Ami said. "If I may—we stayed with Vinzen. He spoke of Yuvsgrend."

"And what did the Dwarf say of the sunken city?"

Ami shrank under the Elder's glare. "He mentioned the source, the greatest of all. He also told us of crowns that protect the wearer from Mind Mages."

"Yes, I have heard of them. Ancient artifacts, lost long ago."

"Why has no one attempted to retrieve them? Vinzen said wearers are protected from the effects of Mind Magic and are able to see the truth of the Quinarium."

Hawel held his chin. "I hear in your voice a desire to go to Yuvsgrend, to retrieve the crowns."

"Yes."

"And what of you three?" Hawel asked, addressing the Humans.

"A Paladin's duty is to the Quinarium," Caudro said.

"Of course it is," Hawel said, staring at Ami. "And you Mages?"

Wynne dug her toe into the ground. "We have to return to Stellburg, and complete our rite."

"Now is the time to think for yourselves," Hawel said. "It was on my word that you were allowed to enter the Nomridian Forest. I acknowledge that I have no further power over you and your acts were of benefit to us. Still, having seen a source for yourselves, I would ask that you consider going to Yuvsgrend. While the crowns themselves are of immense power, there were once whispers among the Dwarves of records detailing the Quinarium's activities. I believe you would find them... illuminating."

"And should we go to the city, and find these crowns and records, what would you have us do?" Dara asked.

"That will be for you to decide."

"I'm going, even if they won't," Ami said.

"I will not forbid it, Aminantskeilara. Though you are a Mage, if you are found in the Human lands, none will vouch for you. You will be entirely on your own."

"As it has always been."

"Hmph." Hawel turned to the Humans. "It will take you a few days to reach Cauldhill. Consider my words. Think of the future of the Fae. Think of your own futures. Remember, service to the Five through the Quinarium is not the only way you might consider yourselves to be the Quinate's Faithful. Reveal the truth, and you will have served in a way few ever can."

CHAPTER 14

Cloudy skies hung low over Cauldhill. As the four emerged from the Nomridian Forest, the patter of rain against rooftops greeted them. Ami wore Human clothing, and they all had on oil-slicked cloaks with hoods pulled over their heads. They plodded through the muddy farmland when a familiar face came out to greet them.

"Are those the young saviors of my farm I see, making their triumphant return?" said Evin. "Is my memory failing, or are there four of you now? Did you always have a Fae with you?"

Ami pulled her hood low as the Humans mumbled and tripped over their words.

"Calm yourselves, you have nothing to worry about. I'm one of the few familiar with your people, young Fae," Evin said reassuringly. "I doubt any of the simpletons hiding behind the walls will give you less than half a moment of notice. Though I would recommend you keep that hood on tight. Ah, you all came at a good time. Rain's a sign of fortune to come."

Wynne bowed. "Thank you. We appreciate your discretion—this is Ami. She was instrumental in our cleansing of the Jackals, and more."

"I should be the one thanking you, all of you! Not a single lost sheep since you cleaned up those Jackals. As for you, madam Ami, whatever your business in Cauldhill is your business. Your people have always treated me with kindness. However, you should keep away from the Confessor."

"Speaking of the terror that is Uldrik," Dara trailed off, pointing to the village.

The Confessor and the Elder bustled along the soggy path with a complement of guards in tow.

"Blasted guards must have called for them! Ami, quickly, with me. To the side of the barn, so they can't see you. You are a fresh farmhand who I swindled into a work contract. Human girl, of course, but shy and you prefer to hide your face. A hideous birthmark, perhaps. Stay behind me, head down, and keep away from the Confessor—he's the one with the ridiculous jewelry. I'll make sure we find your friends later."

Ami handed her bow, belt, and pack to Caudro. The farmer tossed her a shepherd's crook, then pushed her towards the fields. A few minutes later, the party neared within shouting distance.

"You have visitors!" Evin hollered. "Ones whose company I much preferred to yours! Good fortune my new farmhand arrived this morning. We'll be in the fields, away from unpleasant guests."

Dara, Wynne, and Caudro bowed in greeting.

"I am grateful you have returned safely," said Maren.

Uldrik inspected the three. "You wear animal skins on your feet! You dare return to Llendshold, dressed as those heathenous Fae!"

Maren sighed. "Perhaps we can discuss their choice of attire another time? I am sure they have much to tell. It has been weeks since you departed—longer than we expected."

"Weeks without word of their progress. Tell us of the Jackals, and of the rumors of the mana source."

Wynne stepped forward, rain dripping from her hood. "We were instructed to report to the Moderator in Stellburg."

The Confessor's face reddened. "You were instructed to report your findings to the Quinarium. I am an Agent of the Quinarium! I am a member of the Quinate's Faithful, of which you are not yet a part! I am the Confessor of Cauldhill! You are to make your report!"

"And we will," Wynne said coolly. "To the Moderator. Your superior."

"The insolence! I command you to report to me! Two upstart Mages who haven't proved themselves have no place to speak so boldly before a Confessor!" Spit flew from Uldrik's foaming mouth.

Wynne's shoulders slouched at the rebuke.

Dara put her hand on the small of Wynne's back and addressed the Confessor. "We may not yet be fully inducted as members of the Quinarium, but we were given clear instruction: complete our rite, and report directly to the Moderator. Who are you, Confessor, to demand audience before the Moderator? Should we report this to him as we speak of our rite?"

"You stand when you should kneel."

"Ahem, shall we take pause for a moment? It has been a tense time!" Maren said, stepping between the Mages and the Confessor. "Perhaps we should all rest with the wondrous knowledge that our dear Mages and Paladin have made it back safely, and we can revisit this conversation in the morning, perhaps inside a building, should it still be raining. And speaking of Paladins—Caudro, your master is in the Sanctuary, waiting for you."

Caudro bowed. "Thank you, Elder. Unfortunately, our possessions have become intermingled in our travels, and I would share a final meal with Dara and Wynne. If I might be forward, would you please relay to Scireth that I will rejoin her this evening?"

"Ah yes, weeks of bonding deserve a proper farewell!" Maren said cheerily. "You three are welcome at *The Badger and the Hare,* as before. Uldrik, let us take word to Scireth. We will see you in the morning, Dara and Wynne."

The Confessor leaned towards the Mages, hissing through his teeth. "You two had best think clearly and be ready to tell me everything come morning."

In a spacious room at *The Badger and the Hare*, Dara, Wynne, and Caudro stood before a long table littered with their belongings. Ami's belt, bow, and arrows waited at one end. The three had barely shared a word as they sorted equipment and ate stew.

Their heads snapped to attention when the door abruptly creaked open.

"Miss me?"

Wynne grinned. "It's good to see you, Ami."

The Fae shut the door then tossed her cloak off with a flourish. "That farmer friend of yours has quite the reputation. I was worried he might attract the wrong kind of attention, but it turns out his bravado made it easy to navigate the town. Half the inn is laughing with—or at—him."

"I'm grateful for Evin many times over," Dara said, patting Ami on the back as she joined them.

"Do you still plan to go to Yuvsgrend?" Caudro asked, eyes fixed on the table.

"As much as I love you three, I wouldn't be traipsing around Human lands if that wasn't the plan. Alone or not, I have to go."

"Will you be safe in Llendshold?" he asked.

"If you're so worried, come protect me, big man," Ami snorted. "Or if you're scared, convince your friends here. They are near as stubborn as you."

Dara and Wynne looked at each other.

"Our position is not an easy one," Wynne said. "We've spent months and more training, spending every waking moment preparing for our rite. We have to see to the Moderator."

"It's fine, no matter at all," Ami said flippantly. "Ignore the truths you've seen and heard. Run along back to your Quinarium—I'll be on my way tomorrow. And you, big man. What do you intend to tell your master?"

"I will answer truthfully all questions asked of me."

"Good little puppet, aren't you?"

Wynne exhaled slowly. "Ami, aren't you going too far?"

"Did you not hear Hawel? My people are in decline, Wynne. I don't have the luxury of kind words wrapped in ribbon, or soft touches. I am desperate."

Caudro slung his pack on and picked up his spear and shield. "My things are sorted. Ami—I wish you well and hope you might find what you seek. Dara, Wynne—I hope our paths cross again. As They speak."

"So we listen," Dara and Wynne replied.

Caudro marched out without a backward glance.

Ami scurried around the table to face Dara and Wynne. "I see you two have already eaten. Fancy a stroll?"

Dara crossed her arms. "What for?"

"I want to hear what big man has to say to his master."

"Do you think he'll betray you? Tell the Confessor you're here?" Wynne asked.

"He probably wouldn't think of it as betrayal if he's yapping to please the Paladins," Ami said, sprawling across chairs with her feet on the table.

Wynne rubbed her cheek. "Does it matter what the Paladins say? What will you do if Caudro says something about you going to Yuvsgrend?"

"I don't know! But it can't hurt for me to hear what he and his master have to say, especially if they plan to send Paladins after me. It's even more important if I'm traveling through Llendshold alone. You all are in your homeland, but I have to think of my safety. It's a fair ways to Yuvsgrend."

"I'll join you," Dara said. She recoiled at Wynne's disapproving expression. "I'm curious to hear what they have to say."

Wynne sighed. "Fine, I'll come. You two need someone to keep you in line."

The rainy evening had driven most residents of Cauldhill indoors. Still, Dara, Wynne, and Ami plodded through alleys and narrow back streets, finally reaching the steps of the Sanctuary. In the cloudy, moonless night, the imposing building was dark and foreboding. Dara eased a door open just enough to squeeze through one at a time.

Inside, a faint light came from an ajar door at the back. They hurried past rows of seats which lined the Sanctuary like gravestones. Sneaking through the doorway, they tiptoed down a hall, following the sounds of hushed voices. Outside the occupied room, Ami lay on the ground, with Wynne and Dara hovering above. The three peeked through the sliver of a gap between the door and the frame to see inside.

Caudro stood at attention, his back to the three. Uldrik sat with his muddy boots on his desk. Scireth, staring at Caudro, occupied a chair across from the Confessor.

"You did well," said the Paladin. "From your account, it sounds as though you proved formidable in battle. Always good to fight alongside Blood Mages when the opportunity avails itself. You said a Fae accompanied you?"

"Yes, Aminantskeilara. A Fae Mage, our guide and a capable fighter in her own right."

The Confessor spat onto the floor. "Undoubtedly scheming. A Fae spy attempting to gather information about the Quinarium under the guise of aiding you."

"I believe her efforts were genuine," Caudro retorted.

"You are but a young boy. You will learn in time that the Fae are not to be trusted. It would serve you Paladins well to spend more time in Cauldhill, seeing the truth for yourselves."

Scireth picked at a scale of armor covering her leg. "A pointless exercise. The Fae will be of no issue soon enough."

"Within the year, I should think," said the Confessor.

"What do you mean?"

"You are a Paladin now. All that remains is your ceremony in Mordinlet," Scireth said. "I will treat you as such. I'm sure Uldrik would agree there is no harm in telling a Paladin of what is to come—the reason for our existence: holy war."

"And it all begins here, in Cauldhill."

"War?" Caudro stammered, his shoulders hunched. "What war? I thought we were at peace with the Fae?"

"Peace? Peace!?" spewed the Confessor. "The Five would not abide us sitting idly by these heretics forever! They must be brought to heel, be made to see the ways of the Quinate."

"I heard them pray to the Five," Caudro said.

"False! They may pretend to pray as we do, but their words are riddled with lies, falsehoods, mistruths which slander the sanctity of the Quinate. It is we, the Quinate's Faithful, who hear from the Gods themselves through our leader, the Voice, allowing us to act in their name! The Fae may claim they praise the Five, but nothing they do is holy."

"Yes, yes, as you say, Confessor," Scireth said, interrupting the impending sermon. "As for what is to come—we will stage an attack on Cauldhill. We would prefer it to be a hamlet, but such a strike would be unlikely to galvanize Llendshold. If word spreads of an attack by the Fae on the fine village of Cauldhill, it will certainly bring the nation together in battle, unified against our foe."

"Mindfully planned to minimize lasting damage to the village, and sacrificing the fewest number possible," added Uldrik.

"Sacrifices? You mean to let people die?" Caudro hissed. "To attack our own people, pretending it was the Fae? This is treason against our nation! This is heresy against the Five!"

Scireth sat up in her chair. "What do you remember of your lessons regarding Imreia?"

Caudro stood at attention again. "A powerful mage and skilled warrior, and a defiler of the Five. Her family was of high status in Brewardsburg until they attacked Agents of the Quinarium, after which the family was all but destroyed. Imreia survived, a hateful, destructive, dangerous unbeliever, and she continues to do all she can to destabilize the Quinarium."

"You remember well. What then would you say if I told you Imreia is planning to return to Llendshold?"

"That we must be ready to face her."

"And what if I told you that the Fae are her closest allies?"

Caudro blinked rapidly, his mouth shut.

"Why are you silent, boy?" Uldrik fumed. "Your master asked you a question!"

"It's quite alright," Scireth said. "Caudro knows the answer. If we wait for Imreia to attack with a Fae army at her command, we risk a terrible travesty. She has forced our hands. There is no choice but to strike first."

"Unfortunately, not all see the truth as clearly as Scireth and I. We must bring together the might of all of Llendshold in this crusade. The Paladins cannot do this alone."

"What of the innocent people here, in Cauldhill?" Caudro pleaded. "Is there no other way? You all but defended the Fae before we fended off the Jackals. Can we not reason with them, inform them of who Imreia truly is?"

Scireth stood beside Caudro. "The lives of any who die will serve the greater good. Their deaths will be a beautiful sacrifice to be remembered forever. Though we will lose them in life, mana will be harvested from their bodies fueling our Mages, armies will be raised in their names, and the righteous battle will end Imreia's plot. Regarding what was said before you fought the Jackals—I countered our dear Confessor to ensure that my words are not seen as overly biased against the Fae when the time comes to make our declarations. You will learn of rhetoric in time, now that you are a Paladin."

Uldrik nodded. "These few sacrifices will ultimately save many more lives. Think of how many children will become orphans, should we not resolve this threat decisively."

"And I take it your life will not be one of those at risk?" Caudro huffed.

The Confessor leapt from his chair, his fist in the air until Scireth waved him back. She grasped Caudro's shoulder and gave a reassuring squeeze.

"I sense doubt in you, Caudro. Confusion. Anger, even. I sense a wavering in your commitment to your order, to the Five."

Caudro lowered his head. "I walked alongside a Fae. I met one of their Elders. It... it makes little sense for them to attack. They seemed resigned to their status. I don't-"

"The Dwarves seemed docile too, before they rode on Stellburg," Uldrik interjected. "The Quinarium was successful with them, and so too will we be successful in handling the Fae."

Caudro's eyes bulged, but he could not bring himself to speak.

"We have much to discuss," Scireth said. "You served admirably alongside the Mages. We shall make for the Fortress at Mordinlet and continue our discussion there. I am certain you will see the truth in time. Uldrik, I expect we shall hear from each other often in the coming months. I will send you an invitation to Mordinlet when we are ready."

The Confessor grinned. "As They speak."

"So we listen."

Dara, Wynne, and Ami sprinted to a neighboring room, swinging the door shut before Scireth and Caudro marched by. Dara waited with her ear to the door until she heard the Confessor leave and light faded from the cracks around the door. They waited a few minutes more until they were certain they were alone in the Sanctuary.

Wynne lit a candle, revealing a study. Disheveled piles of books and scrolls filled shelves and covered tables, though a few chairs remained clear.

Ami plopped into a seat. She looked up at Dara and Wynne, her eyes glistening. "I have to go to Yuvsgrend. I have to find what the Quinarium did to the Dwarves. I have to find the crowns, I have to... Please. Please help me."

Wynne's heart ached and her head pounded. "They mentioned Imreia again... if she's involved somehow... I don't know... we... it's..."

Tears rolled down Ami's cheeks. "You know. You know what is right, more than anyone else ever does, Wynne. You don't want to admit it, but you know. Please help me. We have to uncover the truth. I swear to you I have heard nothing of Imreia. I'm not loved by the Elders, or most of my people, but I would have heard if the Fae were planning to attack Llendshold. I swear to you it isn't true! Please, help me save my people."

Dara blinked rapidly. She nearly faltered on seeing the doubt on Wynne's face. A longing pulled at her heart, a hope that this would not be the moment they went their separate ways, a hope that she would stay close to Wynne, for at least a little longer.

Dara shoved piles of books off a table and spread a map in their place. "We can lie to the Confessor in the morning, placate him that he sends us off without incident. Though we have to depart heading west—that way, they'll think we're heading for Stellburg."

Wynne breathed in. Her father be damned, as she heard Dara's conviction she knew what must be done.

"There are hills here. They'll provide cover while we head south, before turning east to Yuvsgrend. It shouldn't slow us more than a day. We'll reach Yuvsgrend before the Paladins make it to Mordinlet."

Dara smiled. "Horses will be quicker across the countryside. I reckon we could convince Maren to give us horses instead of going by carriage if we told her it would hasten our trip. Maybe we should ask for four to help carry all our belongings, so we have one for Ami as well? Ami, if you head south on your own, we can convene here, near this pond. Wynne and I should be able to make it there before nightfall tomorrow."

"We should gather all the supplies we can before leaving," Wynne followed. "I bet we can get extra provisions from the Elder, and I'm sure there's a stockpile of mana here in the Sanctuary."

"Thank you," Ami sobbed, pulling the Mages into a hug.

Dara pried herself free from the overly long embrace. "Thank us after we've safely made it to Yuvsgrend. Even on horseback, it will be at least a three-day ride."

CHAPTER 15

Dara, Wynne, and Ami faced the towering stone gates of Yuvsgrend. More than twenty feet tall and cut into the sheer rock face of a mountain, they had never seen its like. Moss and vines covered the entrance, but intricate carvings peeked through the brush.

Surrounding the entry was a brutish lattice of foot-wide and inch-thick steel bars, fastened to the mountain and plunging into the ground. A tree grew where two of the steel bars intersected, its roots wrapping around the metal tightly, defying the lack of soil.

"We spent days riding through wild forests, passing decaying remnants of settlements, to find *this,*" Dara said, patting her horse on its shoulder.

Wynne rode up to the entrance and touched a steel bar. "I was worried we might find guards or enchantments or some other form of protection, but I suppose an impenetrable barrier of steel surrounding immovable stone doors makes those unnecessary. If the Quinarium was certain this barrier couldn't be breached, I wonder, how are we to get in?"

"I'm sure there's a way," Ami said, following Wynne. "Shame Caudro isn't here. We could have used that dolt's head as a battering ram to break our way in."

"Speaking of Caudro, how are you doing, with how that conversation went? I should have asked you about it before. I know you've had Uldrik's and Scireth's scheming on your mind, but we never even spoke about how cruel Hawel was to make you guide us and Caudro, knowing that he is a Paladin. After what happened to your grandfather... Caudro isn't to blame, but still..."

"It's fine. I might have a soft spot for the big man, but I can't really worry about him when I'm on a quest to save what's left of my people in Llendshold."

"What do you mean by that, 'what's left of your people?'"

"I've heard there are Fae living beyond these mountains, far to the east. Who knows if they even look like us, or if it's possible to reach them by the ocean? We are all but alone."

Ami rode back to Dara, who was situating her horse and the packhorse Maren had graciously provided. Wynne and Ami aided in preparations, loading their packs with food, spare clothing, mana, and other supplies they thought might be useful when exploring a flooded city.

"I hope the horses will be alright," Wynne said, tying long leads to a nearby tree. "There's no telling how long we will be in there. That is, if we can make our way in at all."

"I'm sure they will be *fine,*" Ami said in a not at all reassuring tone.

Dara strode over to the gate when a pile of stone drew her attention. She pulled away vines growing above the mound, revealing a giant hole nearly four feet in diameter beside the gate. It was pitch black inside, sloping down at a steep angle.

"This must be one of the tunnels they used to flood the city."

"It should lead us right in!" Ami cheered, strolling over.

Wynne peered down. "It might lead in, but how are we to get out?"

Ami sighed. "We have rope, don't we? We can get out the same way we get in. It might not be as auspicious as the gilded doors the daughter of a Lord is used to, but it'll work well enough. And, with my impressive foresight, I stole one of those little dragonflies from the Sanctuary. Can you send word to Hawel with it, dear Mage of Ilsios? It might take a while, but we can ask that he send aid if we don't make it out in a few days."

Wynne took the dragonfly from Ami. She admired its delicate metal wings as she unfurled a scroll of paper bound to its legs. "Let's hope a bird doesn't eat it."

"Hey, hey you… That's my joke!"

Dara tied two ropes to the nearest steel bar, then flung the coils into the passage. The ropes clattered down, disappearing into the darkness.

Ami held up a lantern packed with a clump of mossy sludge, which gave off a soft green light when ignited. She held it over the entrance and peered inside.

"The tunnel is smooth enough. Hopefully, it'll be an easy slide down."

"I should go first," Dara offered.

Ami tied the lantern to Dara's belt. "As you wish, miss protector lady."

"Not quite the same ring as 'big man' for Caudro," Wynne said. "I'll go second."

"Fine with me. You two hit trouble, then I'll climb right back out."

Dara climbed over the mound of rubble and stepped into the tunnel. Wrapping the rope around her arm, she began her descent. Wynne stepped up after.

"Don't let me get between you two," Ami snickered.

Wynne hurried in, hoping the Fae didn't see her blush. Though dull, the lantern provided enough light for Wynne to see Dara below, sliding a few inches at a time. Wynne paused when she noticed strange grooves in the tunnel wall. She reached out, running her finger over one.

"Dara, have you noticed these marki-"

Wynne lost her grip and hurtled down the tunnel. Sliding ever faster, she gasped when she came to an abrupt stop. Dara held fast, with one arm twisted in the ropes and the other wrapped around Wynne. Dara's heart beat against her cheek. Held tight in her embrace, Wynne never wanted to let go.

Realizing that Dara was supporting them both, Wynne's face burned, and she grabbed hold of the ropes.

"Thank you! I'm sorry, I got distracted by these markings, I-"

"It's alright," Dara said calmly. "I'm glad I caught you. Who knows what waits at the bottom of this tunnel?"

Wynne took hold of the ropes, though she was still pressed close against Dara. "I'm sorry for what I said the other day, at Vinzen's inn. It was too forward. I never should have said anything. I'm sorry if it made you uncomfortable, I-"

"Shut up. Please, shut up. You need to apologize less. I'm the one who should be saying sorry for not responding to you. I was scared, I..." Dara gulped, distracted by how soft Wynne felt, how she smelled of spring flowers. "What I mean to say is I think I feel the same. That I would have missed you. That I'm glad to be here, with you, searching for the truth together."

Wynne leaned close. The warmth of Dara's breath tickled her lips, sending a yearning deep into her heart. The two neared until they were a hair's breadth away, when a loud *zip* came from above.

Ami surged down the tunnel head first, her legs wrapped in the ropes. She came to a stop when her face was inches away.

"Excuse the interruption, but I was wondering if I might pass by? I'm a touch busy, what with saving my people and all that."

"Oh!" Wynne exclaimed, turning away.

Dara quietly resumed the descent; Ami's giggles echoed after.

They had no conception of how far the tunnel would go, but only a few minutes passed when Dara and her lantern slipped out of sight. A slosh and a groan came from below.

"Dara! Are you alright!?" Wynne called.

"I'm fine, but you're about to get wet. There's knee-deep water, and it's cold."

Wynne's feet soon dangled over the edge of the tunnel. Bracing herself, she hopped down.

"Oh! That is much colder than I expected," she grumbled.

Dara steadied Wynne as Ami landed with hardly a splash.

"Brighter than I expected; no need for the lantern."

Luminescent ferns and moss grew all around. The fern stems emitted a deep blue light, brightening to teal at the tips of long, slender leaves, while the moss radiated a pale marigold orange. Delicate carvings adorned the stone, glowing between the plants. The strange light made the chamber appear like it was both dusk and dawn. The cool yet humid air only furthered the oddity of their surroundings.

A shallow set of stairs twenty paces across led upwards to the inside of the main gate, ten yards away. In the opposite direction, there was a dry, raised section of path. With only one way to go, the three waded onward, eager to get out of the water.

Ami plopped onto a pile of rubble and kicked off her boots. "Looks like the stairs head down for a long ways. I'm going to dry my feet as best I can before we move again."

"No complaints from me," Wynne said, following suit. "My boots feel awful. Let me have yours, I'll dry them. I think the comfort will be well worth a touch of mana."

Dara sat with a grin, handing her boots to Wynne. "When I went to the Academy, I swore I would never go back underground. Yet here I am, voluntarily delving into a sunken city with a Fae and the daughter of a Lord."

"You wouldn't have it any other way," Ami laughed.

"What do you think of the workmanship?" Wynne asked, passing her hand over the three pairs of boots. "Waters and time have worn down the stone, but I think the carvings are incredible."

"I can hardly believe I'm saying this, but I would have liked to see them at work," Dara replied. "I hated being in the mines. But here, there's something peaceful about it. Beautiful, even. These walls were shaped with love and care."

Ami snorted. "I have plenty of thoughts to share with Vinzen when I get back. To think the Dwarves are prideful about their dwellings outside of Nomridacai. If they are capable of *this*, what they built there is nothing short of lazy."

Wynne chuckled. "I do wonder about the markings in the tunnel leading down. They were strange. I've never seen markings quite like them."

Dara nodded. "Those tunnels were not cut by the same hands or tools as these carvings. I wond-"

A deep, thunderous murmur interrupted Dara, followed by a sharp clack, as if spears were thrust into stone. Dara leapt up on bare feet, yanking her gauntlet on and pressing a bottle to her lips. Ami and Wynne were up a moment later, staring at the passage ahead.

"Could... could those have been tremors in the mountains? Not something living?" Wynne asked.

Dara clenched her jaw. "I don't think so, but I hope I'm wrong."

"We should move quickly, then," Ami said.

Hastily pulling their boots back on, they headed down the stairs and into the city. The path was easy to navigate, with steps gradually lengthening to nearly ten feet across, yet each was only a few inches high. After a few minutes of quiet, they reached a domed cavern large enough to fit half of Dara's childhood hamlet inside.

Swooping, flowing abstract motifs covered the entire ceiling, an enthralling sight despite the overgrowth and decay slowly consuming the city. Three twenty-foot-wide arched openings dominated the walls. A bronze plated sign was positioned over each: to the left, GOVERN; to the right, RESIDE; and in front, COMMERCE. Rubble completely sealed the district ahead, though the side passages were clear.

"I wonder if the flooding caused the collapse, or something else," Ami said.

"Hard to tell. I hope what we're looking for isn't hidden that way," Dara said.

Wynne made for the passage on the left. "If the Dwarves were at all like Humans, then their records should be in the place from which they govern. I wonder if the source might be there as well?"

"If we find the source, we find the helms," Ami said.

The rumbling sounded again, this time faint.

"We should hurry. I don't like that sound," Dara said, hand on the hilt of her sword.

Dara took the lead. She strode through the wide passage, scurrying over fallen columns and brushing aside dangling ferns. They reached the other side in a few paces, where the enormity of the chamber stunned them all.

More than a hundred yards across, the ceiling was higher than the room was broad. A crystal at the apex cast down dozens of thin rays of white light, which drifted lazily throughout the cavern. Stairs on either side led up and down, with two upper floors wrapping all the way around the chamber. Columns lined both floors, with arched lintels atop and iron sconces between, now cold and dark. Water filled the lower floors, sloshing a few inches below the main level. Light faded as it struck the surface, making it impossible to see how deep the district went. Dara set her pack down by a stair, then walked out to a round platform at the center of the cavern.

Ami whistled and spun about the twenty-pace-diameter platform. "At least the water isn't soaking our feet out here."

Dara's head pivoted about like an owl's. "This is spectacular! I never knew such a place existed, especially not underground. The mines were always dark, dusty. It felt like the tunnels would swallow you up, but this place, it's…"

"Beautiful," Wynne said, her gaze drifting over to Dara.

"Where to begin our search?" Ami said, stroking her chin. "I vote we start at the upper levels, and not down below. I'm not much of a swimmer."

"Did Vinzen not tell you where we should search?" Dara asked.

"He was a child when he last saw Yuvsgrend, and that was some forty years ago. I don't think he knows precisely where to find the final recordings, likely made when he was traveling with the convoy to Stellburg."

"Well, libraries and other record places are often in the upper levels of Sanctuaries and Temples," Wynne offered. "Maybe the Dwarves organized themselves similarly?"

A rumble echoed through the chamber, as if an Ogre had struck an enormous drum. Moments later, crackling, scraping, scratching pierced their ears. Waves crept across the water, splashing over the platform.

"It's near, get ready!"

Dara drew her sword and swallowed a mouthful of mana in a flash; Wynne drank mana and Ami nocked an arrow. They spaced out across the platform, staring into the depths of the waters. Ripples surged again, this time without an accompanying sound.

"Maybe it left?" Wynne stammered.

No sooner had she finished her question than the surface ruptured, and the source of the tremors revealed itself.

The creature's head emerged first. Armored plates surrounded a jaw that clacked and ground together. Its four mandibles spread, revealing a mouth large enough to swallow a horse in a single bite. Fluid spewed forth as it emitted a wet, guttural screech. Six purple eyes on either side of its head jerked every which way. Claw-footed legs slammed onto the platform, propelling the insect-like creature forward. The numerous, tightly packed appendages carried a thirty-foot-long body covered in overlapping black plates. Spines and bristly hairs protruded from between the plates and from the joints along its legs. Its body tapered to a narrow tail with a blunted end.

Ami loosed an arrow, but the projectile shattered against the shell. Dara charged to meet the skittering creature. Sliding beneath one of its outstretched legs, she struck the limb, but her sword glanced off. Spying a gap in the armor by a stationary leg, Dara pushed herself off the ground and thrust her blade into the opening. With a grunt, she pried with her sword and ripped off the segment, sending yellow blood splattering over the platform.

The creature ignored the wound and clattered towards Wynne. The Flame Mage, drawing on the light from the crystal above, uttered a spell as she ran backwards. When the open maw was mere feet away, Wynne unleashed a stream of flames into its face. The creature wailed as it raised its front legs to shield itself.

Dara burst forward, but the creature caught sight of her; a swinging leg sent Dara sliding back across the platform. Ami slung her bow onto her back and cast a spell. Focused on the ceiling, she thrust her open palm to the ground, sending a ripple through the stone. A crack came from above, and a Fae-sized boulder came tumbling down.

The stone crashed into the back of the creature, denting its shell and nearly forcing it to the ground. Dara leapt in, ripping off a second, third, and fourth leg in rapid succession.

The enraged creature spun, flicking its tail like a whip. The blow threw Dara into the air. She crashed into the waters, disappearing beneath the surface.

"Dara!"

Wynne chugged mana, the shimmering liquid dripping down her chin as she gulped. She screamed Ilsios's name and swung her arm in a wide arc, sending sparks flying to sconces around the chamber. Ancient fuel burst into flame, brightening the room. She bellowed again, arm raised and fingers splayed. Pulling her hand to her chest, she clenched her fist, then thrust towards the creature.

Fires in the sconces billowed. Burning white orbs flew out in arcs, bombarding the creature in a torrent of flame.

Faltering under the assault, the creature dove into the waters. It scurried around the platform as flames fizzled above. Bursting out, the creature sent a cascade of water over the platform. Mandibles clacking it skittered after Wynne, when a stone erupted from the ground beneath its belly and knocked it off-balance.

"Wynne, run!" Ami yelled.

Wynne drank more mana and continued her wild barrage. As the distance closed, the creature leapt. Flames burst against its shell like fireworks as it soared, mouth opened wide, ready to swallow the defiant Mage.

Ami dove into Wynne and the two tumbled over the ground as the mandibles snapped shut above. Ami kicked Wynne away as a claw slammed into the ground between them. No longer threatened by the fiery bombardment, the creature reared up and squealed. Ami and Wynne stumbled backwards, crawling and diving to avoid swinging claws as the creature drove them to the edge of the platform. When their backs were to the water, the creature raised six legs high above Ami and Wynne.

Ami drew her dagger, presenting it out in a futile gesture of resistance. Wynne shivered, overtaken by shock and fear. The creature lunged when a splash disrupted the waters.

Dara emerged like a Siren, soaring through the air. The creature clawed at the flying Mage, but she spun between its legs, landing atop its head. Dara slipped the tip of her sword between layers of its armor and thrust until the hilt slammed into the creature. Roaring, she grabbed the handle with both hands and wrenched the blade back and forth. Steel ground against chitin as Dara obliterated the creature's brain. Its eyes went grey as it collapsed to the platform, sending Dara rolling away.

Wynne rushed over, embracing Dara. Chests heaving, they gradually caught their breath and helped each other to their feet.

"I told you emotions running hot makes for powerful magic," Ami snickered, standing atop the creature by Dara's blade. "And that goes for the both of you."

Wynne waved her hand, too exhausted to be embarrassed. "I think we have learned that Quinarium Instructors held back a fair bit about magic."

"That's an understatement," Dara said. "Even Okter either hid or was blind to so much."

Ami pulled Dara's sword free, causing yellow blood to spurt out with a squelch. She leaned close and sniffed. "It's like the Jackals... I can smell the mana, it's intoxicating. Far stronger with this thing."

Realizing she still held Dara's arm tightly, Wynne relinquished her grip.

"It must have either drank from the source or been infused from swimming in the waters. I wonder what happened to it when the city flooded?"

Dara climbed the creature and took her sword from Ami to inspect the yellow blood. "I hope this was the only one of its kind."

Ami slid down the creature's back. "If this was the nastiest thing down here, maybe it scared all the other potential worries away. Let's hope we can search in peace, and not stumble upon something worse!"

CHAPTER 16

Hours burned past as they searched the upper level. Beneath the glow of ferns and moss, they sifted through piles of papers, cracked open books, and unrolled scrolls, reading through all manner of records ranging from trade manifests to tedious ordinances. The majority were too old to be relevant or pertained to local matters, with no relation to the Quinarium.

Dara and Wynne eventually found themselves browsing in the same room. Wynne pulled a book from a shelf and cracked it open.

"How are you faring?"

"Fine, though don't like how cramped everything is," Dara said, reaching and touching the ceiling. "It's a bit like I'm back in the mines. What about you? What do you make of this place?"

"I could spend years in here! An immeasurable amount of lost knowledge, it's all so fascinating... the Dwarves kept impeccable records. I found a book describing a manifestation of flames I had never heard of before, a moving wall of sorts," Wynne said, patting her pack. "A curious use of fire I would never have thought of, but it makes perfect sense in tunnels."

Dara picked up a scroll, but it crumbled apart in her hands. "I was worried about how much reading there would be at the Academy. I thought we might sit in classrooms for hours on end, which sounded impossible after a life spent doing physical labor. Now I wish I had more time to read."

"We spent most of our time in classrooms at the Academy of Ilsios. It sounds as though things were different for you?"

"We spent more than half of each day outside. Training physique, practicing combat with various weapons, even a fair portion of our magic training was in the yards."

Wynne pushed her book aside and faced Dara. "I wonder what will happen to us when we return... if we return."

Dara brushed rotted tomes and loose papers off a table and sat in their place. "I've been wondering the same. It's far easier to keep my mind on the present. Things like that creature are making it easy to ignore what comes next."

"What do you want to do?"

"Find the truth."

Wynne chuckled, hopping onto the table beside Dara. "No, I mean with your life."

Dara's face went blank. "I can tell you what I don't want to be, and that's a miner. I lived every day feeling like an insignificant speck of dirt, and I never want to feel that way again. Maybe it would have felt less awful if someone appreciated us, or if we ate our fill every day. I've been so overjoyed to be gone, yet so consumed by worry I might somehow end up back there, that I haven't much thought of what else I want."

"You said you wished you had more time to read—maybe you'll be a scholar one day. I can see it: old, grizzled Dara, hair all gone grey and a life of adventures behind her, doddering around a library," Wynne giggled.

Dara laughed. "Well, you seem to have my future all planned. What about you? I always saw you as becoming one of the most dedicated servants of the Quinarium, the paragon of the Five, the example we should all strive to emulate."

"I'm not sure if that's possible anymore. All I ever wanted was to help people."

"Couldn't you have done that in Hantsburg? Follow in your mother's footsteps or something?"

Wynne grinned wistfully. "I could have, but I wanted a future of my own. I was certain going to the Academy of Ilsios was my moment, my time to take control of my life and my destiny. Maybe if I was a healer in the Quinarium, all would be perfect, or so I thought. Now here I am, more uncertain than ever. I don't know who I want to be. All I can do is wonder if I'll ever find my place."

Dara looked into Wynne's eyes. "Maybe you already have."

Wynne looked down. "I've certainly found myself in quite the situation! Doubting the Quinarium, the institution I believed with all my heart just months ago."

"I can't imagine how it is for you. Your life was spent connected to the Quinarium. Though I'm one to speak. The Quinarium was my way to escape a life in the mines. And now I've run away from them. I'm lost."

"I think feeling lost is perfectly acceptable when we're deep in the half-flooded remains of an abandoned, underground city," Wynne said with a laugh.

"Wynne! Dara! Come here!"

The two rushed out, following Ami's voice to a room a few doors down. An entry hall with walls covered in carvings led to a round library. It stretched two stories up and down, though the lower levels were flooded; moldering books floated on the water. The main level was damp, and a sticky paste of decomposing books covered the floor. Ami leaned over a handrail at the top floor, motioning for them to join her.

"Don't be shy," she said as they reached the top of the spiraling staircase. "And please accept my most deep, sincere apologies if I was interrupting *something*. I assure you I would only call you for the most important of reasons."

Ami scurried off before either could protest, leading to a pedestal tucked into a recess in the back wall. Upon it was a tome larger than they had ever seen, cracked open to a page two-thirds through. Ami had already placed lit candles nearby, illuminating the pages in a soft orange glow.

"Not ones for subtlety, I suppose. Look at this hunk of a book! I think I found the last page with writing. Until that point, as far as I can tell, it was a mess of rules and codes and other rubbish, mixed in with historical records."

Dara and Wynne huddled over the open page.

"The writing is tiny, and the letters have strange flourishes," Dara said.

"A moment." Wynne dug through her pack, taking out a round lens with a thin metal band around its perimeter. "This will make things a bit easier to see."

Ami chuckled. "You've been carrying that dainty little thing all this time?"

"You never know when something like this might be useful, like right now," Wynne said with a grin, holding the lens close to the book. She flipped back a few pages to where the final section began. "We shall break from convention in this summary ledger for what may be the last words of the Dwarves of Yuvsgrend. These are the writings of Zakera, daughter of Zakera—I wonder if all Dwarves take the name of a parent?—and I make this entry of my own accord, alone, without the authority of...

"Well, this goes on for nearly half a page, the author apologizing and noting how it's poor form to write in this book without there being an assembly of some sort first. I'll skip this bit... continuing on... here. I'll paraphrase. Zakera was quite long-winded, though she was kind enough to summarize the events leading up to this recording. Still quite a few details mixed in here. There is mention of rising tensions with Humans... trade with the Fae slowing once Humans controlled Stellburg... ah! Something of substance."

"Well, get on with it, then!" Ami demanded.

"Right... she says here that at first an accord was struck with the Quinarium, that they might keep a small presence in Yuvsgrend to learn more of the source. Mages and Paladins were sent as peacekeepers, outside of the agreement. When some Dwarves protested, there was surprising disagreement on whether or not the presence of the Quinarium was acceptable—no doubt in part due to the influence of Mind Mages, which only the Priests were able to resist. Further, the Lord of Stellburg said they would bar any trade, including with the Fae, should the Dwarves not agree to host the Mages and Paladins. The Dwarves had no choice but to comply.

"Over time, the numbers of Quinarium Agents increased, but the Dwarves were helpless to resist. Finally, the Lord of Stellburg barred trade with the Fae, calling the passing of caravans between the Nomridian Forest and Yuvsgrend disruptive. The Lord further placed substantial tariffs on Dwarven goods, meaning their trade would all but cease with Humans. Zakera says the Quinarium representatives were the ones who brought word on behalf of the Lord-"

"See?" Ami interjected, wagging a finger about. "I told you, many times now, your Quinarium is not a sweet and gentle institution."

"Let's hear the rest," Dara said coolly.

"The Dwarves knew that such a dramatic change in their economy would be disastrous. In response, they sent a convoy of their most senior officials—along with a few Priests, a small military contingent, and the families of those in the convoy—hoping such a show of seriousness would lead to favorable negotiations. Zakera writes that only a few days after the convoy left…" Wynne's voice cracked. "After the convoy left, war broke out."

"War?" Dara asked.

Wynne gulped. "Zakera describes it in detail. As an army from Llendshold arrived, Paladins and Mages collapsed the Commerce tunnel, which apparently led through the mountain for miles to another Dwarf nation. With most of the leadership in the convoy and the Dwarves having little of an army to begin with, fighting was over quickly. The Dwarves thought they would be taken away, possibly enslaved, but the Paladins, Mages, and Llendshold army left, sealing the doors behind.

"For days, the Dwarves heard cutting and grinding until a giant hole appeared on either side of the gates. Then came the unimaginable flood. The Dwarves fled further into the city, packing into the upper levels as the waters rose for days on end. Food supplies dwindled, and with nowhere to go, they resigned themselves to their fate… the rest is horrible, this says… the children, they didn't want them to starve, they… they…"

Dara took the lens from Wynne and embraced her.

"Was there anything else? After that part?" Dara asked softly.

Wynne shivered despite the warmth emanating from Dara. "At the end, Zakera went on and on, pleading to the Five. That they might be forgiven for what they did. The last line simply asks for the Quinate to save them."

Ami threw over an iron candelabra. "Vinzen was right! The Quinarium did this, along with your Lords! They murdered the Dwarves, all of them! And they mean to do it to my people too!"

A solemn quiet filled the air. Ami slung off her pack and pulled out a square of oiled leather. She closed the giant book and wrapped it inside, then stuffed the parcel into her pack. Dara and Wynne held each other close.

"Oh come now, you two," Ami chided. "Hugs won't change the horrors of the past. You two aren't responsible for this nightmare, nor are you involved in the scheming of Uldrik and Scireth. Cuddle all you want when we're out of here, but I still need your help to find the crowns."

Wynne pulled away from Dara's arms, finding herself suddenly cold. She looked away from the others to the surrounding library. "This is as likely a place as any for us to find out where the crowns are. We should spread out."

Time passed strangely under the constant glow of luminescent plants. Dara cracked open book after book, unrolled scrolls, and read until lines blurred together. Finally, she marched to the center of the room with a smile.

"I think I found it," she called, holding out a book as Wynne and Ami joined her. "This one contains construction records, of all things. They have notes in here about changes made to the Priests' quarters, expanding their rooms in the residence district, with a diagram showing the location."

"Curious," Wynne said, inspecting the page. "This shows regular quarters on either side. The Dwarf Priests lived among laypeople."

"What's strange about that? Fae Mages, Scholars, Elders, they all live with laypeople, as you call them."

"Oh, well, the Quinarium keeps to its own as far as residences and places of worship," Wynne said.

"Explains a lot," Ami said. "Quinarium would be happy to make the Five seem exclusive, only accessible through them. Anyway, let's go. I could use a stretch of the legs after staring at these books. You care to lead, Dara?"

"Of course."

Walking along the perimeter of the governance district, they all stared at the dead creature. Its yellow blood stained the surrounding waters. They hurried away, glad to be free of its sight as they returned to the central chamber.

As they entered the passage to the residences, a crack pierced the quiet.

"What was that!?" Wynne whispered through pursed lips.

"Don't worry, it wasn't anything living," Dara said.

She lifted her foot; a cracked bone lay on the path. Wynne gasped when Dara brushed aside nearby ferns, revealing piles of bones mounded against the walls. She leaned close, delicately tracing one with a finger.

"Is that really necessary?" Ami said.

"There are no signs of scars or any other damage," Dara observed. "These dwarves didn't die in battle."

"It was as the author said." Wynne stepped away. "They either drowned or starved. By the hands of the Quinarium."

"I wonder which it was?" Dara mused.

Wynne sighed. "It doesn't much matter. They met their end regardless."

Ami squinted. "I agree. It was either prolonged and painful or brief and extremely painful, if my understanding of starvation and drowning are correct."

"How desperate it must have been," Wynne said. "Confined to your home, knowing the end is coming, with nowhere to go, nothing to eat, nothing to do. An entire city swallowed up in darkness..."

"Let's go," Dara said, resuming her walk. "Dwelling on it won't help them or the Fae."

They continued down the passage, mindful to avoid stepping on bones. Wynne's mind drifted at the sight of smaller bones. Were they from the hands of adults, or arms of children? She realized she wasn't sure she could tell the difference even if they were Human bones, let alone those of Dwarves. Some bones were tiny, certainly from someone young...

Wynne caught herself just before she ran into Dara. Peering around her shoulder, the residence district came into view.

It was nearly identical to the governance district, including the central platform. The water was substantially lower, with a full level below the main floor clear.

"This time, I'm not going out to the middle," Ami said.

Dara nodded. "No complaints from me."

Wynne started towards a stairway on the left. "From the book Dara found, the Priests' chambers should be on the uppermost level, about a third of the way around."

"So many stairs," Ami groaned. "Why do you Humans, and why did these Dwarves, have such a love for them? Insensible going up and down all day."

Wynne paused. "Ami, there were plenty of buildings in Nomridacai that were quite tall."

"I don't live in any of them. Besides, ours have a comfortable rise with each step. These shallow, long stairs are tedious."

Dara grinned. "Are you perhaps wishing there was a big man to carry you up?"

"If you mean Caudro, then yes. That brainless oaf was useful from time to time, and this would be one of those times I am certain I could make use of him. Besides, I'm the one hauling the record book, half as heavy as each of you it is!"

On reaching the second level, it became immediately clear where the Priest quarters were. Gilded statues of the Quinate protruded from the cavern walls over a pair of bronze doors. Dara expected them to be sealed, yet they swung open from a gentle press, clanging as they reached their limit.

The three stood before a hallway flanked by four doors on either side. Columns separated the doors; a sconce on each burst into flame. Another bronze door waited at the end of the hall, bearing a three-foot-tall feminine face with a blindfold and open mouth. A single word was inscribed above: *SACRIFICE.*

Ami stepped into the hall. "It's Kardef."

Dara shook her head. "Kardef?"

"It looks like Almoya, with the blindfold," Wynne said.

"Kardef, Almoya, different names for the same God. Fae call her 'the one who tends the mind.'"

Wynne nodded. "We say 'That which gives thought.'"

"As I said, different but same."

"Could the crowns be through there?" Dara wondered.

"Only one way to find out," Wynne said as she marched down the hall.

It was the first place in all of Yuvsgrend not covered in ferns and moss. Standing before its face, and despite its blindfold, all felt as though they were being watched.

"Do you feel that pressure in your heads?" Wynne asked.

"Yes," Dara and Ami replied in unison.

Wynne blinked rapidly. "Is it something about this place, or do you think it's of our own creation?"

"I don't think our imagining is the cause if we all feel it," Dara said. "Either way, I hope it subsides after we get this open."

Wynne inspected the door and its surroundings. She noticed two squares on the floor, marked by brass inlaid engravings, and stepped on one. "Perhaps we are meant to stand on these spots?"

"Don't look at me," Ami said. "I was born and raised in the wilds. I'm not well versed in formalities and rituals. You two are the Quinarium Mages."

"Not sure we are anymore," Dara quipped as she stepped on the other spot.

"Well?" Ami asked.

"It's not like they taught us Dwarf incantations at the Academies!" Wynne burst.

"The mouth is open," Dara said, focusing on the face. "I've never seen Almoya represented like this. Perhaps we are meant to speak to it?"

"Yes! What about the greeting? It represents the authority of the Five, and our supplication."

Dara and Wynne faced the door, peering at each other out of the corner of their eyes as they spoke in unison.

"As They speak, so we listen."

They waited in silence when laughter erupted from behind. Wynne glared at Ami. "What!?"

"You said the Quinarium never taught you Dwarf incantations, and yet here you are, reciting Human sayings to a Dwarven door."

Dara crossed her arms and sighed. "Alright then, Ami. What do you suppose we should do? You've spent more time around Dwarves than either of us have."

Ami giggled as she slouched against a column. "Oddly enough, Vinzen didn't talk much about Yuvsgrend. He failed to mention the giant insect-creature-monster thing, let alone the bronze door with a giant face of Kardef sealing it. What a dastardly cur. He should have told me the password!"

Wynne's brow furrowed as she put her hands on her hips. "You are one to laugh while sitting back, not helping. Might I remind you, it's your people we're trying to save?"

"Not helping, but not harming either, am I? And I know what is at risk. It just so happens that I trust you two."

"I would perhaps describe you as distracting," Dara said with a wink to Wynne.

"Fine then! I'll take a nap. You two carry on. Don't mind me over here, snoozing until an epiphany reaches me."

Dara and Wynne stared in disbelief as Ami set down her pack, bow, and quiver, pulled her hood over her head, and lay on the hard stone ground. In seconds, she started gently snoring.

Wynne looked back to the door. "If they had to enter regularly, it must be something simple. What about an offering? Open mouth, ears not shown... could it be that we are to pour mana in? It would be a relevant offering for Dwarf Priests tending the source."

"Possibly. These marked positions are within reach of the door." Dara raised a mana bottle. "Shall we?"

In unison, they poured a steady stream into the mouth. Wynne rushed to cork her bottle when mana dribbled out and spilled onto the floor. She peered inside the opening.

"Nothing in there. That was a terrible waste."

Dara smiled encouragingly. "Better than my first idea of using not only a Human saying, but a Quinarium one."

"So you say, but the effect was the same and words wasted nothing." Wynne grumbled and chewed at her nails. "What about casting a spell? Some Flame Mages provide services in sealing doors and locks with enchantments. This might be the same."

"A good idea, though I wonder if the spell would need to be of Mind Magic?"

"I thought Mind spells only work on living beings?"

Dara tilted her head. "Sacrifice... would it not be more appropriate if the sacrifice were relevant to the one making the sacrifice? Perhaps a Blood spell from me and a Flame spell from you?"

"Let's find out."

They both drank and readied a spell. Whispering to the Gods, they watched each other as they cast their spells, simultaneously stretching their hands out to the door.

A stream of crimson flowed from Dara, while burning white emanated from Wynne. The colors fused into a stream of pale red, illuminating the door. Wynne smiled as the door brightened, the bronze shimmering and wavering. Then, as suddenly as it began, the door went dark.

Wynne's shoulders drooped. "Stupid idea."

"Don't be hard on yourself. We've only just begun," Dara said. "What if... what if the sacrifice is meant to be more literal? Like blood."

Dara drew her dagger and pressed the tip into her palm when Ami popped up like a groundhog from its hole.

"Five above. What madness makes you think that Kardef would want an offering of blood? She is the God of Mind! Blood sacrifice to appease the mind. What do they teach in your Academies?"

"Well, if you are so much better learned, perhaps you could have instructed us before you napped and we wasted mana!" Wynne sputtered. "At least Dara is trying while you lay there, snoring! How can you poke fun when she is willing to spill her blood to get through this door? In no small part to aid your people!"

"Hoping she gets wounded, eh? Eager to patch her up again, are we? Get your hands all over her?"

Dara coughed and avoided looking at the others. "We haven't learned Mind spells, which are what I'm guessing is needed to open the door."

Ami yawned. "I was thinking, right when you were about to cut your own skin open and bleed on the door, that we haven't explored these other rooms. We were a bit hasty, a bit drawn in by the face of Kardef. Maybe instead of going straight to the big imposing door, we should explore the other rooms? Perhaps try to find something that will tell us how to get in?"

Dara shut her eyes tightly and a pained expression took over her face. "Right. Then let's get to it and see if there's anything of use in these other rooms."

Ami trotted away. "I won't judge if you two decide to search together."

Wynne scurried to the nearest door, while Dara went by the entrance. She pulled a brass ring, and the door swung open.

"There are living quarters in here," Ami called.

"I see the same," echoed Wynne.

"As with mine," Dara said.

"Ooh, I wonder if anyone kept a saucy journal," Ami said, her voice fading as she strolled in. "Please do share if you find anything *interesting!*"

Wynne leaned back into the hall, smiling at Dara. "You'd think it was Humans at risk, not the Fae."

Dara shrugged. "I guess it's easier for her to make jokes than to face her fears."

"Fairly said. Good luck!"

Dara tarried for a moment, clinging to the image of Wynne's hair flowing as she walked away. Breathing deeply, Dara entered the Dwarf Priests' quarters.

A single row of beds, eight deep with a small table beside each, lined one wall. Chests were set into the wall opposite the beds. Tattered, half-decomposed remains of a rug ran from one end to the other, and tapestries depicting the Quinate hung from the walls.

Dara went to the first bed and pressed into the cushion. It was remarkably pliable, despite the passage of time. She wondered if the flooding had reached the room, as the rug crumbled beneath her feet, yet the bed was well enough preserved to sleep on. Turning her attention to the nearest chest, she pried open the lid. A ghastly smell of mildew and rot assaulted her nose. Waving away the stench, she peered inside.

Neatly folded clothes were stacked on one side, while the other side was a jumbled mess of belts, jewelry, bangles, odd instruments, and books. Dara gently set the tangle of items on the ground, keeping the strange metal instruments separate in case they had some relevance to the sealed door. She flipped through the books but found them generally unhelpful—a few were history books, while others were filled with poems or stories unrelated to the Priests.

When Dara lifted out the clothing, a thin, leather-bound book slipped to the floor. Curious as to why it was hidden, she gently opened the cover.

"*On Love and Desire: The Complete Manual of Attraction.* No wonder you hid this."

Dara chuckled and readied to toss the book aside when curiosity tugged at her. She sat on the rug and flipped to the first chapter.

"What a silly book. Let's see how ridiculous it gets. *'Are your eyes set on a special someone? Or perhaps you are hoping to improve your personage that the right Dwarf might come sauntering your way? Or are you already paired, but are finding the fling unfulfilling? No matter your reason, read on dear reader, and you will learn all the techniques you need to incite desire, fan the flames of love, touch the depths of a partner's mind, and satisfy their body completely.'*"

Dara pulled the book close, fervently flipping through the pages.

"I found something!" Wynne called.

Dara slammed the book shut and shoved it back into the stack of clothes before throwing the pile into the chest. She hurried out of the room, pulling wrinkles out of her tunic on the way.

"Are you alright?" Wynne asked as Dara arrived. "Your face is flushed."

"Oh," Dara said, touching her cheeks. "I'm fine, nothing's the matter. I didn't want to keep you waiting."

"Are you sure? Your face has been paler than this after battle."

"Let's see it!" Ami said as she sidled into the room. "Dara, are you well? Your face is red."

"I'm fine! Wynne, you said you found something?"

"Yes, a journal from one of the Priests. I'm surprised it lasted this long. It appears to have been spared from the flooding. There's a section in here... the owner was a Priest Initiate of sorts, and describes their frustrations with the duties of their position. It seems that the lower-ranking Priests had to take care of many unsavory tasks, down to scrubbing floors and cleaning latrines. I wonder how they handled a whole city's worth of waste, underground? Anyway, there's a section here about the ritual to open the door to the storage, precisely where we were looking. The author sounds rather frustrated."

"Frustrations aside, what did they say about opening the door?" Dara asked.

"Well, we were right about standing on the two market locations on the floor. And your first inclination was also correct: Priests spoke a chant in unison. The Dwarf was quite embarrassed about frequently making mistakes with this ritual, so they wrote it down... many, many times."

Wynne held up the journal and flipped through five pages, all bearing the same line repeated dozens of times.

Ami snorted. "Good fortune for us that the poor sot was forgetful. So, what's the phrase?"

"Most of the lines are too blurred and faded to read clearly, but thankfully, they left us plenty of examples. 'The blessed of Kardef bow before you. See our minds as we offer ourselves to you.'"

Ami burst into laughter.

"What is there to laugh about? Wynne found our way in. We should rejoice, not laugh," Dara chided.

"The sight of you two, standing there, pouring mana, casting spells, ready to bleed, when all along it was nothing more than a few words needing to be said!"

Wynne scowled. "We can celebrate when it works. With the way this Dwarf rambled, they may well have written the wrong phrase down hundreds of times."

Dara and Wynne stood before the face of Kardef once again. Wynne exhaled slowly, staring at the glimmering metal. She waved, and they recited the phrase. The mouth slammed shut and a faint line traveled from the top to the bottom of the door. The halves slid apart and the three stepped through, gasping at the sight.

Sconces burst aflame, lighting the circular room. Some fifty feet across, shelves lined the perimeter at knee and shoulder height. Unimaginable treasures covered every surface. Jewelry and dishes made of precious metals and studded with gems, pieces of decorative and utilitarian armor and weapons, satchels stuffed with chunks of refined ore and coins spilling out, the sight overwhelmed.

Straight ahead, thin gold crowns were arranged in a neat row, with a placard above stating *Offerings to Kardef.*

Dara spun in the center of the room. "I have never seen such treasures! There is enough here to buy the whole of Cauldhill a hundred times over! Please tell me this is a surprise to you, too, Wynne, that you didn't grow up surrounded by such riches."

"It is beyond belief," she whispered, shuffling through the entrance.

"Well, it will be hard to carry out as much of this as we would like, but we would be fools not to take what we can," Ami said. "Make sure you save room for the crowns, although they do look rather delicate."

Wynne hesitated. "Is it not blasphemous to take offerings to Almoya?"

Ami walked to the shelves, brushing her hand across a sack of coins. "The offerings didn't do the Dwarves any good. At least we can honor them by putting whatever we take to good use."

They roamed the storehouse, examining the offerings in silence. Despite the impracticality of many of the items, they could not resist the urge to touch and hold the treasures, absorbed by the grandeur of it all.

Wynne paused by a strange scepter. It was about the length of her forearm, and made of a blackened bronze. Its grip was wrapped in silvery grey fabric, still soft and pliable. The shaft extended equally in either direction, with spiraling patterns engraved along its length. At one end was a gold-coated flame; at the other, a solid black orb. Wynne noticed an inscription encircling the scepter by its handle.

"What does it say?" Dara asked.

Wynne shivered, pulled from her stupor. "When wielded with a heart true in its purpose, the light of Shidor will outshine all."

"It sounds potent, and fitting for you."

"I've read about using objects as conduits for spells, but I've never tried before." Wynne secured the scepter to her belt using a braided wool rope from the shelf. "Have you found anything?"

"Not yet. It's a shame all the armor was made for Dwarves—I'm more than a touch too large for it."

"Maybe you should give it a try," Wynne said with a smirk. "Something tight-fitting might suit you."

Dara waved and laughed, strolling along the shelves. The sacks of precious metals and jewels soon lost their appeal; instead, she focused on the various pieces of armor and clothing. A domed helmet was polished so smoothly she saw her reflection in its surface. Nearby, a cloak with fibers of silver woven into the trim lay beside a pair of boots with solid gold soles and finely stitched cloth uppers. Then, a dull scabbard caught her eye.

Made of blackened leather with patinated steel trim, it was entirely out of place among the vibrant treasures. The handle, wrapped in a blend of deep crimson and black wool cord, was long enough to grip with two hands. The pommel, in the shape of a teardrop with a rounded point, was cut from a mulberry-colored stone. Dara drew the sword and smiled. The cutting edge had a gentle curve, ending at a fine point. On the back edge, the half nearest the tip was sharp, while the lower half by the hilt was rounded. Along the sides ran a narrow, shallow fuller, stippled in black.

Dara gave the sword a swing, finding its balance perfect. She tried various stances and strikes, taking to the sword as if it were forged for her. She raised the blade to inspect a glint of red in the fuller.

"The Hand of Kahon," Dara said, reading the inscription.

"Kahon must be the Dwarf name for Ramaia," Wynne said, leaning against a shelf as she watched Dara. "You found yourself a fitting item, too."

"I've never held something that felt so... right."

"I know your meaning. It suits you," Wynne said with a smile.

Dara sheathed her new sword. She readied to buckle the scabbard belt around her waist when her hand bumped against the pommel of her old sword. "I don't think it makes much sense for me to carry this anymore. It's covered in markings of the Quinarium."

"Maybe it's time for both of us to consider a different future."

Dara let her Quinarium blade fall to the ground and adjusted her new sword while Wynne walked over to Ami. The Fae held a rectangular gold talisman with pyramid indents across its surface. She rotated it back and forth. When viewed from one side, it displayed the face of a man; from the other, a woman; from below, a mountain; from above, a circle.

"Curious thing, that."

Ami nodded. "I'm not quite sure what it is, but these images are enthralling. I think I'll take this back to Vinzen."

"Find anything for yourself?" Dara asked.

Ami's face went blank. "I don't need anything except for the crowns and the record book."

"We should see to the crowns, then," Dara said.

A mischievous smile crept across Ami's face and she winked. "Maybe I'll pinch a bit of gold too. Couldn't hurt if there's a war; I've heard they're expensive."

Dara and Wynne helped Ami stuff her pack with gold ore and gems, taking a few pouches themselves at the Fae's urging. With their packs as heavy as they dared to fill them, they approached the stand of crowns.

The bands were thin and less than half an inch wide. Smooth lines ran across their surfaces, intertwining like tree branches. In the center, wrapping around each crown, was a narrow groove which emanated a soft lavender light. There were thirty crowns, far more than they had originally thought.

"Delicate things," Wynne said, kneeling close. "Strange they carry such power."

"Great power can sometimes be found in unexpected places," Dara said, staring at Wynne.

"Profound today, aren't we? I wonder what has incited such a *fire* in you, Dara." Ami snickered.

"Could there be some ceremony we are to follow with the crowns?" Wynne asked.

"No patience left in me," Ami said, selecting a crown that looked her size and slipping it on. "Ahem, let's see if I can be as poetic as Dara. Feels light as a leaf, floating on the wind."

Dara clenched her jaw and crossed her arms.

"Do you feel anything?" Wynne asked, inspecting Ami's face.

"It's like my body is being embraced by mana. I promise you, no joking this time! It's different from when we drink mana... it's like the mana is surrounding me. How spectacular! Try one on for yourselves!"

Dara and Wynne were skeptical of Ami, yet her description was apt—once the crowns were situated, an electric sensation rippled across their skin.

"Incredible," Wynne said.

Dara stretched and adjusted her shoulders. "It's beyond words."

"If Vinzen is to be believed—and he has never lied to me before—these will protect the wearer from Mind Magic. It sounds like they also fend off the addiction to mana which the Dwarf Priests might have been prone to, with the amount of time they spent tending the source."

"I wonder if they enhance the wearer's magical ability as well?" Wynne mused.

"Protecting from Mind spells alone makes them powerful artifacts," Dara said.

Wynne slid off her crown and ogled at the treasures. "It still seems disrespectful to loot this place."

Ami sighed. "This is a sunken city, a place of death. I think the Dwarves would be rather glad to know we will make use of their cherished offerings. Besides, I'll return some of the crowns and gold to Vinzen and his people. I'm sure that will smooth over any irritation caused by our well-intentioned burglary."

"You should take most of them," Dara offered. "Wynne and I won't be able to go around handing these out in Llendshold. I'm sure the Fae and the Dwarves will put them to good use."

After gathering all the crowns and stowing them in their packs, they readied to leave. Glancing over their shoulders by the exit, a deep longing in their hearts told them to go back, to revel among the treasures. Dara wrenched herself away and stepped over the threshold first.

"Ami, Wynne, we did it. We found the records and the crowns!"

The two exited the storage room when an unseen bell clanged.

The ground quaked. All three fell to their knees as treasures crashed in the storehouse behind them. The doors slammed shut and the mouth of Kardef groaned open. A whining ring filled their ears.

As soon as it had all started, the tremors and the sounds ceased.

"I take it we weren't supposed to remove all the crowns?" Dara said, rising to her feet and helping the others up. "Or maybe it was the offerings?"

"I'm not sure about the offerings, but the crowns must have come and gone regularly," Wynne said. "Maybe there was a procedure, something we didn't follow."

Ami waltzed towards the exit. "Whatever we did may have deviated from the proper procedure, but we have the crowns. I'd call our venture a success."

Before they reached the end of the hallway, a splashing sound came from outside.

Ami's face went pale. "Something's in the water."

"Could it be another one of those creatures?" Wynne said, grasping a mana bottle.

Dara drew her sword. "Whatever is making these sounds is smaller, but there are a lot of them. I can't imagine anything still inhabiting Yuvsgrend will be friendly. Let's go!"

They ran out and peered over the stone railing. Half-decomposed, bloated Dwarves lumbered out of the water, their skin a sickening bluish-grey. They moved in staccato, jerking back and forth. Pearly white crystals protruded from their bodies, piercing through the tatters of clothes and tangles of moss draped over them. Water drained from their bodies as they hobbled onto the central platform and funneled towards the stairway.

The Dwarves groaned and gasped in a guttural, hollow, grinding, squelching cacophony.

Wynne cried out. "My head! It's like I'm being ripped apart from inside!"

"The crowns!" Dara yelled. "Put them on!"

Throwing on the crowns, the three fled around the perimeter of the district. Dara skidded to a stop when they reached the stairway. At the bottom, a mass of risen Dwarves waited.

CHAPTER 17

Dara slammed back a mouthful of mana and braced herself. The first of the gurgling Dwarves raised a club-like arm covered in a solid mass of crystal. Dara evaded the fist as it smashed into the stair, cracking stone. She countered with a flurry of strikes, leaving deep gashes in the Dwarf's moldering flesh.

The Dwarf clambered on as if Dara's strikes were less than pricks from a needle. Dara grabbed her sword with both hands, screaming as she beheaded the attacker. The body fell to the ground, yet it still attempted to crawl until advancing Dwarves stomped it into a pile of rotting flesh and bone and crystal.

Dara kicked and hacked at the Dwarves while Ami sent arrow after arrow into the throng, but the Dwarves pressed up the stairs.

"This way!" Wynne shouted.

Three ropes waited, tied off to the railing. Wynne took hold of one and leapt, swinging in a wide arc over the flood of Dwarves. She landed behind the throng and rolled over the path, coming to a stop near the exit. Dara and Ami followed soon after, tumbling in a heap by Wynne. She moved to help them up when Ami scrambled on her hands and knees towards the oncoming Dwarves to grab a fallen crown.

Dara leapt over her, dismembering the nearest Dwarves. No matter how many she cut down, more arrived to take their place.

"Dara, run!" Wynne called out.

A disc of white flame, more than ten feet across, arced around Dara. It sped through the advancing mob, igniting countless Dwarves before fading. Dara glanced over her shoulder to see Wynne, her hair flying back as if a gust of ocean wind blew in the cavern, scepter raised high. The flaming end shone pure white, as if the fires of Ilsios burned inside. Dara's awe was short-lived, as the spell of immolation merely slowed the horde.

Dara rejoined Ami and Wynne as they fled into the central chamber. Wynne stumbled, exhausted from her spell. Ami stood between Wynne and the Dwarves, taking a deep drink of mana. She punched the ground, sending tremors through the stone. A section of the passage crumbled, crushing the nearest Dwarves.

Exhaustion pulled at the three, whispering in their ears and beckoning them to give up, to lie down, to accept their fate. Memories of the mines flashed before Dara, of running, fleeing as monsters' growls echoed through the tunnels. Helplessness, hopelessness, and fear coursed through her veins.

"I refuse!" she screamed, emptying the last of the mana from a bottle. "Ramaia, boil their blood!"

Streams of red fragments, like a thousand wispy feathers caught in a gale, streamed from Dara's fingertips and into the Dwarves. Their skin bubbled and burst, sending a bluish goo splattering over the stone floors.

A fresh pack of Dwarves clambered over the fallen. An arrow pierced cleanly through one's eye, but it charged on, unhindered.

Dara, Wynne, and Ami pushed and pulled each other up the stairs towards the exit, desperate to further the distance between them and their pursuers. Wynne glanced backwards; the Dwarves advanced quickly and soon would overtake the three.

Wynne pushed Dara and Ami further along the path, then faced the Dwarves. She downed a mouthful of mana, relishing the heat and brightness flowing through her body. Eyes closed, she raised the scepter. Calling on Ilsios with all her heart and mind, she waved in a circle.

Flames billowed in a ring from the floor up the walls and across the ceiling. Wynne thrust the scepter forward, and the flames surged forth, engulfing the tunnel and sending Dwarves tumbling down the stairs.

Wynne collapsed in place, the warm embrace of mana faded. Tears streamed down her cheeks at the sight of charred Dwarves rising and resuming their pursuit.

"Is there no end?"

"It's almost like there's a whole city of them!" Ami said as she and Dara hooked their arms under Wynne's.

Urging each other on, they made it to the level section of path where they had dried their boots. Ami waved Dara and Wynne on, tilting a bottle of mana back. She mumbled a spell, then touched the ground. Boulders and rubble vibrated, wobbling towards the stairs. The chunks of stone rolled down, smashing into the Dwarves, but it did little more than stymie the flow.

"I'm out of mana!" Ami said.

Dara shook the bottle at her hip. "I have barely a sip left, and the bottles in my bag are spent."

"I'm out as well," Wynne gasped.

Dara grimaced. "Then there is nothing else we can do. Run!"

Ami drew her bow in desperation, loosing arrows to slow the Dwarves as they hobbled up the stairs. The three trudged through the flooded passage. Behind, Dwarves splashed and floundered, but as more piled into the water, they began treading on each other, using their fallen as a walkway to hasten their pursuit. Dara looked at the others; Ami's quiver was empty, and Wynne's face was drained of color.

Dara drew her sword.

"There are too many! Dara, we have to run!" Wynne cried.

Dara's eyes glistened. "Go! Please... go."

The Blood Mage cut and hacked and kicked wildly, screaming like a Siren. Ami pulled at the flailing Wynne, forcing her towards the exit.

A Dwarf struck Dara in the shoulder. Dwarves leapt in, throwing her into the water. Wynne cried out when a burst of light illuminated the tunnel. A gale wind sailed over Ami and Wynne, then crashed into the Dwarves surrounding Dara. Crystals and dismembered parts of Dwarves flew through the air.

A woman charged by faster than Dara thought possible. She dove into the melee, cutting and slicing with a long, slender sword. A flurry of spells punctuated her strikes; a group of attackers went flying from another wave of air, followed by crystals exploding from inside the Dwarves and sending shards rocketing through the tunnel. Finally, the woman squeezed her fist, and the remaining Dwarves collapsed into the waters.

As ripples subsided, silence filled the tunnel.

Wynne and Ami rushed to Dara, helping her to her feet. Stunned, they stared at their savior.

The Human woman was of an unassuming build, though her face had the look of a person who was not old but had lived a hard life. Her hair was pulled back tight. High cheekbones and sharply angled brow framed her teal eyes. A scar ran from her slender jaw up and over her nose.

She wore and carried an unusual ensemble. A thick padded gambeson, dyed a rich earthy brown, ended below her knees. Smooth steel plate armor protected her shoulders, elbows, knees, and neck. Padded leather boots rose over her calves. A Mage's gauntlet covered her left hand, while a thick leather gauntlet covered her right. A bandolier wrapped across her chest, holding five mana bottles. Her belt was adorned with various pouches, a dagger, and a buckler.

The woman sheathed her sword and grinned.

"Who are we to thank for saving us?" Wynne inquired, her head hanging low.

"I presume you are Wynne." The woman's voice was bold and deep, rich and soothing, like hot tea on a wintry day. "That makes you, Dara. And you, Ami. You're welcome. As for whom to thank—you may call me Imreia."

INTERLUDE

"Is the space sufficient, Okter?"

Okter paced around the room, inspecting every detail. It was spacious, larger than his old office, with ample shelves hosting tomes, artifacts, bags and jars of reagents, rows of mana bottles, and an array of weapons. At one end, a wide desk was placed inside an arc of tall windows, which offered a commanding view of the landscape. A forest stretched to the right, while to the left, open fields led to towering mountains. The room lacked decoration; there were no paintings or tapestries or other curiosities that Okter preferred to surround himself with, but it was, as measured by his demanding expectations, sufficient.

"My Lord, thank you—both for coming personally, and for arranging such a study. When I came to Draethhold, I never expected so gracious a reception. You honor me with this incredible gift, which I assure you is far more than sufficient."

The Lord smiled. "I see unique potential in partnership with you, and hope this to be the beginning of something truly great. I, and my peers, believe investing in you will allow our entire nation to benefit from your ambitions."

Okter sat at the desk and slid off his gloves. In place of his right hand was an ethereal skeleton, shrouded in a lilac haze. He uncorked a mana bottle and filled a gold-rimmed glass. When he took a sip, the haze condensed and solidified.

"Your gesture is most appreciated. I will be of support whenever, and however, there is need."

The Lord's gaze dwelled on Okter's purple hand. "I understand you have some personal motivations that lead you to provide such assistance."

Okter slammed his ethereal hand onto the desk. "I will see the Adjudicator's error corrected. Shortsighted, perverse, twisting the words of the Five into her own, she believes herself beyond reproach. She thought that taking a hand would prevent the oppressed from overthrowing their oppressor, that it is the hand which is necessary to take action. I expected an Adjudicator to know that true power lies in the mind, and it is the voice which gives the mind reach."

The Lord pressed the cork back into the mana bottle. "The level of control they maintain over mana is still problematic, seeing as our sources ran dry long ago. We will continue to smuggle what we can, and much will be diverted here."

Okter swirled the mana in his glass. "I will be judicious in its use, but do not forget my objective, beyond correcting the Adjudicator's error: where they see mana as a tool for control, I see its potential as a pathway to freedom. One I will gladly share with the people of Draethhold."

"All in time. As you mention sharing of mana... are you prepared to take on a student, or do you require more time?"

"I am always ready to teach those who are willing to learn."

"If I may, allow me to introduce my child." The Lord turned to the door. "Rhoslin!"

A young girl shuffled into the room. Head down, her long, smooth black hair covered her face. She dressed plainly, wearing a light tunic in the style of Llendshold, bound with a leather belt. Okter rose to meet her; she was barely as tall as his shoulder.

"Rhos has a genuine fascination and love for all things magic. The mystical arts are unfortunately fading in Draethhold, thanks to the Quinarium, but her interest remains strong." The Lord squeezed his daughter's shoulder reassuringly. "I openly admit to my crime of nepotism in presenting my child to you, but I can think of none more suitable to be your student."

Okter lifted Rhoslin's face by the chin. Her narrow lips and eyes were set between gaunt cheeks. "What I find most important is desire. I care little for what drives the desire, but it is essential that desire burns as furiously as the Flames of Ilsios. I see that desire in you, Rhoslin. I will accept you as my student, as long as you are willing to follow my every instruction."

"Your word is my command, sir." Rhoslin bowed deeply, her voice thin and strained.

Okter grinned. "There is no need for such formality with me. Be attentive. Be focused. Excellence demands effort. Be ready to push yourself until failure, then push yourself until you break, then push yourself further still. You will be frustrated. You will be angry. You may hate me at times, and yet through my instruction you will be awarded mightily, should you persevere. If you agree to this, I will help you become powerful beyond the dreams of any Quinarium Mage."

Rhoslin's face brightened, and she nodded hungrily.

Okter grinned. "We begin tomorrow, at dawn."

CHAPTER 18

Imreia pressed the butt of a skewer into the dirt, positioning a fish over a crackling fire to her liking. The sealed gate of Yuvsgrend shone in the moonlight, a short distance away. Their horses neighed, joining the singing of night animals; the chorus of crickets and owls had been most welcome on exiting the sunken city. Across the fire, Wynne and Ami sat close on either side of Dara.

"The artifacts you carry—I assume you found them in Yuvsgrend. I can teach you how to unlock their true power." Imreia tore off a piece of fish and pinched it gently before taking a bite. She chewed the morsel slowly. "You need not fear me, regardless of what the Quinarium may have told you. On that thought, I have to admit my curiosity. What are they saying about me these days?"

Wynne cleared her throat. "Commentary about your nature aside, we overheard a Confessor and Paladin claim you are readying an army of Fae to attack Llendshold."

Imreia laughed boisterously. "I am sure they are scheming gleefully, drumming up fears of an overwhelming invasion carried out by the mighty Fae. Though, I admit I count the Fae among my allies. Dwarves and the Humans of Draethhold, too."

"They mean to eradicate my people," Ami said. "We won't be allies of yours for much longer if we are all dead."

Imreia nodded with raised eyebrows. "An unfortunate truth, and an end which I hope does not come to be. I presume it was these worries of genocide which took you to Yuvsgrend?"

"Yes," Ami replied. "We came for the crowns of the Dwarf Priests, and to find proof of the Dwarf genocide. It would seem that everyone in Llendshold was taught the Dwarves disappeared of their own accord, after what you call the Second Battle of Stellburg."

"Why would you work to protect the Fae?" Wynne interjected.

"Because they are more an ally to me than most all of Llendshold."

"Who are you, truly?" Dara stared at Imreia. "If the Quinarium speaks falsely of you, then what is the truth?"

"I am Imreia Keserian, the rightful Lord of Brewardsburg."

"LORD!?" Wynne shouted.

"I see the Quinarium—along with the Earls, Lords, and possibly Regents themselves—continue to spin tales about me and my family. Allow me to tell you the truth, as I lived it. Should we ever find ourselves beside a Mind Mage, you are welcome to have them verify the truth of it all.

"My parents were the Lords of Brewardsburg, and I, their firstborn. Through decades of hard work, we transformed Brewardsburg from the lowest of the five cities to the most reputable, and my parents were favored to be crowned the next Regents of Llendshold. They did all this without reliance on the Quinarium, which enraged the Adjudicators and the Voice of the Five. They began a crusade against my family, claiming we were worse than lacking in faith, that we were heretics. As such, the seated Regent called upon the other Lords of Llendshold and the forces of the Quinarium to march on Brewardsburg, murdering my family and most of our supporters, from Earls to

Servants. The few fortunate enough to not be killed were exiled. I barely escaped."

"My mother never mentioned..." Wynne murmured.

"Mother? I heard you are the daughter of a Lord. Where do you hail from, Wynne?"

"Hantsburg."

"You are of the Pharadrax family. Your mother has a deserved reputation for being a pragmatic Lord. The distance between our cities was a small kindness, as soldiers of Hantsburg were not involved in the massacre in Brewardsburg, and this happened before she was named Lord."

"I don't care so much about your past as I do about the present," Dara said. "How did you come to know who we are, and that we would be in Yuvsgrend?"

"You aren't Vinzen's only friends," Imreia said. "When I heard of you passing through his inn, and that he believed you might make for Yuvsgrend, curiosity took hold of me. Imagine my surprise as I spoke with more of my allies—among them a particular farmer in Cauldhill—and they confirmed seeing you three. I asked myself: who could these young Mages be, setting off on their own, in defiance of the Quinarium? Who could this young Fae be, bold enough to sneak through Llendshold? I simply had to meet you."

"Probably more dangerous for you than Ami to be in Llendshold," Dara remarked.

"Most certainly. While there is technically no prohibition on Fae in Llendshold, it would have been most unwise to flaunt her identity. Ami chose correctly to conceal herself. As for my travels, the night is my friend. The Quinarium spends a great deal of time preaching about beasts in the dark, when the light of Ilsios is gone. I travel with many horses that I might make good use of the night. Perhaps the thundering of my horses' hooves has contributed to the rumors?"

"And what do you think?" Wynne asked.

"Of what?"

"Of us."

"I'm impressed. You all survived an encounter with the Risen Dwarves. Even experienced delvers of ancient tombs and ruins would have been unlikely to see the sky again."

"You had to save us," Dara said.

"Ahem!" Ami interjected. "Wynne managed to learn a host of new spells merely by reading a book. And we also slew a monster down there. Wild creature, over a hundred feet long, towering on a hundred legs!"

Imreia chuckled. "Yes, I saw the carcass. Though you embellish, the creature was undoubtedly a formidable foe. I noticed the final blow from Dara—the back of the head was a good choice. It was a great show of skill from you all to slay such a creature."

"We weren't skilled enough to flee the Dwarves," Dara said, gazing into the fire.

"Oh, don't be hard on yourselves. You three are young and did well to last as long as you did. The Risen... such a strange phenomenon. I saw them once before, at the site of a crashed Quinarium ship laden with mana. Humans, that time. I never imagined them in such numbers."

Dara inched closer to the fire. "When I was younger, in the mines, another child struck a sandy bit of rock. It gave way, and he fell into a pit filled with water. It took days to get him free, and when they pulled out his body, it was... grotesque. How is it the Risen Dwarves didn't rot away to nothing but bone?"

"And what caused them to be covered in crystals?" Wynne added.

"I believe the answer to both your questions lies in the source. It would require studying to confirm, but when the flood mixed with the mana source, it must have infused the bodies of the dead. I can only assume the crystals grew for the same reasons.

Mana often acts in inexplicable ways, as you have seen. It is good fortune you made away with both the records and the crowns, despite the appearance of the Risen."

"A foolish mistake to take them all," Wynne said. "I think taking them caused the Dwarves to wake. We nearly died because of it."

"A true fool is one who acts in defiance of the knowledge they carry. You did not know then, and we still do not know now, what caused the bell to ring."

"Why did you take so long to help us?" Ami demanded.

"I saw your work on the creature, which made me believe you three were capable enough to handle whatever might come your way. I thought it prudent to wait by the entrance, where you were certain to pass. None could have predicted the Risen, and in such numbers. I came as soon as I heard. And despite my claimed tardiness, you all showed yourselves well—especially given the limited training provided by the Quinarium."

Wynne scoffed. "We learn more of that institution every day."

Imreia leaned close by the fire. "Tell me, how much do you know?"

"Of what?" Dara asked facetiously.

"The Quinarium."

Wynne took a deep breath and exhaled slowly through her nose.

"Enough to doubt their intentions. Enough to distrust their aims. Enough to drive us to abandon our rite and assist Ami." Wynne trembled with rage and tears welled in her eyes. "Enough to... to... enough to abandon our faith."

Imreia snorted. "Abandoned your faith? You are a precious thing. It is entirely possible to remain faithful to the Quinate while rejecting the inadequacy and the lies of the Quinarium. As you have defied the demands of the *Quinarium,* I have a proposition for you."

Dara sat up tall. "Will you present us with a false choice, where there is only one possible outcome? Or are we free to agree or reject as we wish?"

Imreia chuckled and shook her head. "Quite the challenge. While I appreciate your caution, remember that I saved you. I wish you no harm and you are welcome to reject my offer. I will even help you reach the Fae and vouch for you, if need be."

"What do you propose?" Wynne asked.

"Join me." The corners of Imreia's mouth slowly curled upwards. "If only for a few days, join me. Wear your crowns. Experience the truth as is only possible when seen with your own eyes. I am not asking for your loyalty, your partnership, or anything else—not yet. All I want is for you to come with me, and see."

Dara tossed a fresh log into the fire. "See what?"

"Extraction."

Wynne shook her head at the way Imreia dramatically stretched the word. "Are you speaking of the Harvest Ceremony? What of it? It is a common procedure, and one I've seen many times."

"Tell me what you saw."

Wynne was perplexed, but entertained the request. "It is always with an aged or ill person. They lie on an altar, loved ones surrounding them to celebrate their passing. Then, Quinarium Agents prepare bottles and fill them with a spell. Mana flows, and the person falls into their final slumber. It is a simple and peaceful thing, the least of my worries with the Quinarium."

"Come with me. See what *really* happens."

The fire crackled and spit as Dara, Wynne, and Ami looked amongst themselves.

"I have no love for the Quinarium and need no convincing of their ills." Ami said. "I know what I need from what happened to my grandfather. I heard enough from Uldrik and Scireth. I need to warn the Fae and meet with the Dwarves, too. They need to see the records. I need to be there for my people."

"Dara?"

"Wynne, I... I have spent enough of my life being ordered around by people claiming to be acting for my good, only to be used and left hungry. We have a chance to see the truth. We should take that opportunity. Think about what the Siren said, the Fae, what we heard in the Sanctuary... this might be your chance to forge your own path, to be someone more than the daughter of a Lord."

"By abandoning everything I've ever known."

"Progress cannot be made without sacrifice."

Imreia's words cut like a cleaver through an overripe squash.

"What do you want from us?" Wynne asked.

"I want the same thing for you as I want for all—I want you to see the truth of the Quinarium." Imreia marched before the fire. "It is my crusade. I must bring light to the inequities of the Quinarium, rattle the foundations of their false righteousness, and secure a safe and bright future for all of Llendshold!"

"What is your part in this future?" Dara asked.

"I will not deceive you. In tearing down the Quinarium, I aim to recover my family's seat as Lord of Brewardsburg; to achieve this, I will recruit any and all who are willing to support me. I do not expect you to consider joining me at this moment, but travel with me for a few days. You are already nearing a week late in reporting to Stellburg. What difference would a few days make, should you reject my offer?"

"Wynne, what do you think?" Dara asked.

"Can we take a moment to say goodbye to Ami?"

Imreia smiled at the tacit agreement. "More than a moment. Take as long as you wish. I'll prepare a map for Ami, showing the safest route back to the Nomridian Forest."

Dara, Wynne, and Ami walked along the woods until the crackling of the campfire faded.

"Are you sure about her?" Ami asked. "I haven't heard mention of Imreia among the Fae, yet she speaks casually of us…"

"I am far from certain, but I can't turn away from this opportunity," Dara said. "Even if we do return to the Moderator, we're in for it as late as we are. I need to see the truth first."

Wynne nodded. "I fear Imreia. I have never seen or heard of anyone with power like hers. But you're right. What we read of the past was horrible, and I need to find out what is happening now. This may be our only chance."

"I hope your people can put the crowns to good use. The Dwarves, too," Dara said. "Should we give you the rest of the crowns? We only need one for each of us."

"Keep the ones you have. I'm sure you'll find plenty good use for them." Ami kicked her toe into the dirt. "I can't thank you two enough. I never would have found the records or the crowns without you. I would have been another corpse littering the floors of Yuvsgrend, if I even made it inside. Five above, I hate depending on others, but I must admit I've become dependent on you. I will truly miss you, and hope to see you again one day."

Wynne pulled Ami into an embrace. "Travel safely."

Dara wrapped her arms around them both. "Be well."

"Would it be untoward if I closed by saying 'as They speak'?"

The three broke into laughter as Imreia walked over. She held out a map to Ami, with a path marked and notes at various points along the way.

"Here you are then. It should be an easy enough journey for one such as yourself, Ami."

Ami twirled back, bowing with a flourish before mounting her horse and riding into the dark.

Imreia turned to Dara and Wynne. "As for us, we may as well get situated for the night. You were likely the first visitors to Yuvsgrend in near half a century; I doubt any will wander by, though I'll scout around to be certain. You get yourselves comfortable. And perhaps put on some fresh tunics... you reek."

After changing, Dara and Wynne sat on bedrolls beside each other in the warmth of the crackling fire. A pot of stew bubbled joyfully by the coals. The fresh tunics were a welcome change, though it felt strange to wear garments given to them by the Quinarium. The gravity of what they had agreed to further weighed heavily on both. Still, when a gentle breeze sang through the nearby trees, they could not help but feel at ease, if only for a moment.

Wynne pulled her legs to her chest and rest her chin on her knees. "It's hard to believe all that we've been through."

"Some rite that was," Dara snorted. "I wonder what the others had to do. It's like you and I were singled out for who we are... or should I say, who we were."

"Do you think our rite was a punishment?"

"You and I do make an odd pair. A miner studying the ways of Ramaia, a Lord's daughter trained under Ilsios... maybe the Quinarium would have rather we failed. Sending us into the Nomridian Forest, battling Jackals, they gave us a task better suited for a company of Paladins and Mages."

Wynne smiled. "If only they knew what would come of it all."

"Following Imreia, of all people. If only we could see the face of Uldrik when he hears of it," Dara smirked. "That dastardly Confessor. I don't have ill will towards most in the Quinarium, but him? I would gladly see him get his due. And Imreia... she was incredible in the tunnels. I never dreamed of moving as she did, commanding magic as she did."

"Don't speak as if you are anything less than exceptional," Wynne said, punching Dara's shoulder. "When that creature was hovering over Ami and me, you flew out of the water. I am still in awe, seeing you soar through the air and land on its head. How did you manage to cast a spell while underwater?"

"I gurgled it."

They broke into laughter at the absurdity of the admission. Dara sighed and leaned back on her elbows. "I guess it was like you, with the Jackal Denmother. I went unconscious when I hit the surface, but woke when I choked on water. At first I panicked, but then I saw the shadow of the creature. I couldn't stand the thought of it hurting you."

"And Ami."

"I was thinking only of you."

Wynne's heart raced. "What about when we were fleeing from the Risen? You would have died had Imreia not arrived."

"I gladly would have, if it meant saving you."

Wynne and Dara locked eyes. Their faces glowed in the light of the flickering fire. A log cracked and split, brightening the night for a moment.

"Can I ask you... if you imagine us to be the people we were that first day of our rite, if we were those people today, would you have been willing to sacrifice yourself? Based on how you acted, I don't think you felt quite the same back then."

"I'm not sure what I would have done," Dara said with a grimace. "I suppose that's not exactly reassuring. What I mean to say is that I judged you poorly. After the Moderator announced your heritage, I was worried you might be like the others from the Academy. They never saw me for who I was, for what I was capable of; they only saw where I came from. If I'm honest, I was also nervous because I found you beautiful."

Wynne faced the fire, hoping its light would hide her blushing cheeks. "You don't have to lie. My mother and father always worried about finding me a partner, saying that I was the plainest of my brothers and sisters. Too short, not enough poise, lacking the dignity, my face-"

"Why would you say these things?" Dara sat tall. "You are all the things I wish I was. I spent my life in the mines, the sun a distant stranger. I've seen it more these past weeks than I would in an entire year as a child. My skin is forever pale, yours is rich and vibrant. My hands are rough and brutish, yours are soft and tender. I can never see past what is right in front of me, while your mind is a treat, always thoughtful, thinking of more. You, Wynne, are beautiful, and anyone who says otherwise is either jealous or a fool."

Wynne's mouth hung open in shock while Dara spoke. She pulled her mouth closed and swallowed. "You've always been distant. I never thought you would see me this way."

"I'm distant because I'm scared." Dara retreated, hunching low.

"What would you possibly have to be scared of? Until we met Imreia, I have never seen any your equal."

"I'm not scared of fighting, Wynne. I'm scared of love, because I've never felt it before. It's only something I've ever seen. It's like I was always on the outside, looking in through a window at love shared between others... Not even my parents... my parents... When I left for the Academy, my parents didn't even say goodbye. Their backs were turned before the carriage driver climbed into her seat. My whole life, I have felt like a burden to the only people I have ever sought love from. And when I started to feel something for you..." Dara wiped tears from her face. "I'm sorry, I shouldn't cry. Okter always said tears are for children."

Wynne crawled over and sat beside Dara, then rested her head on the Blood Mage's shoulder. "Okter is wrong. Crying is for everyone, no matter their age. If you want to cry, then it is right to cry."

Dara's eyes glistened; she exhaled slowly as Wynne held her hands and their fingers intertwined. "Our time together has been chaos unimaginable. But through it all, I know that when I'm with you, I feel something *more*. I'm scared of losing this, of losing you. I never want this to end."

"It's the same for me."

Wynne lifted Dara's chin, bringing their faces close together. Dara brushed away a lock of Wynne's hair, then cupped her cheek. Their lips neared as they burned with an insatiable need to feel each other's touch. Wynne inhaled and pressed forward when a twig snapped in the woods nearby.

Dara and Wynne flew apart.

"Don't let me interrupt," Imreia said, strolling over to the fire. "I smelled the stew and a furious hunger drove me back. As capable as I am in a fight, I am a horrible cook and have had little more than roast fish and dried provisions these last few days. We'll need to be well-rested and well-fed for the journey ahead—shall we eat?"

Imreia slowed her horse at the top of a small hill by the edge of a forest. It was an unpleasantly drizzly morning, yet she beamed.

A small hamlet—comprised of twenty homes, a smithy, a few farm buildings, an inn, and little else—waited in the field below.

Dara and Wynne could not comprehend Imreia's joy. The two were on edge; torn between their unquenched thirst for time together and anticipation of the Harvest Ceremony, their mood only worsened now the hamlet was in sight.

"Good, good." Imreia closed her eyes and smiled at the sky as raindrops bounced off her skin. "The Quinarium Agents should arrive soon. Keep your crowns on and hoods low. The rain is a fortunate friend today."

"You don't need a crown?" Wynne asked.

"I have my own methods—ones which I am sure you are capable of learning, but we don't have the luxury of time for instruction. Nor do we have the substantial mana necessary for frivolous training. Speaking of mana, keep your bottles hidden. We don't want to attract attention."

"What of our clothes? These are Quinarium tunics."

"It's a hamlet, Dara. Back when you worked in the mines, would you have recognized a Mage, were it not for their gauntlet and mana bottles? Your tunics will hardly be enough to draw notice. We are simple delvers, searching for a ruin when we lost our way. Blessed are we to be in the hamlet as the Quinarium arrives for a Harvest Ceremony."

Residents flurried about the muddy streets of the hamlet like bees about a hive. On a typical day, three strangers riding in on horses would be cause for much ado, but their arrival drew little more than the occasional stare.

As if annoyed by the inattention, Imreia waved down a passing man.

"Excuse me, good sir. What is going on in the hamlet today?"

"The Quinarium is coming!" the man cheered.

"Whatever for?"

"After some months of declining health, our Elder has done the most wonderful thing. She has offered herself for the Harvest Ceremony! No waiting for her. She wanted to ensure her body would provide well. As They speak!"

Imreia grinned broadly. "So we listen, my friend. So we listen."

Imreia halted outside the inn and dismounted.

"Is it wise for us to spend time among the residents here?" Dara whispered. "Should we not be more cautious?"

"Nonsense. We are delvers. An inn is precisely where we should stop first."

Wynne grabbed Dara's arm after Imreia entered and pulled her back.

"She's enjoying this."

Dara nodded. "From what little she's said, I think any opportunity to expose the Quinarium is going to excite her, but this seems..."

"Perverse. If harvesting is such a heinous act, then why is she giddy? We should be mindful of her," Wynne counseled.

"I agree, though I think she will hold to her word. If the coming hours go poorly, we will go our own way."

Dara squeezed Wynne's hand, then followed Imreia.

Locals packed the inn, chatting loudly over mugs of ale. Imreia was already seated at a table, raising her mug high whenever a cheer sounded out. At her urging, Dara and Wynne sat and picked at bowls of stew, unable to bring themselves to revel with the locals.

Imreia was halfway through her second mug of ale when the door to the inn flew open.

"They're here!" a woman shouted.

Chairs and tables crashed to the ground, while ale and food splattered across the floor. The innkeeper said not a word of the mess, pushing and shoving residents out into the hamlet. Imreia waited for the inn to quiet; when the three were the only ones remaining, she emptied her mug and set a few Guilders on the table.

"Shall we?"

They stepped out as two carriages bearing the symbol of the Quinarium rolled to a stop. The drivers hopped down to open the carriage doors. An Officiant, wearing a bright tunic which stretched to his ankles, was joined by two Assistants, a Paladin, and a Mind Mage. They all grimaced and groaned as their shoes sank into slick mud.

Residents quietly ushered the Agents of the Quinarium to a crude structure tucked against a nearby building. It consisted of four posts with a tan linen sheet hanging above and a raised bed beneath. Though the rain had lessened to a gentle mist, the structure was soaked and dripping.

The Officiant touched a post and faced the crowd of nearly one hundred, the entirety of the hamlet. "Thank you, thank you all. You have prepared well for our coming. It is a blessed day when we are called to bring one closer to the Quinate. Your Elder is to be honored, no, revered, for her decision! You all would do well to follow in her footsteps. There is no better way to show your love for the Quinate than to offer yourself freely. All you who have gathered today will see the beauty, the joy, the gift that is to become one with the Five!"

The door to a nearby building opened, and the crowd erupted in cheer, with Imreia among the loudest. The Elder hobbled out, assisted by two others. Her tunic, aged and threadbare, barely reached her knees. She stood as proudly as she was able, waving to the boisterous onlookers. A cough overtook her, and blood stained her sleeve. Dara spied the Officiant scowling, though he quickly hid his expression as the Elder tottered over.

The Paladins helped the Elder onto the bed. She clutched the hem of her tunic, convulsing from another cough. A young man rushed out with a cloth to wipe blood dribbling from her mouth, but the Paladins pushed him back.

The Officiant held his hands up in a call for quiet as he approached the crowd. Behind him, the Mind Mage took a drink of mana and cast an unintelligible spell. A wave of purple light flew out from the Mage's fingers and through the hamlet. Despite the grandeur of the spell surging through the onlookers, not a single person noticed.

"What was that?" Wynne asked Imreia.

"Quiet. Cheer for the sacrifice, don't draw attention. What you saw was the beginning, and you only saw it because of the crowns."

The Officiant returned to the Elder's side, pulling on a gauntlet of his own. He smiled and addressed the residents. "And so begins the most beautiful passing. As your Elder gifts her life in the name of the Quinate, I will ensure the essence of her soul is preserved. As They speak!"

"So we listen!"

A smile crept across the Elder's face as the Officiant whispered into her ear. She closed her eyes and exhaled slowly.

"Let the Gods hear your praise!" urged a Paladin.

While the crowd shouted anew, the Assistants took position on either side of the bed. They presented open bottles as the Officiant recited a long spell and placed his hand over the Elder's head.

A boom ripped through the hamlet, drowning out the applause. Dara and Wynne fought the urge to cover their ears, though the residents were unbothered. A grey cloud formed a few feet above the Elder. Her face contorted as she groaned, her body quivering. The cloud billowed and crackled as if lightning burst inside. The Elder's chest suddenly lifted from the bed with a crack. She shrieked as her body contorted, bones snapping, joints bending in every direction.

"Please! Five above, help me, please! Mercy! Mercy! Mercy!" she screamed over and over, her voice ever more shrill and thin.

Blood flowed from the Elder's body into the cloud as her skin tightened and wrinkled. The swirling crimson mass above her glowed and pulsed. The Assistants raised their bottles while the Officiant pressed his hand directly over the Elder's screaming face. Droplets of mana condensed on the edge of the cloud and funneled into the bottles. As the liquid passed through the air, ash fell to the ground all around. The flow was slow at first, but increased in intensity, the onlookers cheering gleefully all the while.

The Elder's feet kicked in desperation as the bones in her legs snapped.

After five agonizing minutes, the cloud finally calmed and dissipated. The Elder's twisted corpse lay motionless. The Assistants quietly sealed mana bottles while the Officiant addressed the crowd.

"Such is the beauty, the joy, the peacefulness that is bestowed by the Quinate through the hands of the Quinarium!" The Officiant patted the shriveled shoulder of the Elder, her face frozen in a silent scream. "See the restfulness, the tranquility on her face? This is an end which cannot be rivaled. Now that her soul has been elevated, sent to swim through the sky with the Five, allow us to put what remains of her to rest."

A joyful parade formed, with the corpse of the Elder carried at the front, followed by the Quinarium Agents and a long tail of residents. They marched out of the village to their graveyard on the other side of a broad hill, not a soul noticing when Imreia, Dara, and Wynne slipped away.

Once the noise of the celebration faded, Imreia faced Dara and Wynne.

"And how did you enjoy the extraction this time?"

Wynne plopped onto a box. She wavered for a moment before bending over and hurling.

"How could this be?" Dara asked, rubbing Wynne's back. "How could they do this to so many people, and so brazenly? Why have none have ever risen against them?"

"This is but a taste of their deception. From the records I have uncovered through the years, it appeared the Quinarium first acted as grave robbers, testing their spells on the recently dead. Realizing they extracted greater quantities of mana the more recent the death, they sought a fresher source: the living. As going around and murdering whoever they pleased was a touch impractical, and the process takes some effort, they concocted this ceremony, hidden with the power of Mind Mages. The slow escalation results in the acceptance as it is today."

Imreia looked up to the thinning clouds. "I thought extraction the best example of truth to share with you. This is, however, but a sample of the Quinarium's ways. The Test of Mana—which you both underwent—is claimed to be a potentially fatal test. In truth, none will ever die from drinking mana, regardless of how unattuned your body might be. The Quinarium has designed the bottles used in the test to contain a small capsule of poison. If the bottle is turned in a particular way, the poison will pour inside, killing the imbiber."

"Why?" Wynne asked, returning to her feet.

"Power."

"What power could possibly come from killing children?" Dara fumed. The cries of Adan's parents at their farm outside her hamlet flooded her ears. "Especially those wanting to become a part of the Quinarium?"

"Oh, it's quite simple, my dear." Imreia leaned casually against the wall. "Poor children, thankfully not you, but those like yourself, are sacrificed to strengthen the idea that only the Quinarium is capable of controlling this powerful, dangerous substance. A gift, but one which must be tended by masters.

"As for the wealthy children, they die for a decidedly different reason: to send a message to their families. If the Quinarium believes a family is attempting to circumvent their control, they will kill one of their children. As clear a message as a letter written in blood that the family has offended, and if they do not fall in line, then they will all suffer a similar fate."

Wynne ground her teeth. "What then-"

Imreia threw off her cloak and pulled on her gauntlet in a single motion. Unsure of the reason for her alarm, Wynne and

Dara followed suit. Imreia adjusted her bandolier, positioning her mana bottles at the front once again. She took a deep drink, then stepped out into the hamlet.

Dara and Wynne hurried after to see two Paladins at the edge of the hamlet. Three carriages roared into the street, the drivers cracking their whips. A complement of ten Paladins followed on horseback.

As the carriages skidded to a stop, the door of the first opened. A man sauntered out, his white tunic dragging on the steps. He took off his silver mask, revealing deep-set eyes beneath bushy eyebrows, a slender nose, and thin lips.

"Ah, so we have found our wayward Mages," said the Moderator of Stellburg.

Chapter 19

Mud squelched beneath the Moderator's boots. Behind him, an imposing force assembled. The Paladins dismounted and joined their compatriots, forming a line of shields and spears. Two archers climbed atop each of the carriages, arrows nocked and at the ready, while four Mages pulled on their gauntlets.

"You two miscreants abandoned your Rite of the Faithful, abandoned the orders of the Quinarium, and in doing so, have abandoned the Quinate!" lectured the Moderator. "Your defiance is heresy. Your path to becoming a part of the Quinate's Faithful has forever ended, a fate you sealed long before you stood beside the monster that is Imreia."

Dara squinted, recognizing two of the Mages as none other than Jodrie and Ffionin, the worst of her tormentors from the Academy of Ramaia. "You expect fealty when all you have done is deceive us!"

The Moderator laughed. "Deceive you? Who are you to speak of deception? The only deception is from the two of you, acting in the name of the Quinarium, all the while scheming to undermine the mandate of the Gods!"

"The extraction!" Wynne screamed. "We saw the truth of it!"

"Extraction? You malign the beauty of the Harvest Ceremony with such a name. And why speak of truth when there are no lies in the ceremony?" the Moderator said. "Ah, I see the crowns on your heads. You will tell me how you came to acquire those, but that is for another time. As for the harvest, there are no lies. There is no more beautiful way to embrace death. We shield the minds of the observers for their safety. It is a protection, a kindness! You would have learned all of this, as these loyal Mages behind me have, had you fulfilled your duty and completed your rite. All would have been shown to you in time, yet instead you chose ignorance!"

"As expected, Dara turned out to be a failure," Jodrie interjected. "She never should have been allowed into the Academy of Ramaia."

"A miner, if I remember," chortled Ffionin. "I always knew you would end up underground once again—I didn't realize we would have the good fortune of putting you there."

"I do not recall asking for your opinion," the Moderator said, silencing the Mages.

Anger brewed in Wynne on seeing Dara wince at the jabs. "And what of the people who you extract mana from? Do they not deserve to know what a horrific end they will meet, should they volunteer? They tortured the Elder!"

"Horrific?" The Moderator paced back and forth in the street. "There is no greater act, no more meaningful sacrifice one can make than to dedicate your life to the Quinate, to the Quinarium, the institution which you have abandoned! We ensure the safety, the stability, the peace in all of Llendshold, in the name of the Quinate and in service of the Regency! That you would call an act of the Quinarium *torture* tells me all I need know: you are a traitor, Llewelyn Pharadrax, as are you, Dara. You will face the Five's judgement in the court of the Quinarium!"

Imreia picked at her teeth, then spat into the street. "You speak as if we must be in some Quinarium construct to be in the presence of the Five. Face their judgement in a court... Are they not always present? Or have your lessons changed? Or perhaps it is that you intend to judge these two Mages by the standards of Humans? Humans wielding claims of godliness, all the while corrupted and hungry for power, seeking only to benefit themselves."

The Moderator threw his mask aside. "Do you know who I am, Imreia?"

"Another fool who has convinced himself he speaks with the authority of the Five. What am I to care? There is little difference between all the puppets within the Quinarium. You being a Moderator does not make you any more significant than a single grain in a field of wheat."

"I was there, the day your parents died," the Moderator said with a sneer. "It was a beautiful sunny day, blessed by the Quinate. We captured your mother and father alive. I was the one to harvest mana from them. When the process is involuntary, it is magnitudes more painful. You were already on the run, but I wonder, did you hear their screams? I made sure it took *hours*. The Quinate has blessed us, as today we end the last of your cursed family."

Imreia yawned. "Forgive me. I was unsure when your prattling would end. It is a shame you Moderators don't get an Enforcer to follow you around. I would have enjoyed a challenge."

Wynne's heart raced, realizing Imreia intended to fight.

"Are you blind, or merely stupid?" the Moderator seethed. "Do you not see the force accompanying me? You may as well kneel and accept your death, all three of you. A blessed day indeed. I will be certain to ascend to the rank of Adjudicator once I deliver your head to the Voice!"

"If you want to live," Imreia bellowed with a wave at the Paladins, archers, and Mages, "run. You have my word, I will leave you be. However, should you choose to stay, consider yourself to be living on time borrowed from the Quinate, as I will end you all."

Chills ran up Dara's and Wynne's spines at the veracity of Imreia's vow. The Moderator paced while Imreia stood still as a statue. A bead of sweat dripped down Wynne's face despite the air being cool. Her fingers tingled, as though the mana she drank was itching with desire to be unleashed in a spell.

"There are so many. What are we to do?" Wynne said beneath her breath.

"I believe Dara has a personal matter to attend to?" Imreia replied.

"Yes—I will take care of the Blood Mages."

"Excellent. The other two appear to be of Earth and Air—a trifle. Wynne, you stay with me and all will be fine. Though, please don't hurt the Moderator. He is mine."

Imreia cast a spell to infuse herself with speed before the Quinarium Mages finished uncorking their mana bottles. She cast a second spell, concluding it with a swift punch into the mud. A fissure ran forth, sending clods of dirt flying. The ground split like lightning, rattling beneath the Quinarium forces.

An archer recovered and drew back his bowstring when a dagger thrown by Dara pierced his neck. As the archer fell from the carriage, Dara dove behind a nearby building, on her way to flank the Quinarium forces and reach the Blood Mages.

Wynne swung her scepter, hurling an orb of white flame at a carriage. As the vehicle burst into fire, the horses charged away, sending the archers atop tumbling to the ground. Paladins marched forward, their shields raised and spears lowered. Wynne took a drink of mana as Imreia blitzed past the Moderator and headed directly for the Earth and Air Mages.

Before either could cast a spell, Imreia shrieked with an outstretched hand. Air pulled from their lungs, the two Mages grasped at their throats. She dispatched each with a single strike, then faced the Paladins. Meanwhile, the Moderator fled to the remaining carriages and the cover of the archers, calling on the Paladins and Blood Mages to stand between him and Imreia.

Dara sped out from behind a row of houses. Two Paladins scurried forth and blocked the way to the Blood Mages. Dara slid beneath a spear and kicked aside the nearest Paladin's shield. She grabbed his belt and pulled herself up, thrusting her sword into his armpit, driving the blade into his chest through a gap in his armor.

As the first Paladin fell, she rolled over the shield of the second. Before the Paladin could turn, Dara sliced behind their knees, sending them wailing, falling into the mud. Jodrie and Ffionin stood with their swords raised. Dara glared as blood trickled down her blade.

The three charged in a fury, the clanging of steel echoing through the hamlet. The Blood Mages darted back and forth, disappearing into a nearby field. Wynne moved to follow Dara when arrows slammed into the building beside her. As the missiles flew in, she slipped behind a stack of barrels.

Wynne peeked out to see the Paladins form a circle around Imreia, approaching in unison with their spears lowered. Archers released their bowstrings, sending arrows flying. With a wave of her hand, Imreia froze the arrows mid-flight. She closed her fist, then pointed, sending the arrows hurtling back. The missiles found their mark and two of the archers crumpled atop the carriages.

Wynne rushed forward with her scepter raised. She called on Ilsios and the end of her weapon glowed pure white. When three Paladins peeled off to face her, Wynne unleashed a gout of flame. As the stream sailed towards the Paladins, the Moderator roared a spell of his own. The Paladins' shields glowed white as the flames struck. They cheered when Wynne's spell was deflected, then broke into a charge.

Wynne stumbled backwards when Imreia appeared, soaring through the air. She landed atop one Paladin and plunged her blade through the back of their neck. Before the other two could raise their shields, she was upon them.

Imreia grabbed hold of one Paladin's spear, wrenching it aside and thrusting it below the breastplate of the other Paladin, burying the tip in their belly. She turned back to the first, slicing their throat. Imreia stomped on the spear haft, breaking it in two, then plunged the weapon in until only the splintered end was visible. The impaled Paladin fell to their knees, prompting Imreia to kick aside the lifeless body.

"Come on then, Wynne. There's more to take care of."

Imreia marched back towards the Moderator when an arrow struck her thigh. She groaned, dropping to her knees. Spying the archer, she pointed as she yelled, then pulled her fist to her shoulder. A gust flung the archer into the air as Imreia planted her sword, point up, on the ground.

The archer's screams were cut short as they landed directly on Imreia's sword. She pushed the body off her blade, then snapped the arrow shaft, leaving a stub protruding from her leg. Wynne flung an orb of flame at the carriages, sending the last two archers diving for cover.

Imreia rose as the remaining Paladins surrounded her. They kept their distance, spears at the ready. Wynne moved to provide aid when arrows struck nearby, forcing her to hide. She swallowed back mana and prepared to fight again when a white light illuminated the hamlet.

Wynne peered out to see the Moderator screaming, hand raised to the sky. A column of fire and crackling lightning fell to the earth like a meteor, striking where Imreia stood. White ribbons bounced between the Paladins' shields, creating a web of flame and lightning. Wynne stared, stunned.

The Moderator stumbled back, mana dribbling down his chin, cackling as the blaze faded.

"Where has your haughtiness gone, Imreia? Where has your confidence gone, Imreia?" The Moderator grinned as he exhaled in exhaustion. "You thought us insufficient? Tell me of the might of Ilsios and Seraeus combined, wielded by a Moderator! Tell me, Imreia! What have you to say!?"

A gasp sounded from the carriage above the Moderator. Imreia knelt atop the vehicle between the last of the archers, who clawed at their slit throats. The Moderator scurried away as the Paladins attempted to regroup. Imreia drained a mana bottle then threw it aside. She murmured a spell as she punched the carriage.

Thousands of splinters erupted from the side of the vehicle. The fleeing Moderator pulled a Paladin in front of himself as wood shards rained down on them. Splinters pierced gaps in armor, killing a few of the Paladins and maiming the rest. The Moderator squealed in pain, his legs peppered with fragments of the carriage.

Imreia waved to Wynne, still atop the tattered vehicle. "Why don't you go see where your friend has gone off to? I think the fight is about gone from these ones."

"Dara!" Wynne ran for the fields.

Imreia hopped down and faced the last four bleeding, shaking Paladins. They huddled by the Moderator, who was crawling away in the mud. She took a drink of mana and strolled forward.

"I gave you a chance to leave."

She whispered to Ramaia and the Paladins' hands bubbled, the blood inside boiling. They screamed and dropped their spears and shields.

"I told you what was to come."

The nearest Paladin fell to their back, hands outstretched in a plea for mercy. Imreia plunged her sword into their neck.

"And now, see how I hold true to my word."

Imreia lunged forward, swiftly ending the last of the Paladins.

The Moderator gasped as he squirmed in the mud, desperately dragging his bloodied legs. Imreia grabbed him by the shoulders and flipped him over. She kicked the Moderator's hand when he lunged for his dagger, breaking his fingers. He yelped, clutching the mangled digits to his chest.

"What have you proven, Imreia?" the Moderator cackled. "Your family's insolence was punished appropriately, in accordance with the laws of the Quinarium. They deserved their end! You deserve no more than the same! The Five will not be denied their retribution!"

"Arrogant to the last."

The Moderator attempted to wriggle away on his back. Imreia stepped on the wood splinters in his legs, pinning him in place.

"Do what you will!" he shrieked. "But one day, you will fall before the might of the Quinarium! Your end is coming!"

"So you already said, you disgusting, insignificant, vile little worm."

The Moderator screamed, his eyes bulging and tongue sticking out of his mouth. Imreia brought her sword above her shoulder, beheading him with a swift strike.

"At last, some quiet. Now where have Wynne and Dara gone off to?"

Driven by fury, Wynne cursed herself as she ran—accusing herself of barely assisting Imreia at the expense of leaving Dara to face two Blood Mages, alone. She finally reached a field of already harvested crops. Dead stems protruded from the ground, cut at knee height. The once tidied rows had been kicked into disarray, the cause immediately apparent.

At the far end of the field, Dara was locked in a duel with the two Blood Mages. They tore across the field in a fury, their desperate strikes punctuated with drinks of mana. Dara was clearly the best of the three, but each time she found an advantage against one, the second would drive her off.

Wynne sprinted as fast as she was able, fueled by desperation, her legs aching and lungs screaming. She watched the melee as she closed the distance.

Dara finally gained the upper hand, kicking Ffionin squarely in her chest. When Jodrie dove in, Dara ducked beneath his sword, cutting his thigh as she rolled past. Ffionin countered, slashing Dara across her back. Dara roared through the pain, lacerating Ffionin's side.

Slow to rise, Dara did not see Jodrie charging. Before she could turn, his sword pierced through her shoulder. Wynne cried out as Dara's sword slipped from her hand and she fell to her knees, her arm dangling.

The two Blood Mages stood side by side. They raised their swords together, ready to deliver the final blow. Wynne screamed, her throat burning.

Jodrie and Ffionin stumbled back, their weapons knocked aside. Dara squinted, a blazing white barrier of flame surrounding her. As the light faded, she saw Wynne, scepter raised.

Wynne gulped back mana. Speaking feverishly, she waved an open hand over the scepter. A white blade appeared, enrobed in curls of yellow flame. Wynne held the weapon out, challenging the Blood Mages.

Jodrie cackled. "Do you see how she holds the sword?"

"That scepter will make a fine trophy," Ffionin replied. "But what of Dara?"

"She isn't going anywhere. Let's deal with this one first."

Wynne charged, screaming, her sword raised high and tears falling from her eyes. The Blood Mages cackled, easily parrying her first swing. They stalked in a circle on opposite sides of Wynne, like sharks ready to feast. Time and time again, they casually knocked aside Wynne's strikes, laughing all the while.

"I'm bored," said Ffionin. "Let's finish—"

A wet crunch interrupted the Mage's words. Ffionin's head rolled forward and her body fell aside, Dara's sword protruding from her chest.

"Ffionin! No!" Jodrie cried. Blood vessels threatened to burst from his forehead as he shook with rage. "That was a nice trick, saving Dara. I admit, I never expected her to be able to throw a sword, either. That was a mistake on her part, though. She can't save you now!"

Wynne desperately swung her blade, but sparks flew as Jodrie deflected the sword of flame. He grabbed Wynne's shoulder, then plunged his sword into her stomach.

The scepter fell to the ground, the blade extinguished. Pain overwhelmed Wynne. She looked up to the sky, spotting a fleck of blue between the clouds. It reminded her of the ocean, of home, a place she wished she could have taken Dara one day. As Jodrie cackled in her ear, Wynne imagined Dara's face over his shoulder, growing ever closer. She wished she could reach out and touch her, feel the warmth of her skin.

Dara soared, coming to an abrupt stop with a crack as her elbow struck the back of Jodrie's neck, shattering his spine. She kicked his corpse away and caught Wynne with her good arm, slowly lowering her to the ground.

Wynne lay on her side, coughing and squirming and clutching at the handle of the sword. Dara's tears pattered against the side of the blade as she hunched over Wynne.

"You should have run," Dara said, cradling Wynne's head in her lap.

Wynne smiled meekly. "You survived."

"I..." A storm of fear raged in Dara as she touched Wynne's cheek with a trembling hand. "There's so much more I want to say, that I have to say."

Wynne's eyes fluttered shut. "At least we had this time together. At least we saw the truth."

Dara shook her head. "Please, please don't let this be the end. Please don't go."

"Odd request, that. Wynne is going to have a hard time going anywhere with a sword sticking out of her belly."

Imreia trotted over, the broken arrow still sticking out of her thigh. She knelt beside Wynne and examined the wound.

"Is this what they teach these days at the Academy of Ramaia? The placement of this blade... I assume he did mean to kill you, and not simply inflict pain? A Blood Mage worth half a bottle of mana would have gone for the neck, or at least the heart or the spine. But here?"

"Can you help her? Will she be alright?"

Imreia nodded lazily. "I'm sure Wynne is in excruciating pain, but she should survive. I'm sure you're in excruciating pain as well, but we'll get to you in a moment. What a pair you two are. See, this is why I usually travel alone."

Imreia drained a bottle of mana from her bandolier, then whispered a spell calling on Ilsios. She placed a glowing hand on Wynne's stomach, forming a circle around the sword with her thumb and middle finger. Wynne cried out as Imreia pulled the sword, but once the blade was free, the wound closed and her breathing eased.

Dara pulled Wynne close with her good arm.

"Thank you, Imreia."

"I assume this was not the day you expected. Five above, you're a mess too, Dara. Your arm is dangling like a bunch of herbs set out to dry. Let me get you situated, then we need to hurry. Although Quinarium Officiants can prattle to the dead for hours, I expect the residents will be returning soon. I'm not sure about you, but I would much rather not be involved in cleaning up the hamlet. I am assuming, of course, with the Moderator dead, that you do not intend to make for Stellburg?"

CHAPTER 20

A gentle evening wind carried away the last of the clouds. Imreia leaned against a tree at the top of a hill, watching as a horde of Quinarium and Llendshold forces descended on the hamlet. Dara and Wynne, half-covered in bandages, huddled close by a small fire; a veritable herd of horses, taken from the Paladins and the carriages, crowded the nearby woods.

"Are you sure it's safe for us to have a fire?" Dara asked.

"And for us to be this close to the hamlet?" Wynne followed.

Imreia waved her hand. "We are plenty far away. If they can see our fire half a day's ride away, in the night, then they're truly blessed by the Five. Besides, we have struck fear into their hearts, and fear is a powerful motivator indeed. A Moderator beheaded. Four Mages dead, along with a complement of Paladins and archers. The guards and Paladins will be reluctant to stray into the darkness. I believe them as likely to crawl and hide beneath their beds like scared children as they are to venture this far from the hamlet."

"You'll have to forgive me if I can't share your lighthearted-ness," Dara said. "You escaped with a modest wound, but Wynne and I are entirely helpless in our current condition."

"I find levity a necessity in times such as these. A cloud-ed, overly dark mind can easily misguide," Imreia counseled. "Though I must admit, your caution is warranted. It is caution, more than ability, that has kept me alive all these years, and yours is appreciated. For you, Dara, I will scout the area again and make doubly sure the camp is safe for the night."

Once Imreia disappeared into the darkness, Wynne rested her head on Dara's good shoulder. Dara closed her eyes, relishing the warmth, the gentle pressure, the sounds of Wynne's breathing. She put her arm around Wynne and pulled her close.

"What have we done?" Wynne muttered, staring into the fire.

"Why do you ask that?"

"We fought alongside Imreia... we killed Agents of the Quinarium. I don't regret the death of the Moderator, but the others... were they so different from us? We followed the Quinarium's lead without question. We swore to serve the Quinate through the Quinarium, and despite what we've learned, it feels somehow wrong."

"They gave us no choice," Dara replied. "If we didn't fight them, they meant to kill us, or worse. With all we've seen and heard... I also am sad for their deaths, but I have no regret for what we did. The words of Hawel, Catarin, Failure, Uldrik and Scireth, the records of Yuvsgrend, and the sight of the extraction today, they all tell me what I need to know: the leaders of the Quinarium have abandoned the Quinate in favor of their own lust for power and control."

Wynne nuzzled further into Dara. "Had things not gone as they did, if we had a simpler rite, do you think we would have gone along with the Quinarium? Supported the extractions, even?"

"I might be simple enough, desperate enough, to be convinced. Every day in the Academy, I feared losing what I had, so much so that I might follow their orders. But you? Never."

"You seem certain about me," Wynne said coyly.

"Am I wrong?"

"I'm not sure." Wynne closed her eyes and exhaled. "My life revolved around dedication to Hantsburg and the Quinarium in equal parts. It's hard to see the truth when you're raised blind."

"I guess it was a small blessing in some ways to be born poor and ignored."

"Not ignored anymore," Wynne said, squeezing Dara's hand. "What do you make of Imreia? Do you think we can trust her?"

"While I think she has motivations beyond what she has shared, her actions speak loudly. I believe her motivations to be true."

"I'm surprised."

"Why?"

"You've been slow to trust. I thought you would be more hesitant to follow her."

Dara blinked. "I've seen both the Quinarium and the Lords, Earls, and Elders of the Regency abandon people. Leaving us hungry, uncared for. Perhaps it's my desperation speaking, but Imreia saved us twice and has made no demands of us in return."

"Yet, at least," Wynne said, her voice trailing off.

"I take it you think less positively of her?"

"I think we should be cautious, is all. Everything she is doing is as much her own benefit, to take back her title, as it is to tear down the Quinarium. But you're right; she saved us."

Dara rested her cheek atop Wynne's head. "Speaking of saving, I wonder what has become of Ami and Caudro."

"I'm sure Ami will make it back to the Nomridian Forest. Caudro, however... he's a bit thick at times. That conversation with his mentor and the Confessor, it's the first time I've heard his adherence wavering. Scireth spoke with false kindness, and I hope Caudro realized it."

"He's a big, strong man, as Ami would say," Dara said with a chuckle. "I'm sure he will be alright."

Wynne smiled. "I wonder if he realizes he cares for her."

"I'm not one to speak, given how I've been with you, but Ami was quite forward with her affections. He really is a dense man, isn't he? I wonder if the other Paladins are all so indoctrinated. If we showed them the truth, would any of them take off their armor and leave the Quinarium? I at least hope Caudro will. Well, perhaps if he is reminded of Ami, he will be convinced."

"Listen to you, sounding like a proper leader."

Dara blushed and grinned. "When I was younger, on the rare occasions when I played with other children, I always let them be the Lords and Moderators and other people in high places. Even pretending to rise above my station was painful, as when I went home, I had to face the reality of another day in the mines. I was scared... but now? Now I have a chance to do something. To be someone."

"Shine the light of Ilsios upon all of Llendshold."

"What's that?"

Wynne smiled wistfully. "Something a particularly kind Instructor said to me. That if I wished to honor her, I would 'shine the light of Ilsios upon all of Llendshold.' I wonder if Sionan would leave the Quinarium if given the opportunity? Or if she is already aware of what they do?"

"I hope there are many who will leave the Quinarium once they learn the truth, or realize there is a path to freedom. There have to be people with inklings of what's going on, people who want to break free."

"Have you thought of what comes next? Do we follow Imreia?" Wynne's brow furrowed. "Is following her what we want, or is it our only choice, now that we're fugitives?"

"I believe following Imreia is the best we can do," Dara said. "And you're right that the Quinarium will likely be hunting us. We're a threat to their precious control. Still, even if she has other motivations, I agree with Imreia that the Quinarium must be dismantled. She says she wants to retake her seat as Lord of Brewardsburg. We don't have to follow her there. Once the Quinarium is no longer as it is, we can have a future of our own, whatever we want it to be."

Wynne clung to Dara's arm. "I wonder if I'll ever see my parents again, or any of my family. My father... while I might want his approval, I don't think I'll miss him. But my mother, my siblings... we're alone, aren't we?"

Dara leaned forward to face Wynne. "I can't imagine what you feel, and I can't begin to replace your family. But I have been alone my entire life. I was alone as a child. I was alone at the Academy. And now, finally... If nothing else, at least we are together. Maybe one day I can be that doddering, grizzled old scholar, living on the coast, with you."

"Am I enough for you?" Wynne asked tearfully, averting her gaze.

Dara drew Wynne back in by her chin and stared into her eyes. "Wynne, you will always be more than I ever need."

"And you, for me, Dara."

Dara eagerly leaned forward, but they bumped into each other before their lips could touch.

Laughter overtook Wynne as they rubbed their foreheads. Dara turned away for a moment, then gazed back at Wynne; her eyes glowed in the light of the crackling fire, filled with longing. The two sat for a moment, hesitant, as earnest desire brewed inside.

Unable to resist any longer, Dara reached out and cradled Wynne's cheek. Wynne rested her palm against the side of Dara's neck, her fingers pressing into Dara's tender skin. Wynne suddenly grabbed hold of Dara's tunic and pulled her in.

Inching forward, their eyes closed as their lips finally met. Dara inhaled, astonished at the softness, the delicateness of Wynne's touch. Smiles crept across their faces as they eased back and stared into each other's eyes, relishing the shared expression of satisfaction. Wynne bit her lower lip, then took hold of Dara with both hands.

They embraced each other tightly as they kissed again. A burning passion rushed through Dara and Wynne, washing away their pain, their exhaustion, their fears. Intoxicated by the taste, their hearts pounded and they breathed deeply as if to drink in the desire that coursed between the two. The world around them faded from existence along with all their worries and uncertainties, and in that moment, all was well.

When they finally pulled apart, a comforting warmth lingered. Eyelids slowly parted and they smiled, shy yet flushed with excitement.

"You two sound worried about what comes next," Imreia boomed. Dara and Wynne turned their heads to find Imreia standing by the edge of the fire. "I will not force you to follow me, and you have options should you wish not to. You could seek refuge in Draethhold—they are most welcoming of Mage refugees. Or perhaps you could go to the Fae. You were kind to Ami. They might take pity on you. The Dwarves would certainly accept you after the recovery of their records and crowns. But allow me to tell you further of what I intend to do, what I would be glad to do with you at my side."

Dara grimaced as she sat upright. "Were you listening to us?"

"Of course I was. Watching, too. I haven't survived this long by trusting without verification. As for what comes next. Today was but a taste of the true Quinarium. I asked you to come and see the extraction, that we-"

"You knew what would happen, didn't you?" Wynne said coolly. "You knew the Quinarium was coming. Were you the one to inform them that we would be there, in the hamlet? It had to be you, otherwise the Moderator couldn't possibly arrive in such a timely manner. It must be two or three days' ride from Stellburg."

"Clever, Wynne." Imreia smiled gleefully. "You are correct. I admit to my scheming. And yet, I did not expect you two to become so... involved. I thought you would flee from battle and I would provide a demonstration."

"You tricked us!" Wynne shouted. "You ask for our support on the back of your own deceit!"

"I disagree," Imreia said, pausing with a finger to her lip. "I provided you an opportunity to show me where your hearts lie. Now that I have seen and heard what you believe, I wish to further that opportunity.

"You saw for yourselves the atrocious nature of the Quinarium. They murdered a sick woman instead of helping her. They commit the same crime hundreds of times every year, and defile the bodies of countless more recently deceased. You can flee, but if you wish to stop this madness, if you wish to stand up to the Quinarium, if you wish to show yourselves to truly be the Quinate's Faithful and agents of the Gods on our world, then join me. I will tear down the Quinarium, expose it for all to see, and free Llendshold from its grasp!"

Dara took hold of Wynne's hand. "I agree that this is a poor start, but partnering with Imreia is our best chance to help Ami and the Fae. We can't allow there to be a second Yuvsgrend. After what we saw there, you know they will burn the entire forest to the ground."

Wynne's head drooped. "Honesty or deceit, I suppose it matters little. I have Quinarium blood on my hands."

Imreia chuckled. "Wynne, despite the prowess of your magic and the excellent usage of Flame, I don't think you killed anyone. My apologies, an inconsequential detail, especially considering my aim is not to spill blood. I wish to show people to the light, the beauty, the joy of the Five when not bound by the hatred which fills the Quinarium. Nor, as Dara noted, can I sit idly by while they commit a second genocide. I believe the Quinarium is preparing something truly hideous, and we must expose it. We must stop their machinations before they can cause more harm. If they succeed and the Fae are gone, then I have no doubt their eyes will turn south to Draethhold, and yet another war will consume our world."

Dara held Wynne close as she addressed Imreia. "You saved our lives twice. I am indebted to you."

"I think nothing of it, as should you. I brought you here, and as such, you are my responsibility. As for Yuvsgrend, it was also my choice to intervene."

"No matter what you say, the debt still exists," Dara said with a shake of her head. "Your acts of deceit, especially when done while decrying the deceit of the Quinarium, reflect poorly upon you. I will not pledge myself to your quest for the title of Lord of Brewardsburg—however, I believe you are our best way to stop the madness of the Quinarium. I would see my debt repaid, and will aid you in tearing down the institution."

Imreia beamed. "And you, Wynne?"

"I have conditions."

Imreia bowed facetiously. "Of course, my Lord. Please present your conditions, that I might consider them thoughtfully."

Wynne glared. "First, we must do everything in our power to assist Ami and the Fae and stop the scheming of Uldrik and Scireth."

"Hardly a condition when I already have a more established relationship with the Fae than you. But, of course. I swear to you, we will not forsake the Fae as we look to cleanse Llendshold of the Quinarium."

"Second, we find Caudro. His mentor is the Paladin Scireth. She said they would return to the Fortress at Mordinlet. I will not abandon him to whatever she has planned."

"Caudro, the Paladin Trainee who accompanied you through the Nomridian Forest?" Imreia sat by the fire across from Wynne and Dara. "While I cannot guarantee I will go myself in search of him, he sounds like a potential ally. A Paladin leaving the Quinarium... a powerful symbol indeed. I will lend you my support in finding him."

"Third, we prioritize exposing the truth of the Quinarium, not causing harm. I will not seek conflict when we can instead help people see that, as you said, turning from the Quinarium is not turning from the Five—no matter what the Confessors and Moderators and Adjudicators might say. And, as Dara, I pledge myself only to stopping the Quinarium, not to restoring your title."

"You saw my methods today. I was genuine in my offer to those who opposed us. Had they left, I would have honored my word." Imreia sat tall, gazing at the night sky. "I cannot reclaim my seat in Brewardsburg on a path stained with blood. Such a position must be won through love and truth and kindness, which is all I ever hope to bring to Llendshold. I assure you both that path is my own, not yours, and I will not coerce you into marching on Brewardsburg."

"Finally," Wynne said, staring at Imreia, "the trickery ends today. You will treat us as your equals. As partners in this all. We have lost our home—we are all but bound to you. Show us the honesty we have hungered for. Show us the respect we have earned. We cannot build a future on a foundation rife with deception."

Imreia bowed. "You have my word. I assure you, my deceit was for my own safety, that I might understand you before trusting you. And now, I both understand and trust you. Are those your demands? We are in agreement then?"

"I have one condition of my own," Dara said.

"And that would be?"

"Wynne and I... we are in this together, as one."

Imreia walked to the edge of the fire's light and looked out over the valley.

"So it shall be: Dara and Wynne, as one. You have completed the Rite of the Faithful, and in doing so, proven yourselves worthy. Though we may have days, months, possibly years of struggle ahead, we will toil in the name of the Five. Tomorrow is a new day for you, and for all of Llendshold. Stand proud, Dara, Champion of Ramaia. Stand proud, Wynne, Champion of Ilsios. You are the purest of the Quinate's Faithful, and you will be their heralds in Llendshold, the bringers of their righteous word!"

ABOUT THE AUTHOR

Brendan Corbett grew up in a military family, always on the move. Books, particularly fantasy, were both stabilizing and the ultimate escape, companions to other worlds that could journey with him even when friends could not. As an adult his career turned away from the arts, though a wide range of experiences have brought him back to his love of writing.

He now resides in Oregon with his wife, son, dog and two cats. While writing consumes much of his time, you might also find him at one of his ever-growing list of hobbies, including cooking, gardening, hiking, gaming, archery, and woodworking.

Keep up to date with Brendan by signing up for his newsletter at his website, authorbrendancorbett.com, or by following him at one of the following:

instagram.com/authorbrendancorbett/

bookbub.com/profile/brendan-corbett

goodreads.com/author/show/6473803.Brendan_Corbett